ASH FOREST

(AND THE KING'S GOLD)

ASH FOREST

(AND THE KING'S GOLD)

Stephen R. Pratt

Ash Forest (and the King's Gold) by Stephen R. Pratt

Published by Ocean's Light Publishing

http://stephenrpratt.com/

First Edition 2020

Cover, chapter and map art by Vito Leo

(IS) Paperback ISBN: 978-0-6488300-2-3

To Tasha and Chloe,

for taking me on the adventure of a lifetime

ACKNOWLEDGMENTS

My eternal gratitude goes out to my darling wife, Tasha Pratt, for your inspiration, passion, wisdom, patience, and guidance, and for charging forward with me every step of the way.

To Tony White and Timothy Wade, for their eagle eyes, valuable feedback, and great humor.

And to the readers who purchased this book, enjoyed the adventure, and contributed to its success.

TABLE OF CONTENTS

Ashville

CHAPTER ONE

They Came with the Rising Sun

A scruffy thirteen-year-old boy emerged from the luminous fog and made his way toward the babbling creek. He had no friends, no parents, and no name. But he had a knife, and for this morning, that was going to be enough.

He lived in a quaint village called Ashville. Nothing much ever happened here, and that's just how the townspeople preferred it. They didn't like anything odd, and perhaps that's why they didn't like him. "He shouldn't be alive," "He must be cursed with dark magic," he would sometimes hear them say. And although he had no formal name, the townspeople called him the Feral Boy, among other mean things.

He had been making his way to the northern grove to look for food when he noticed something in the creek that was very odd and sparked his curiosity. Its turquoise waters glittered as usual, as dawn's light shimmered across the surface, but there were more intriguing flashes of vibrant silver farther beneath. The fish were all swimming downstream at a frantic pace, away from the nearby waterfall, and away from town. The Feral Boy had never seen anything like this before and stepped in for a closer look. This was not a seasonal thing, and the crystal clear waters did not smell contaminated. So what was causing this? He did know that sound traveled faster through the ground and water than the air, so perhaps they sensed something ominous approaching. But surely this was not the case. Nothing exciting ever happened in Ashville, and nothing daunting ever came this way. He turned and made for the grove.

***

Farther east, beyond the horizon and the long green grasslands, a dust cloud rose from a steep, gloomy ravine. Thunder seemed to rise from the earth with it. Never stopping. Just growing louder. And closer.

It was the sound of power and rage. The sound of four hundred men on horseback, galloping at high speed in four columns through the narrow gorge, side by side, with the Four Generals leading the charge. They were the greatest warriors from the four corners of the earth. The fair skinned Baertics from the Realm of the Far North, the square jawed Harromae from the Kingdom of the Sun, the dark skinned Yurrandar from the Empire of the Wild Plains, and the olive skinned Cuttorians from the Dominion of the Deserts. Each wore ornate armor indicative of his region, forming an eclectic mix of chain mail, cane-armor, leather, furs, and fine silk. But they all wore the same cloaks of blood-red cloth, anchored over their broad shoulders and fluttering wildly behind them. With this simple piece of attire, they appeared as one. For indeed they were united, serving one very infamous King.

They entered the clearing of grasslands and quickened their pace. The Flag Bearer cut his way to the front and raised his pole high. Its black cloth unraveled to reveal the motif of a fist

2

clenching a wreath of thorns. Beyond a distant hill, they could see the peak of the waterfall that acted as a beacon for the place they were charging toward. Ashville.

***

At the northern tip of Ashville, the Feral Boy strolled into the heart of a dense grove beneath a majestic waterfall. A coil of thin rope hung in his left hand, with a tarnished bronze grapple hook tied to its end. He flicked back his mop of dark hair and carefully examined the branches overhead, resplendent in the colors of fall. He began spinning his hook, which hummed as he increased the speed, faster and faster. He released it and sent it upward with a whoosh. The hook hit a cluster of hazelnuts high above with a loud smack, and they fell to his feet. A perfect shot.

He pressed his foot onto one of the hazelnuts that had a small crack on its upper shell, then drew a short, bronze-bladed knife from the holster on his left thigh. The holster hung from his belt and was cinched firmly in place by another strap lower down that wrapped around his leg. He pressed the blade through the crack in the hazelnut and tried to gently pry it open, but the bronze tip snapped with a loud crack, and the force of the movement caused him to lose his balance momentarily.

He examined the broken blade with a sense of frustration. Sure, it was old, but he was hoping to get much more use from it. Regardless, even though it no longer had a tip, its jagged edge might still serve a purpose. He sheathed the knife with a sigh.

He spotted movement in the grass, and his eyes quickly fixed on two lines of purple caterpillars, marching side by side, coming together to form a single line. A swarm of bright red

3

ants and yellow ants were launching a vicious attack on one caterpillar that had haplessly drifted off the back. *It seemed someone was having a worse day than him*, the Feral Boy thought to himself. He stared for a moment, caught in the moroseness of it. Then his hand darted out, grabbed the caterpillar, and brought it close to his mouth. He gently blew the ants away and placed it back in the line. And away it merrily walked with the others. Now, if only his knife problems could be solved so easily.

The Feral Boy marveled again at the coloring of the caterpillar and contemplated taking it home, like a pet, curious to witness its evolution into a butterfly. But he felt a sudden pang of sadness. He had tried keeping a pet once before, when he discovered an injured, young bird. It had died a week later. He always wondered if he should have left it alone. He had no experience caring for an injured animal and should not have tried. Maybe it was just bad luck for the bird. Or maybe what the townspeople sometimes said about him was true: he was so wild that he was evil.

As the Feral Boy pocketed his hazelnuts, he noticed movement beyond the trees, at the town's front gates. A wagon was approaching, drawn by a weary horse.

At the reins was Efscott, a forty-year-old bearded man with a jovial, round face that was punctuated with smile lines around his eyes. Beside him sat his pretty daughter, Prudence. Twelve, blonde-haired, rosy-cheeked, and with a reserved nature that most people would mistake as shyness. Shy indeed. She looked like someone who came across as timid at first but would quickly throw a bucket of water on you if you so much as dropped a frog in her pocket.

The Feral Boy was transfixed by her. Not by her beauty so much, for beauty was actually a rather common thing. But there was something radiant about her that he couldn't define. And seeing as he wasn't the type to waste a good frog, he probably had nothing to worry about. He locked the flap down on his knife sheath by fastening a slim button through its eyelet, grinning when he spotted a large branch on the ground that had a perfect shape for a task he had in mind. He picked it up and made his way out of the grove, keeping a wary eye on the approaching carriage.

***

Guarding the main entrance were two men in rocking chairs, who were fast asleep. Not exactly the town's best and brightest, at first glance. But upon meeting the rest of the townspeople, you might think again. One was short and rotund, the Tax Collector, who loved to hear his own voice and rarely paid attention to what others had to say. The other, Sir Sudley, was a tall and gangly man with a placid calmness about him. He must have been over seventy years old, and it was he who woke first.

Sir Sudley rose slowly and shuffled over to the gate. It was a fragile old thing that had been tied together in sections with pieces of cloth. Under Sir Sudley's sleepy eyes sat a bulbous nose, flamboyant mustache, and easy-going smile. He wore an old bronze-plated armor vest on his torso and a faded purple scarf around his neck. The bronze-bladed spear he carried was severely chipped and tarnished. It had clearly not seen any action in years. He opened the gate and waved the carriage in.

The Tax Collector begrudgingly heaved himself up to his feet, eyeing the disheveled wagon with contempt as it wobbled in. He tried to step forward, but his chair was still fixed tightly to his overly plump buttocks, causing him to stumble. The Tax

5

Collector quickened his steps frantically in a bid to regain his balance while spinning his hands wildly around in circles. But instead, he tripped and fell flat on his face with a thud, then took a deep breath, grunted, and pushed the chair away. It dislodged with a pop.

Efscott brought the carriage to a halt and nodded a salutation, making sure not to smile too much for fear it might seem he was laughing at the Tax Collector's expense. "Good morning, sirs! We wish to settle here. Long term," said Efscott in a polite tone.

The Tax Collector scowled as he rose to his feet and dusted himself off. "Five silver coins gives you the best views, four silvers gives you ..." His voice trailed off when he saw the single bronze nugget in Efscott's hand. The Tax Collector groaned and snatched it up. "One bronze nugget. Head to the back! All the way. Just past the poo-wagons." He pointed to the south end of the village. "Also known as Bottom's End," added the Tax Collector.

Efscott cast an apologetic glance to Prudence, who simply smiled and shrugged. He chuckled, then turned to address the Tax Collector. "And where would I find your Chief?"

The Tax Collector was already waddling away and gave a dismissive gesture toward town. "Edge of the Empty Heart," he grumbled.

Efscott nodded politely and gazed vacantly toward town, then flicked the reins and moved slowly down the gravel road that was flanked on both sides by quaint, single-level cottages. Most were built with log walls and were capped with sod roofs of lush green grass. Some of these had succulents scattered across them in a variety of brilliant colors, making the rows of homes seem like an undulating garden of sorts. Some of the less spectacular cottages used shingles on higher-pitched roofs but still had ornate gardens filled with herbs and colorful flowers. Efscott turned warily over his shoulder and noticed a lithe figure slide out from behind a straw bale and move toward them.

It was the Feral Boy. He wiped his nose with the back of his left hand and gestured to the cottages. "The Blacksmith's their Chief. That's who you want. Follow the blackest pillar of smoke. That's the town square. They call it the Empty Heart because there's a lot of space." He pointed to a dense plume of chimney smoke coming from a cottage at the edge of the creek. A water-driven paddle wheel churned slowly around beyond the rear wall. This part of town was notably less congested and even prettier.

"Thank you," replied Efscott.

The Feral Boy eyed Efscott thoughtfully, noting that despite his gentle appearance and a bit of a potbelly, he had strong arms and stalwart hands. Most probably a tradesman of some sort. This disappointed him because it meant they were not carrying anything of significant value. But perhaps they had some expensive tools. *Maybe a good knife*, he thought to himself. The Feral Boy looked over at Prudence, who was eyeing him with equal wariness.

She was brandishing a tiny blade in one hand and held a small wooden bird in the other, carved into shape from many hours of diligent work. She put the knife and wooden bird down by her side with an air of self-consciousness. No surprise. The art of carving small things from wood—whittling—was something girls usually didn't do. It was considered quite a manly interest. But if you were the daughter of a carpenter, for example, that might be less peculiar. Which meant that the carriage probably did contain tools. The Feral Boy grinned.

"And what is your name?" asked Efscott.

The Feral Boy was caught off guard. No one had ever asked him this before. He felt a heat rush through his cheeks as they turned slightly red, and he shrugged.

The Feral Boy noticed Prudence looking at him, studying him. She was paying attention to his right arm, which made him feel uncomfortable. He smiled at her, and Prudence smiled back, but quickly averted her gaze.

"Goodness, does he ever bathe?" she whispered to her father. She brushed a strand of hair away from her face and straightened her posture.

The Feral Boy puffed out his chest and maintained his pace alongside them. There was something about these two he liked. They seemed different. But a seed of doubt immediately crept into his mind: maybe they would quickly become like everyone else he ever met. The world never took long to show its revulsion of him, nor to conclude that he was less than nothing. Why would they be any different? Even the swagger in his stride changed to more of a plodding one. But perhaps his little trick had worked. He was trying to look as normal to them as possible, so he could set a good first impression, which he had heard was important. But his trick was soon to be harshly unveiled.

Their carriage passed a group of several children who were playing a game in which they tapped an acorn to each other on wooden paddles. The children stopped and approached the Feral Boy. Brunt was the largest and oldest of them. He was sixteen and heavyset with rough hands that had been hardened from years of working with metal. He was the Blacksmith's son. And although he told everyone that the small scar on his chin was from a shard of metal hitting him while he was working, it was actually because he fell out of bed one night while having a nightmare about being chased by a giant carnivorous butterfly.

Brunt poked the Feral Boy's shoulder with a finger that looked as solid as granite. "Hey! Run back to your trees, monkey-cripple!" He leaned in closer and whispered menacingly into the boy's ear. "Thief!"

The Forest Boy ignored Brunt and kept walking beside Efscott's carriage, but Brunt wasn't giving up so easily. He hooked his paddle inside the Feral Boy's right arm and yanked hard, ripping the entire limb out of the long shirtsleeve, sending it flipping through the air and tumbling to the ground. The Feral Boy's trick had been unveiled.

He wasn't so normal after all. Brunt and his friends laughed hysterically while Prudence stiffened in shock. She gave a slight start. It was clearly dawning on her that the arm was fake—the Feral Boy had been using a branch as an artificial limb inside his sleeve. He only had one arm. His left one.

The Feral Boy bent over to pick up the branch, and Brunt delivered a swift kick to his butt, sending him sprawling onto the dirt. "Keep an eye on this one," Brunt declared to Efscott, "he's only got one arm. But he steals like someone with four." Brunt winked mischievously at Prudence, then turned and jogged away with the rest of the children and returned to his game.

The Feral Boy felt his face glowing an even warmer tinge of red than before, partly from anger, but mostly from embarrassment, which was relatively new for him. For some inexplicable reason, he had felt a compulsion to impress this girl. Clearly his plan did not work, and the result was a rather new shade of shame.

He pulled himself to his feet and grabbed the branch with his left hand. His only hand. It looked as if he was considering throwing the stick at Brunt, who had scampered away, but his attention was quickly averted by movement in the distance. The surge of indignation that felt like a wave of hot energy rushing through him suddenly gave way to curiosity. To the east beyond the hills, a large flock of birds fluttered skyward from the trees on the horizon. He frowned. Efscott followed his line of sight and also noticed the birds.

***

Back on the plains—still unbeknownst to the townspeople—the army of four hundred advanced quickly. Two horsemen galloped up beside the Generals. They carried the army's gold standard of the fist and thorns. Four giant wolves, also wearing armor, ran alongside them in tight formation. The three grey wolves were terrifying beasts, but none of them were as menacing as Armageddon. He was the largest of them all, with thick white fur, piercing blue eyes, and huge fangs that became exposed as he growled. It was a loud, guttural rumble that could have been easily mistaken for thunder. He meant business. The Four Generals drew their swords, and the sound of clanking metal resounded as the army of four hundred men behind them did likewise.

CHAPTER TWO

Sharp Blades

Back in Ashville, the Feral Boy stepped behind Efscott's carriage. His right sleeve hung limp, and it appeared as if his left hand was jammed deep in his pocket. Through a gap in the rear door, he spotted two bronze chisels in a toolbox. One had a chipped blade, and the other was shiny and elegant in design. He felt his heartbeat quicken. While the tool was not brand new, it was clearly well made and would be very useful. His left hand slid serpentine-like through a gap between his shirt buttons and into the carriage. His left sleeve, obviously now with the branch inside it, remained firmly lodged in his left pocket. It was clearly a ruse to make people think his arm was by his side and in clear view, when in fact, his arm was inside the body of his loose-fitting shirt. He retrieved the shiny chisel and deftly pocketed it within the waistband of his trousers under his shirt. He pulled his arm back inside his shirt then pushed it back down his left sleeve, driving the branch out with it. He had performed the operation quickly and smoothly, and no one had noticed a thing. He stepped casually around to the other side of the carriage, with the stick now in his left hand and his right sleeve still hanging limp.

Coming in quick, an acorn hurtled through the air, straight toward the Feral Boy. Just before it cracked into his head, he dodged it, and it flew past, missing him by an inch. In the distance, the group of children erupted in laughter. Brunt grabbed another acorn from the ground and hit it with his paddle. This time it was aimed straight at Prudence, who raised a hand to protect herself and braced herself for the painful impact.

Lightning fast, the Feral Boy reached out and caught the acorn in the hand-like extremity of his branch. He flipped it up high and prepared to smash it back at the group, who all instinctively ducked in terror. Instead, the Feral Boy let the acorn drop into his palm. Efscott eyed Brunt with a stern glance as the Feral Boy casually examined the blue speckled acorn. He held it up for Prudence and Efscott to see. "The ones with blue spots taste best," he said with a grin.

Prudence frowned. Ashville was clearly doing very little to impress her. Brunt and his gang stood back up, appearing chastened by their failed provocation. "Freak!" screamed Brunt while puffing out his chest and pulling his shoulders back.

The Feral Boy strolled away toward the creek, looking unperturbed. He glanced back over his shoulder at Efscott and Prudence and spotted movement again in the corner of his eye. But it wasn't an acorn this time. High in the eastern sky some two miles away, a flock of birds darted swiftly northward. He examined their formation and noticed something odd: they were flying higher than usual. It seemed something had frightened them. And it was heading this way.

Efscott noticed the concerned look on the boy's face and, following his line of sight once again, also spotted the birds. He turned to ask a question, but the boy was gone.

***

The Blacksmith's workshop extended from the front of his cottage. The walls were dotted with many tools of various shapes and sizes. Some were made of tarnished bronze, but the ones displayed proudly in the front of his workshop were made of dark iron. They glistened in the morning light through the billows of steam that rose from the fire pit, fed by the enormous bellows that the Blacksmith pumped with vigor.

Efscott sluggishly alighted from the carriage that was now parked outside. He stretched his neck and back as soon as he got to the ground and took a deep breath. Prudence bounded down effortlessly and tethered their horse to a fence post. She stretched her arms above her head, arching her back, then bent down to pick up a small purple flower that had been lying randomly on the ground, already plucked from the earth. Pinning her other hand to the ground, her legs suddenly flipped into the air and flung over her head as she carried out a cartwheel, landing gracefully and walking nonchalantly ahead.

The Feral Boy watched all of this from behind a pile of charcoal beside the Blacksmith's workshop. He sometimes found discarded nails in this area, which proved to be handy, but this time he found himself intrigued once more by Prudence. He had seen other girls perform this cartwheel trick and thought of them as showoffs. But this girl managed it with such effortlessness and grace.

Taking in her surroundings and sniffing the flower in her hand, Prudence looked delighted to find a lush herb garden in the neighbor's yard. The air was alive with the peculiar combination of molten metal from the Blacksmith's workshop and sweet, pungent plants. The Baker's wife Driyetta was picking some of the dill in her garden and caught Prudence's eye. She was a large woman who looked like a ball of dough set upon tiny feet. Prudence smiled but was met with a scowl.

"You'll be keeping your hands off my herbs now, you understand that?" grumbled Driyetta, glaring at Prudence, who nodded.

"That's fine," replied Prudence softly. "I have my own anyway."

Upon hearing the accent in Prudence's voice, Driyetta eyed her with even greater suspicion. Prudence turned away and surveyed the other cottages around her with the usual dreaminess of a young child in a new town.

The Feral Boy studied Prudence as she gazed casually down the street, eyeing the various locals engaged in some form of disagreement. Arguing over prices, bickering over borderlines between cottages, complaining about the smell wafting in from their neighbor's steamed cabbage.

The Feral Boy had heard other travelers mention that the people of Ashville were a mean-spirited bunch who were unkind to each other and took even less liking to newcomers or anyone remotely different. No doubt this was what Prudence was discovering about her new home. She looked quite dejected, and at first, the Feral Boy felt a pang of sorrow for her, but this soon changed to a feeling of slight annoyance. Was her life so privileged that this was all that it took to sadden her? They had a large carriage, and surely it was filled with a lot of good food. And they had each other. Most likely, the town would soon embrace them, more than it ever did him. So what right did she have to be unhappy?

Efscott rummaged around the back of the carriage, leaning in through the tarp and searching anxiously in his toolbox. His fingers ran over the space where the shiny chisel once lay. He looked frantically around the tool kit and under it, then sighed in disbelief upon realizing that it was definitely gone. He despondently picked up the bronze chisel instead.

The Feral Boy found his hand automatically going to the handle of the shiny chisel to ensure that it still sat securely in his waistband, feeling it through the cloth of his shirt that concealed it. He shrank a little farther back from his vantage point, trying to keep from everyone's view. Especially Efscott's.

With a beautifully carved chair held in his other hand, Efscott approached the imposing Blacksmith, who continued hammering hot metal on his anvil. Upon seeing Efscott's bronze chisel, the Blacksmith snorted. "The Bronze Age is dying. We usually use iron now."

Efscott nodded, slightly abashed, then gestured to his chair and gently set it on the ground. He beamed with pride, knowing full well that the Blacksmith and Chief could only appreciate his excellent craftsmanship. He brushed some invisible dust from the top of the backrest.

The Blacksmith leaned forward and scrutinized it, particularly the joints and then the ornate etchings of trees and birds that adorned the backrest. "This is fine work. Very fine. We could do with a good carpenter around here."

Efscott motioned to the chipped bronze chisel in his hand. "Seems I have lost my best chisel, unfortunately. And this one is in need of a new blade. Though I must confess, I cannot pay until I find work."

The Blacksmith turned away in disgust. "If you have no money, you have no business here."

Efscott stiffened slightly. "Our journey was long, and we spent all we had, but if—"

The Blacksmith returned to his bellows. "You'll get no favors from anyone in this village, Carpenter. Beg for money in the gutters, if you must." He pumped the handle firmly, and the kiln belched out flames.

Efscott nodded. "I see," he said softly as he retreated.

Back at the carriage, Efscott placed the chair down and withdrew a small sack from behind the tarp. He seemed mortified in front of his daughter to be in this state of powerlessness and beggarhood. He approached the Blacksmith again, drawing out two apples and a loaf of bread. "This is the only food we have. Perhaps you would accept it as a down payment?"

The Blacksmith eyed the chair beside the carriage. "And the chair?"

Efscott nodded sadly, and the Blacksmith grabbed the food and chisel from him, placing them down on a nearby bench.

Brunt sauntered in, pulled off a piece of the bread, and smirked at Efscott as he bit into it. Brunt approached the bellows and pushed the handle down to stoke the flames with the familiarity of a pro, addressing his father with his mouth still full of bread. "They were talking to the Feral Boy." Bits of food flew from his mouth as he spoke, but he continued, "Little Urdin!"

The Blacksmith shot a cautionary look to Efscott. "He's probably diseased, so be careful. Little savage. No manners."

The Feral Boy felt his body become rigid and his blood run cold. But it wasn't from the insult he had just overheard—he had been called much worse than this before. It was something else. The discarded nails on the ground by his feet were vibrating ever so slightly from an unseen force. He now understood why the birds had been fleeing erratically through the sky. Something ominous was definitely heading this way, and fast. In a flash, he considered his options and whether he should warn the others. The Blacksmith and Brunt would probably throw something at him, and it wouldn't be the bread, which would actually be useful. He could warn Efscott and Prudence. But what if they discovered he had stolen their chisel? He needed to act now. They were on their own, he decided, as he turned on his heel and darted away.

Brunt took another large bite from his bread and sneered mockingly at Prudence, with his cheeks stuffed full.

But Prudence's mind was elsewhere. Like the Feral Boy, she noticed an odd movement in her vicinity. The Blacksmith's tools were vibrating ever so slightly upon the walls. A deep rumble grew louder. Everyone else became aware of it now.

Driyetta dropped her dill and placed a hand on her chest. "Oh dear," she squeaked.

The Blacksmith was perplexed as he gawked up at the clear skies. "What thunder is this?"

"That's not thunder," replied Efscott, looking more concerned. He hurried to the carriage and pulled Prudence closer. He peered over the rooftops toward the eastern gates but couldn't see anything. He recognized this sound though. "Horsemen! Coming fast! How large is your defense-army?"

The Blacksmith turned pale. "Ummm ..."

****

At the front gates, the Tax Collector swayed gently on his rocking chair in a state of half-sleep. An orange leaf floated down and landed on his chin. He giggled and declared with a croaky voice, "Oooh, the first leaf drops! Fall is coming!"

Sir Sudley stared in horror beyond the gates. "So is something ... bad."

Four hundred warriors charged over the hill, bearing down on them at a frightening pace, with a cloud of dust and grass billowing up behind. The Tax Collector sprang up with his chair still firmly attached to his buttocks, then waddled frantically toward some straw bales and dove behind them.

Sir Sudley rose and apprehensively lifted his spear. It shook within his trembling grip. He wasn't sure if that was from his fear or the growing vibrations through the ground caused by the encroaching army. He realized with dismay that he was holding the wrong end in front of himself. They were just forty yards away now. He turned his spear around frantically, but the pointy bronze tip fell off with a pop. They were so close—he could see the wild whites of their eyes—and his knees wobbled.

The lead Horseman leaped over the gate with ease, straight over Sir Sudley's head. The old Guard's eyes rolled back into their sockets, and he fainted with a high-pitched, quivering groan. His back hit the ground with a smack, and his legs whipped upward.

The next two horsemen smashed the gate off its hinges with their iron hammers, and the remainder of the army charged in, passing Sir Sudley in its four-column formation.

The army rumbled toward the center of town, but a pack of five riders broke away and headed for the creek, beside which a group of terrified children stood.

A wild black stallion with bright red eyes led the pack. It was ridden by a cloaked figure that held a wooden staff tightly in one hand and the reins in the other, hunched upon a saddle made of scaly hide. It was the King's Witch, a necromancer of the Black Witch Order. A red snake about five feet in length hung around her neck, limp and relaxed but very much attentive and alive. The hood of the Witch's robe flew back, revealing her face. Her skin, mottled with Baertic scar-tattoos, was pale to the point of appearing almost blue; her blue eyes so fair, they almost seemed white. Her long, grey hair flailed in the wind as she galloped past the shrieking children. She led the riders across the creek, sending up plumes of white water, then charged up the embankment toward the vast, foreboding woods that overlooked the town: the Ash Forest.

The four columns of horsemen continued their charge through the village, setting fire to the roofs of some cottages and terrorizing the townspeople in a wave of synergistic destruction. The dumbstruck Potter watched wide-eyed, raising his bushy eyebrows, while his hands stayed immersed in clay. The townspeople called him Potty the Potter because he seemed a bit confused about everything. He raised a trembling finger and hollered, "Ummm, you're supposed to pay at the gate!"

General Pound, the Baertic commander, swung his broadsword at a timber support beam, cutting it in half, and General Yan, the Harromaen commander, sliced through the shaft on the opposite side with his slender, razor-sharp sword. The beam parted with ease, and the straw roof collapsed onto the Potter, whose head popped through the middle, creating an eruption of straw.

The tall, muscular Pig Farmer proudly lifted his pitchfork and braced himself for a fight. But as the attackers drew nearer, he gave it a second thought, tossed his weapon away, and sprinted off in the opposite direction. A blur of movement to the side prompted him to spin. Armageddon had leaped over a hut to shorten his route and had gone airborne. He was a silent blur of shiny armor and white fur hurtling through the sky. The colossal wolf pounced onto the Pig Farmer, pinning him to the ground with a loud smack and an explosion of dust.

CHAPTER THREE

The Necromancer

In a flurry of screams and yells, the invading army made swift work of taking command of the town. The only local who came remotely close to putting up a fight was Sir Sudley, who still lay unconscious at the front gates. This army of four hundred had previously been victorious in defeating forces ten times their size, partly because of their ability to attack swiftly, which deprived their enemy of an organized defense. But it was their elite skills in fighting that made them particularly formidable. They were natural-born soldiers who had spent their lives fine-tuning their rare skills. Conquering the town of Ashville, that had no discernable army of any sort, made this the most leisurely afternoon of work they had ever had.

The dust settled, and the horsemen slowed their pace, surrounding the village and corralling the townspeople into its center. The Flag Bearer was listening to a group of the townspeople who pointed frantically at the Blacksmith. The Flag Bearer turned and slowly rode his horse up to the terrified Town Chief. Efscott pulled Prudence in behind him as the Flag

Bearer drew nearer, lifting his flagpole high, then thrusting it into the ground between the cobblestones, an inch from the Blacksmith's feet.

General Pound sheathed his sword and took off his helmet, an intimidating looking thing with polished steel wings upon the temples, a slender nose guard, and an angular cheek guard. He was a thuggish brute with wild red hair, a thick beard, a broad face, and a commanding presence.

He regarded the Blacksmith coolly and brought his agitated horse slowly toward him. The other three Generals came behind Pound and also took off their helmets: General Dinara from the Dominion of the Deserts, General Pularax from the Empire of the Wild Plains, and General Yan from the Kingdom of the Sun. They were all battle-hardened men who carried themselves with confidence and calm, yet their eyes had a sorrowful emptiness to them, a stare of men who had spent their lives searching hard for something without finding it.

General Pound bellowed out to the townspeople with a gravelly northern accent. "Listen up now! Can you hear me in the back there?"

The townspeople at the back of the crowd nodded obediently. Except for the Shoemaker. He was a bit of a jester who prided himself on making everyone laugh. "What?" he yelled.

Pound hollered louder. "I said, can you hear me in the back?"

"Yes, please. With two spoons of honey!" replied the Shoemaker, who quickly turned his back on Pound to hide the fact that he was giggling uncontrollably at his own joke.

Pound calmly grabbed his bow, stood high in his stirrups, aimed an arrow, and fired. Swish-thunk! It flew over the heads of the crowd and lodged itself into the Shoemaker's buttock! A bird-like yelp escaped his lips, and his knees quivered. The townspeople behind him stopped laughing.

"We can hear you! We can hear you!" they shrieked.

Pound sat back into his saddle and continued. "This village is now the property of his royal wonderfulness, King Luxurous Bankamine!"

He gestured toward two Royal Guards at the end of the road, flanking the main gate, pounding away on large battle drums. And through the main entrance came a sight that caught all the townspeople by surprise.

Three dwarves ran at a vigorous pace, pulling a giant carriage with a gold throne upon it. Sitting in it was King Luxurous. He was a tall, long-faced man in his forties, with a well-groomed beard, blonde hair, and cold blue eyes. He wore an ornate, jewel-studded gold crown. To his right, on a smaller throne, sat a thin-lipped, fifteen-year-old boy, Prince Perfeyn, his son. And on another small throne to his left lay a leather bag. Two Royal Guards stood behind the thrones, with ceremonial spears.

The panting dwarves pulled the carriage over the top of Sir Sudley, who lay motionless on the ground. Their feet and wheels missed him by inches. They continued their charge down the main street and drew the carriage up behind the Four Generals, gasping and sweating profusely, but quickly regaining their breaths. Around their necks they wore iron collars that were chained to the carriage's wooden yoke.

The townspeople were stunned into silence by the oddity of it all. The Shoemaker would have typically made a joke about now, but having an arrow embedded in his backside was enough to give him pause.

Luxurous rose slowly from his throne and placed his left hand on the pommel of his sheathed broadsword, then strode to the front of the carriage with an air of pompous ceremony. Upon reaching the end, he placed his right hand on the leather grip of the broadsword and unsheathed it with a resounding metallic chime. The gold blade was ornately designed and studded with jewels.

The townspeople cooed and leaned in closer, except for the terrified few standing closest to the King who retreated slightly. Luxurous held the sword proudly above his head. Pound grinned as he surveyed the wonder in the eyes of the townspeople. "And behold," barked Pound, "he is the holder of the legendary Gun Ronin. The sword they call the King Maker!"

The townspeople gasped.

Luxurous smiled. "It talks to me too!" he declared with the grandiose manner of a bad actor. Because he had done it so often, this melodramatic timbre in his voice had actually become his conventional way of speaking over the years. His ordinary dialect, therefore, was a pompous theatrical performance.

Luxurous brought the flat of the sword's blade to his ear. "And it says that 'none should ever challenge me, for I am King, the ruler of all worlds!'"

The townspeople responded with more gasps and excited mumblings.

Luxurous smirked, sheathed the sword, and returned to his throne. He leaned toward his son. "You see, my boy, you make the people love you by terrifying them."

Prince Perfeyn nodded. "Because then you can control them?"

"Yes, like silly little puppets," his father replied, wiggling his fingers. "The gold controls their minds. The legend of Gun Ronin controls their hearts. And terror unites it all."

Prince Perfeyn eyed the waterfall pensively. "And the wishing well, Father? When you leave the town under my command, the wishing well will be mine, yes?"

"Yes, yes, my son. What's mine is yours. All in time," replied Luxurous.

A young girl in the crowd craned her neck upon noticing movement below the royal carriage. A shadow glided behind the bars of a large cage that was bolted beneath the vehicle. Eyes blinked in the darkness. And the owner of those eyes—a huge albino crocodile—dove out between the bars of the cage and snatched in its massive jaws a toy princess from the young girl's hand. The crocodile devoured the morsel of cloth and down instantly, sending feathers flying from its mouth with each chomp. Prince Perfeyn grinned sardonically at the child, who backed away, wide-eyed and mortified.

Luxurous peered toward the field beyond the village wall and the solitary figure standing in it, dressed in royal garb. His name was Minus, a weasel-faced man with a facial tick, a weak sense of hygiene, but a strong talent in accounting. He was the King's Treasurer, among other things.

Minus snatched up a dark grey stone from the soil with glee and held it above his head victoriously. "Good news, Sire!"

Luxurous smirked and turned to the Guard. "Bring me the Witch."

***

The Witch currently stood at the top of the grassy hill, with the village behind her. Using her wooden staff as a walking stick, she hobbled cautiously toward the edge of the forest. The snake around her neck hissed and recoiled as if intimidated by the woods, and the Witch stopped. The four Royal Guards behind

24

her also halted. What they all heard next could easily have been mistaken as the growl of an ominous animal but was actually the sound of something far worse: carnivorous vegetation, moving swiftly toward them.

Out of the woods, a plant lunged for the Witch. It was a gigantic Venus Flytrap and was known to the townspeople as a Venus Mantrap. Or as the Baker called it, "The Poop-Your-Pants Plant." Its head was the size of a pony with coarse, green, leather-like skin, set upon a twelve-foot-tall malleable stalk that groaned, roared, and rumbled as it moved. Its monstrous jaws opened, revealing sinewy pale teeth that snapped viciously just an inch from her face. It could not reach her, though, and came to an abrupt halt, anchored by the roots that pinned it to the ground.

The Witch barely flinched, standing her ground and grinning disdainfully. Another Venus Mantrap lunged out from the woods and also snapped furiously. But it, too, could not reach the Witch. Both plants snapped viciously again, then hissed and slowly withdrew into the woods.

Without stepping any closer, the Witch reached up to one of the smaller trees on the forest's edge, grabbing its nearest branch, and with a firm twist, snapped it off. A soft breeze whistled through the woods, and the trees seemed to groan as if in protest. The Witch scrutinized the branch, then returned her steely gaze to the woods, as if she sensed something else deeper within. She blinked purposefully, and dark lines suddenly emanated from her pupils, like black veins, getting thicker and longer, quickly purging the whites of her eyes and rendering them as dark as glistening black glass.

Inside the forest, unbeknownst to her, someone else stared back. The Witch's snake hissed, and the eyes within the forest widened with fear and then retreated.

The Royal Guardsman galloped toward her, hooves thumping, and armor rattling. The Witch's train of thought seemed broken by this, and her eyes returned to their usual pale color. The Royal Guardsman stopped several yards behind her. "It is time!" he announced.

The Wishing Well

The townspeople stared, transfixed, as Luxurous and the Witch waded into the middle of the creek at the top of the town's waterfall. They were knee-deep in the crystal clear water that spilled gently over the edge just six feet away from them. The waterfall was not formidable in appearance, but it certainly made up in beauty what it lacked in power. Its curtain of water unfolded over the precipice, hitting the occasional extrusion of rock on the way down. It collided with the creek base in a surprisingly quiet whipping of white water, where speed and stillness met, where air and water became one, like mist.

The Witch approached the edge of the waterfall, and Luxurous followed with some trepidation. They both stopped just four feet from the sheer drop. From here, they had a stunning view of the town and countryside below, including the Ash Forest to the west. But farther to the west, beyond the Ash Forest, was a mystery. Even from this height. The woods began on flat soil then gradually extended up to a slight hill. Beyond its furthest edge hung an ever-present fog and a low-lying bank of clouds, obscuring the world beyond.

The Witch still held the branch she had taken from the Ash Forest and rubbed her thumbs over the bark in contemplation. Her voice was croaky yet commanding, and although it seemed soft, it traveled far with ease. "The wood is good. The water is well. The ground is sound. Now I cast my spell."

The townspeople had all gathered near the base of the waterfall and watched with great anticipation. The portly Potato Farmer, who had thin, wispy white hair and a bright red nose, was particularly impressed. "She's very good with the rhyming, isn't she?"

The Feral Boy watched them all from the grove where he sat casually in the branch of a tree that swayed gently in the breeze, happily eating his acorns. He was a very adept climber, which was surprising given that he only had one arm, but his skill in listening was even greater still. The Feral Boy was a genuinely curious person, and a life of being scorned by almost everyone left him with no chance to interact with others, and so he had developed a habit of watching and listening. He found that he learned many things this way, and sometimes this helped him survive. The Feral Boy also remembered hearing some stories about ambitious emperors and their invasions, which never ended well for the people whose town was conquered, so he was confused about why the townspeople were not more concerned. Did they know something he didn't? Or were they in blissful denial? Perhaps he should be more worried as well.

Through a narrow gap between the tree trunks before him, the Feral Boy could make out the royal carriage on the other side of the creek, very close to the base of the waterfall. Prince Perfeyn sat upon it on his gold throne, seemingly listening to the proceedings. One of the guards who had an unusually thick jaw and short neck stepped in and gave a respectful bow, speaking clearly and amiably. "Sire, I thought it might be best if we moved the carriage back, so you are not splashed by the water."

Perfeyn turned to him in a slight daze. "What?" he blurted, with a degree of irritation.

The Guard repeated himself, but Perfeyn sighed heavily and gazed up as if in a daydream. "If I was standing on the top of that waterfall," Perfeyn lamented, "I'd give a speech first. Something powerful that also struck terror into the hearts of all these peasants. Then I'd go ahead with the big show. Don't you think that would be grand?"

The Guard nodded politely. "A grand idea, Sire. I'm sure the King would approve too, Sire."

Perfeyn frowned. "Now … please repeat yourself. You have a very boring voice, and because of this, I did not notice you the first time you spoke, and I did not care about your message the second time you spoke. This is your third and last chance. Or I shall have you whipped."

The Guard grew a little pale and gave another obedient bow, then spoke even louder while maintaining a very congenial tone. "Of course, Sire. My apologies, Sire. I was suggesting it might be best to move the carriage back, so you did not get wet, Sire."

Perfeyn sighed again. "We're fine here, you idiot. Look how high up they are. That's a long way."

"Yes, Sire, it's just that water does travel downward fairly easily—"

"What? Why are you still talking?" barked Perfeyn.

The slightly mystified Guard nodded dutifully and backed away. "Very good, Sire. Nothing more to add, Sire."

Perfeyn turned, and through the narrow gap between the other Royal Guards surrounding him, he surveyed the distant grove with a penetrating gaze. It was hard to tell from this distance, but it seemed to the Feral Boy as if Perfeyn was staring straight at him. It was a gaze he felt uncomfortable to be under, so he leaned his branch in the opposite direction and eased himself out of Perfeyn's line of sight.

Overhead, at the top of the waterfall, the Witch pointed her branch skyward and craned her neck back, continuing her ceremony with earnestness. "Magic in water, magic in spell, here I create a wishing well!"

The townspeople bustled with curiosity, and the Barmaid turned to her husband, declaring in her usual squeaky voice, "Oh, a wishing well! That'd be nice."

Brunt, like everyone else, was fascinated by the proceedings and turned to his father. "Is she a real witch?"

The Blacksmith folded his arms and cocked his head. "Magician, probably. Real witches are much taller."

The Witch thrust her hand down, pointing her branch at the water between her and Luxurous, and with a thunderous crack, a bolt of lightning struck in the same spot, sending up an eruption of water and steam.

The spray of water hit everyone below, including Perfeyn, who cowered as the downpour struck. It was followed by a shower of small dead frogs, bouncing off heads and shoulders to the yelps of the townspeople and Perfeyn. The Guard, who had warned him about the risky proximity to the waterfall, shrank back behind another to stay hidden, just as Perfeyn spun, glaring, with his fists clenched so tightly that the knuckles whitened.

More dead frogs floated over the waterfall and down the creek. They drifted past the Blacksmith, who was standing on the bank. Brunt shot an inquiring look to his father, who shrugged in return. "Not a witch … just … lucky guess with the weather, that's all," grunted the Blacksmith.

The Witch lowered the branch in her hand, bringing it to chest height. "Snake is our medicine, good comes from bad," she declared with a snarl. The snake on her neck lashed out and bit the branch. "Ash branches waken and move like the mad!"

Her eyes turned jet black again, and her hair flailed up from the mysterious ensuing winds! Suddenly the branch in her hand twitched, then writhed like a snake. She grinned, then growled ferociously and spat a fireball onto it, about the size of a plum, and the wiggling stick erupted into flames.

The townspeople all gasped. Brunt was wide-eyed. "Woah!"

He looked up at his father, who nodded sheepishly. "Yeah, probably a witch," mumbled the Blacksmith as he pursed his lips. "A very short one though."

The Feral Boy adjusted his position in the tree, standing up and craning his neck to get a better view of the Witch and Luxurous. His heart was pounding harder in his chest. There was something terrifying yet compelling about all of this.

The Witch threw the wiggling, fiery branch into the water, and it dissolved in a violent flash of green light. She carefully took a glistening black bottle from her pocket and pulled the cork top off it.

She tipped the bottle carefully over, allowing a single drop of liquid to fall from it into the creek waters that still glowed green. She recorked the bottle, pocketed it, and stepped back. "Make your wish, oh mortal man!" she said and nodded to Luxurous.

Efscott inclined his head, frowning. "A mortal who is granted one of the three wishes by a Black Witch," he said softly as if talking to himself. "They say that you must eat a golden apple for this."

Brunt heard him clearly, though, and turned to his father again. "Can I have a golden apple, Father? So I can make a wish?"

Efscott shot him a cautionary glance. "Don't be so quick, child. All who eat the golden apple die."

"Then why is he alive?" asked the Blacksmith.

"Who knows," replied Efscott.

Luxurous reached into the leather bag on his shoulder and withdrew a glistening grey rock—the same chunk of lead that Minus had retrieved from the field—then stretched out his arm and dropped it casually into the green circle of water between himself and the Witch. In a way, it was a bit of an anticlimax. No grand gesture, just a dull plop. Even the townspeople below were disappointed. It sat motionless on the bed of rocks twenty inches under the surface.

The first small bubbles that emanated from it were unnoticed by the townspeople. But it didn't take long before the black stone glowed red-hot, and the water around it began hissing and frothing. The townspeople were once again transfixed by the ceremony. Luxurous took a deep breath. "I wish for gold!" he whispered.

His softly spoken words traveled over water and rock, and the townspeople below heard him clearly, as if the waterfall amplified this message.

The Witch kept her black-eyed gaze on the glowing stone between her and Luxurous, then pointed the top of her staff toward it. "Ashes to ashes, now dust to dust. Man's gold we make. In gold, shall we trust."

Luxurous reached into the water and picked up the same rock he had dropped, but it was no longer a dull grey chunk of lead. It was solid gold. He held it above his head, and the townspeople gasped. And for the record, this was already the highest amount of gasping the townspeople had ever done in one day—ever. They simply weren't accustomed to things out of the ordinary.

"What is it, Father?" asked Brunt, regarding Luxurous's gold nugget with wonder.

The Blacksmith was lost for an explanation. But Efscott was able to provide it instead. "Turning lead to gold. No magic trick here. Alchemy!"

"Black magic," Prudence added nervously. Her body was rigid, and her eyes were wide and attentive. "This Witch has the powers of a necromancer. And she is strong."

The Blacksmith was awestruck, and his voice softened in contemplation. "The gold made by man and magic! Man's gold. I've heard of this. It is even more precious than real gold," he said with a tone of wonder. "Stronger than even iron, they say … stronger than even iron …" his voice trailed off.

Luxurous stepped onto a large rock protruding beyond the waterfall's edge in the center of the creek. From this vantage point, everyone could see him. Minus entered the stream and stood behind him on his left, knee-deep in the creek water. The Witch stood behind Luxurous, on his right, her eyes returned to their normal state.

Luxurous held the gold rock between the fingers of both hands and lifted it above his head. And despite being a man with a whiny voice, he had an incredibly imposing presence. This was a man who felt he owned the world. And in a sense, he did. "I am wonderfulness itself!" he declared. "And I bring wonderful things. And in case it's not very obvious, I have conquered you today, for you are a *little* people."

There was a mixed look of indignation and defeat upon the faces of the townspeople. But none dared to protest. Luxurous continued, "But don't think of yourselves as my moronic pathetic slaves. More like … people who will do lots and lots of work for me. Because in a way, this wishing well is yours as well as mine. But you must work for it. You will not see your families much. But let's be honest, families are annoying, and gold is grand!"

The Feral Boy did not take great offense to these words because he didn't really consider himself to be one of the townspeople. But he was curious to see how others would respond to it.

The looks on their faces made it clear. They were absolutely stunned, as well as insulted, confused, and horrified. They probably wanted to gasp but were just too dumbfounded. Was their world turned upside down? Made better? Made worse? They weren't sure. They had never seen anything like this. And regardless of how they felt, they were clearly powerless to do anything about it. It was evident that they should just go along for now and be obedient.

Luxurous handed the gold rock to Minus, who placed it into the leather satchel. "Do as I bid, and I shall not kill you!" declared Luxurous.

His cool demeanor changed to a slightly awkward one, as if he was struggling to find the best way to conclude his speech. He cleared his throat and yelled, "So … thank you! You can all go back to your usual peasant business now. Any questions?"

The Baker raised his hand. He was a stout man with tiny dark eyes, a gentle plump face, and was always curious to learn new things, which was sometimes of detriment to himself.

Luxurous pointed to him. "Yes?"

"Umm … why do you have three dwarves pulling your giant carriage?" asked the Baker.

The King raised an eyebrow, and the people standing around the Baker backed nervously away for fear that someone might send an arrow in the direction of his rotund buttocks.

Luxurous replied in a very matter-of-fact way, "I like sad things." And with that, he shrugged and turned with a melodramatic flick of his cloak, then retreated from the waterfall's edge.

The townspeople eyed each other with disbelief, and the Blacksmith mumbled to himself, "Not the best speechwriter, is he?"

"Well, at least he's quick," replied the Potato Farmer.

The crowd dispersed, but the Blacksmith, Brunt, Efscott, and Prudence remained. Brunt eyed more of the dead frogs that floated past them in the babbling waters. He whispered to his father, "Didn't the last of the wizards write that the king who created gold would bring death to all land and mankind?"

The Blacksmith sighed and shrugged. "Maybe. Or it could be a spelling mistake on their prophecy scroll. They probably meant to say 'bring *dearth*' not 'bring death.' And dearth means scarcity. And King's Gold is very scarce indeed. Plus, prophecies are often …" he searched for the word, "missin-terprefide! That's it, missin-terprefide. I'm sure this King means well. He seems nice enough."

He looked over to a skeptical Efscott. "Welcome to Ashville, Carpenter," grunted the Blacksmith.

Brunt and the Blacksmith turned and strolled away. "Besides," said the Blacksmith to his son with another sigh, "there's not much we can do about it anyway."

Efscott took a deep breath. "Come, Prudence. We have much to do."

The Feral Boy bounded gracefully down from his tree, landing quietly on the soft damp grass. His eye was drawn to a slight movement beyond the grove. Above the eastern horizon, a dust cloud was rising. It seemed that more surprises were heading this way. The Feral Boy could tell by the formation of the billowing dust that the pack creating it was even larger than the army that had just arrived, but slower and more cumbersome. He was curious to know what it was, but something told him this was not the safest vantage point. He turned and made his way out of the grove.

CHAPTER FIVE

What's In A Name

Efscott slowly walked up the embankment, approaching the Ash Forest. He could see three horsemen higher up and farther to the right. They were close to the edge where the ground leveled out, about thirty feet away from the forest's tree line. They watched over the town below as a thousand carriages moved in, ferrying stone blocks that were being unloaded near the base of the waterfall. The giant wolf, Armageddon, stood guard with the horsemen. He was almost the size of a horse—a monster of a thing. The third Horseman, Busk, chewed on bread and cheese, grinning with cheeks full of food. "It's a pretty place to conquer, isn't it?" he said reflectively.

Behind, within the darkness of the forest, a pair of eyes watched them. And from these shadows, a thin rope suddenly shot out. A small tarnished hook was on its end. It latched onto Busk's saddlebag and whisked it away. It was dragged immediately into the forest, without a single person realizing it. But Armageddon noticed, just as the bag was swallowed into the woods.

The first Horseman nodded sleepily, still contemplating the comment from Busk. "Yeah. It's a very ... quaint town."

The others nodded. Armageddon growled, bared his fangs, and stood with the fur on the back of his neck rising. He prowled menacingly toward the tree line where the bag had been pulled in.

Busk elbowed the Horseman beside him, Grub, who was in charge of the attack wolves. Oddly enough, he didn't even like animals, especially Armageddon, who had a particularly feisty nature. Grub took more joy in inflicting pain on them, proclaiming that it made them more ferocious. The truth was, he just liked hurting animals.

"You better get him back," warned Busk. "The Witch says there's danger in that forest. The townspeople call it the Forest of Death. Say it's full of monsters. They won't go into it."

Grub surveyed the forest with an evil glint in his eye. "Monsters, hey? Well, I wouldn't mind seeing *that* fight." He chuckled and coaxed Armageddon onward. "Go on, boy, in ya go. What's in there, hey?"

Armageddon was still fixated on the tree line. He knew something lurked within.

In the hope of sending Armageddon into the woods, Grub snatched his bullwhip and unfurled it with a firm flick, cracking the tip upon Armageddon's back leg. Armageddon yelped and cowered while glancing back over his shoulder at Grub with sorrowful confusion.

Lightning fast, a giant Venus Mantrap lunged out of the forest and swallowed Armageddon whole with a loud snap. It immediately drew back into the woods with serpentine speed. The men recoiled, wide-eyed, and their horses whinnied in terror, reeling up onto their hind legs.

Busk looked pale and struggled to control his horse. "Let's move a bit closer to town, hey?" he suggested in a high, quavering voice.

"Yeah, just a bit closer," blurted Grub, as he kicked his heels into his horse's ribs and galloped down the hill, with Busk and the first Horseman following at breakneck speed.

The first Horseman looked over his shoulder, reflecting for a moment. "Fiercest wolf I'd ever seen. Gone in a flash."

"Good riddance anyway," snarled Grub coldly. "Stupid mutt didn't know how to take a beating."

They passed Efscott, who stood motionless, horrified by what he had just witnessed, his toolbox still rattling in his trembling hand. He began to turn away, then stopped. His eyes fixed on his carriage … home. As the color returned to his face, he regained his composure and made for the forest, albeit with a look of great apprehension. As he got closer to the forest's edge, he slowed, surveying it with even greater scrutiny.

A boy's voice suddenly rang out from within. "You shouldn't come any closer!"

Efscott stopped. He couldn't see who was speaking and addressed the disembodied voice through the forest's patches of eternal green, purple, and yellow.

"I'm in need of timber," said Efscott.

"Why?"

"To help the townspeople rebuild their roofs. It might rain tonight."

"The townspeople are stupid and cruel," snapped the voice. "Maybe they should all be rained on. Washed away."

Efscott pondered his next response carefully. "I must admit I am sometimes stupid myself. And indeed, the world has far too many cruel people. Kindness is hard to find, I'm afraid. And therefore, all the more precious."

"You should go back to your home!" insisted the boy, who was clearly not swayed by Efscott's appeal.

Efscott spotted a Venus Mantrap moving its head slyly between the trees on the forest's edge and toward him. It was twelve feet above the ground and about thirteen feet away from him. It growled, and Efscott took a few quick steps back. "Good day then," he stammered, then nodded despondently in defeat and turned for the town.

From within the shadows of the Ash Forest, the eyes that watched him slid out from the darkness. It was the Feral Boy.

He sighed as if unsatisfied by his win over Efscott, then turned his attention to the large Venus Mantrap that had swallowed Armageddon. Muffled whimpers and sporadic movement came from within the giant green jaws, as the wolf tried in vain to escape.

The Feral Boy stepped nimbly from a tree root to a boulder. He stretched up and grabbed the lower jaw of the plant and forced his fingers through its tightly sealed lips. He locked his left hand onto the lower lip and pulled with all his might. It growled with growing displeasure. The scuttling of many tiny feet swelled from a concerning noise to a vile tactile sensation as an intrusion of large cockroaches scurried over and up the boulder and ran up his legs. They continued up to his neck, biting hard and repeatedly. The Feral Boy instinctively brushed some of them away but quickly regained his composure, focusing on prying open the plant's jaws even more fervently. The cockroaches kept biting, but he ignored them and pulled harder. The Mantrap was not giving up its prey quite so easily though. It growled with disdain and shook its head violently, knocking the Feral Boy off the rock. He hit the ground hard with a dull thump.

He wheezed as he tried to inhale while slowly pulling himself up to a seated position. The air was knocked from his lungs, and his back still rang from the sting of the hit. He grabbed a pile of leaves and threw them at the Mantrap with indignation. The plant would always lock its jaws after nabbing its prey, and the subsequent upturned mouth from this now gave it the distinct appearance of having a mocking grin.

A sense of panic came over the Feral Boy. He knew that before the night was over, Armageddon would run out of air in the Mantrap's tightly sealed mouth, after which he would be slowly digested. And while the plant had beaten the formidable battle wolf fair and square in its own bid to survive, the Feral Boy still hated the sound of the wolf's sorrowful whining. It was crying for help, and those who were meant to care for it had abandoned it, which struck a deep chord with the Feral Boy. And while he had never felt pity for himself in his solitary life, he now felt something particularly odd: overwhelming compassion for something else. It swept over him like a hot wave and brought with it a sense of great urgency.

***

In the village, the drivers of the carriages continued to drop off their cargo of stone, and hundreds of soldiers worked together in chain gangs to move it. They dragged the granite to the base of the waterfall in teams of twenty men. The three dwarves worked in a group by themselves, pulling equally large blocks. The earth trembled and groaned under the force of all the construction.

The Potato Farmer watched with intrigue when General Pound walked past him, supervising some of his men in the construction. "Goodness," said the Potato Farmer with a

41

nervous chuckle, "it's lucky we weren't recruited to help. It looks like hard work."

"Of course you were not recruited," barked Pound. "You're a bunch of numpty buffoons. And have you ever built a castle?"

The Potato Farmer sheepishly shook his head.

"Of course not," snapped Pound, and with a mischievous grin, he added, "besides, they've got something else in store for all of you lot. Best to save your energy, lad."

Pound moved on, leaving the Potato Farmer, who now looked decidedly anxious.

The Witch barked orders at all the warriors and pointed the way with her gaunt index finger. They moved with slow, deliberate measure, and yet the fruits of this labor unfolded with unusual swiftness. It was a contradiction of time.

Construction was impossibly fast. It would typically take a year for such a creation, but with the supernatural powers of a Black Witch, it was made in less than a day. The massive split-level castle took full shape around the waterfall before the sun even touched the horizon.

Another gang of soldiers completed digging a moat around the castle's base, and the three dwarves pulled the King's carriage to its edge.

Water from the waterfall was channeled through aqueducts in the castle. Some of this was directed to the mouths of two large, stone gargoyles perched on the front wall, above the gaping solitary entrance. From here, the gargoyles vomited a constant stream of water into the moat.

Five crocodiles were coaxed out of their cage beneath the King's carriage onto a plank of wood, where they slid down into the moat with a mighty splash.

The townspeople marveled at the speed and enormity of it all. And as the sun sank beyond the horizon, the look of hope on many of their faces also disappeared. No doubt, it was becoming clear that from this day onward, they were no longer in control of their own lives.

***

At the front gates, a figure lay motionless in the dirt while the bustle of activity continued around him. It was Sir Sudley, still unconscious from his fainting spell. A butterfly fluttered down and settled on his large nose just as his eyes flickered open. He lifted his head, and it flew away. He rose sluggishly to his feet and stretched, then leaped back in shock upon seeing the town's latest home, a giant castle that enveloped the entire waterfall. It was proud, austere, and imposing. Nothing about it welcomed visitors. It was not only a reminder of Luxurous's power but, more importantly, that everyone outside the castle did not have any.

"Quick, aren't they?" said the Tax Collector as he sidled up to Sir Sudley, rubbing his chin. "They call it prefab granite. They have a Witch! She's a handy little minx."

Sir Sudley looked over his shoulder. Most of the townspeople were busy repairing their roofs. The Shoemaker limped past with a bucket of water in his hand and a bandage on his buttocks. The creek was now only half full.

The Tax Collector pointed to the moat. "Creek's been cut off. All the water goes into the moat now."

"Not all of it," said Sir Sudley, "otherwise it would flood." He pointed to the castle's circular tower and the flume of steam rising from its center. "They're boiling it," hushed Sir Sudley.

"What for?"

"I wonder myself." Sir Sudley stiffened upon recognizing the shape of the gold capitals that were being hoisted to the top of the columns perched upon the castle's flat rooftop floor. It

43

was the King's standard. The wreath of thorns clenched within a fist. "The Golden Fist. King Luxurous!" croaked Sir Sudley.

"You know of him?" asked the Tax Collector.

Sir Sudley nodded and yanked off his purple scarf. A giant scar was visible on the front of his neck. "He gave me this."

"He cut you with his sword?"

Sir Sudley blushed and gestured to the scarf in his hand. "No, he gave me the scarf; I actually cut my neck, shaving." He stared pensively into the purple folds of the weathered cloth. "It was his scarf. But he took something far more precious from me."

***

The Feral Boy could see Sir Sudley and the Tax Collector as he ran toward a pile of straw bales. This was the most challenging straw to steal because the chances of getting caught were highest. The Tax Collector was also a good shot at throwing stones, making it particularly hazardous. But it was the best straw for the task he had in mind. The Feral Boy stayed hunched over to avoid being noticed and trod lightly, reaching the bale. He was close enough to hear them now, even over the sound of his own labored breathing, which he tried to subdue. He began to tug at some of the straw, but the bales were recently packed, which meant they were pressed firmly together and bound by several ropes, making it hard to pull anything out.

"I was practically a boy," mumbled Sir Sudley. "I had been picking mushrooms in the field when the young Luxurous's carriage pulled up."

"You say you met him when you were a boy?"

"Well ... no. More like an older boy."

"Like ... how old?"

"Like ... twenty-five."

"You were a man?"

"Yes," Sir Sudley confessed, turning crimson, "I was a man."

"And he was ...?"

"About ten years old."

"Oh."

"But it's hard to overpower even a boy when he's the future King."

"I expect so."

Sir Sudley continued gazing at the castle, but with a degree of detachment. "He saw my puppy dog and asked me what his name was. 'His name is Skarfy,' I said. And then he laughed and said we should swap. 'Your Skarfy for my scarf,' he said, and he threw his scarf in my face and grabbed my little boy."

The Feral Boy raised his head and peered over the top of the straw bale. He paused for a moment, then returned to tugging harder on one of the ropes that bound the straw bale together, all the while hanging on each of Sir Sudley's words.

"He walked away with Skarfy, and the Black Witch came up to me." Sir Sudley's voice trembled, and his brow beaded with sweat. "She stood perfectly still, just staring at me as if waiting for something. I was terrified. I did nothing. And then ... I feebly asked young Luxurous if I could keep Skarfy instead. He turned and stared at me with the coldest of gazes that I will never forget. 'No,' he said calmly, 'he's white and fluffy and will make a perfect pair of mittens that I can polish my gold with.' And then he smiled."

"Goodness," hushed the Tax Collector.

"I couldn't believe my ears," said Sir Sudley. "I begged him to take anything else from me instead, but he refused. When I asked him why he needed to take Skarfy, young Luxurous replied very matter-of-factly, 'Because I like sad things.' And then I discovered why the Witch had been standing so close to me: a single tear ran down my cheek, and she reached forward and scooped it up with her fingernail, then dropped it into a small black bottle.

"So they took your dog and your tears. Not a good day for you, really, was it?"

"No," lamented Sir Sudley. "But I kept the scarf as a reminder to myself that one day I would ..." his voice trailed off as if he was searching for more appropriate words "... that one day I would do something to appease my guilt. Something worthy of Skarfy's memory." His gaze lifted again and fixed on the castle. "I never got my revenge though. I just got ... old."

"I wonder. What sort of a person likes sad things?" the Tax Collector asked pensively. Then he piped up with a burst of enthusiasm with his next bit of news. "Oh, the Witch granted him a wish too."

"I know. He wants gold," said Sir Sudley, who was heaving the damaged gate back onto its hinges by himself. He proceeded to mend its broken beams with well-tied strips of cloth. Tying knots was a skill he excelled at, acquired from many years of maintaining the dilapidated gates.

"Yes, gold," said the Tax Collector, who hadn't raised a finger to help and now rested his hands on his ample belly. "That's exactly what he wants. But they say you have to eat the golden apple to be granted this wish. But it's poisonous. Deadly! Wonder how he did it?"

"Tricked his twin brother into it," said Sir Sudley as he came to the Tax Collector's side, brushing the dirt off his hands.

"Oh!"

"When they were nine years old."

"Ohhh! I guess *that's* the sort of person who likes sad things."

They watched in silence as the final gold standard was heaved onto the last column. The sun was beneath the horizon now, and the town was blanketed in the ambiance of dusk. But the grandiose fist-and-thorn wreath had the vantage point of height, which meant that they still caught the day's last light from a sun that had already departed. The horizon's shadow rose up the standards, swallowing up each of the bright gold thorns until it reached the highest one and seemingly ascended into the nothingness of air.

The Feral Boy yanked a second rope loose on the large bale, finally giving him easy access to the tufts of straw. He reefed a large handful out, sweating and panting from the effort. The top layer was damp, and he was going to need dryer strands for his task. The Feral Boy discarded it and dove his hand deeper in.

The Tax Collector spotted him first and yelled, "Boy! Get away with you! Shoo! Shoo!"

The Feral Boy grabbed one last dry handful and hurried away, keeping his head low in case any stones were thrown his way.

The Tax Collector frantically searched for something to hurl, but the stampede of horses had pounded all rocks tightly into the soft earth. He huffed and puffed with frustration, and turned a disapproving glance at Sir Sudley.

"Why do you never help me scold him?" asked the Tax Collector. "Every strand of straw has some financial value, no matter how small."

Sir Sudley watched the Feral Boy retreating into town. His face was impassive. "I think that life has scolded him enough," he said softly.

CHAPTER SIX

Beneath the Book's Cover

T he Feral Boy grabbed a branch and some twine from the ground and continued slyly through the shadows of town, as dusk turned to night. He passed five Cuttorian horsemen, who were oblivious to his presence, and although the Feral Boy treaded with urgency, he listened intently.

The first Warrior grumbled as he shifted on his saddle. "I miss my mama's home cooking. And I don't really like the way the King talks to me. It's like he doesn't …" his voice trailed off as he searched for the right words.

Omar nodded. He was a massive monster of a man. "Doesn't appreciate that you've got feelings?" he proposed in a sympathetic tone.

The other warriors stared at Omar in astonishment. The first Warrior now found the words he had been looking for. "Doesn't have a larger financial vision for us … is what I was going to say."

Omar became notably uncomfortable. The second Warrior added dryly, "Anything you want to tell us, Omar?"

Omar shrugged bashfully.

Their voices faded in the distance as the Feral Boy stepped onto the road. Using his teeth, he tied the tuft of straw to the tip of the stick. He approached a group of the Baertic horsemen, with the pudgy-faced Busk among them.

"Truth is, burning down people's houses just leaves me feeling a bit empty, lately," lamented Busk. "I mean, I enjoy it, but what does it all mean? Besides, I'd really like to write my book."

The horsemen beside him nodded. The second Horseman looked a bit confused even though he was nodding. "What's a book?" he asked with some trepidation, for fear of looking foolish.

Busk replied proudly, "It's like a scroll but much fancier. It's the latest thing in the West. It has a cover too. It tells you what's inside before you even open it." The Feral Boy hurried passed them. Again unnoticed.

***

At the far end of town, just past the poo-wagons, stood Efscott's shack. It was small but quaint, and surprisingly sturdy, a simple thing of cloth and timber extending from their carriage, which served as the rear wall and storage area.

Efscott hammered some wooden shingles on the roof of the cottage next door. A little old lady, Mrs. Sudley, walked out of the front door and marveled at the work he had done. He descended.

Mrs. Sudley smiled meekly. "Please, I have a spare turnip. I insist you take it."

"Are you sure?" asked Efscott.

"I insist. I would give you more, of course, but the soldiers took most of our food. I have enough for my husband and me."

49

Mrs. Sudley handed the turnip to Efscott, which he took, nodding gratefully.

***

Inside Efscott's shack, Prudence stirred a small pot that sat on a clay oven. Efscott entered and handed her the turnip. "A turnip and a carrot." She muttered with a grin. "We'll eat like kings tonight, won't we?"

Efscott shot her a gentle, scolding glance, and she yielded politely. "I know—appreciate what you have."

She placed a lid on the pot and examined the stove's fire, which was getting lower, then peered over at the large basket nearby that contained only one small branch. She rose and ambled outside.

Across the road in one of the rubbish heaps, she found a discarded window shutter and enthusiastically picked it up, then made for home. Nearing her door, she noticed a figure emerging from the darkness farther down the road. It was the Feral Boy jogging in her direction. She paused.

"Watch out for him," came a voice nearby. It was their neighbor, Mrs. Sudley, sweeping the front doorstep of her cottage. "He's a cheeky one." Prudence stared fixedly back at the Feral Boy, and Mrs. Sudley eyed her with a grin. "But you like him, don't you?" added Mrs. Sudley. "You better be even more careful then," she said with a chuckle.

Prudence straightened her dress and stood a bit taller. "I don't particularly like him at all," she blurted. "He's terribly scruffy. And I don't have any time for thieves or cheeky boys."

"Oh yes, he is all that," added Mrs. Sudley with a grin, "never prone to self-pity though. A rare thing to find. He's a creature of the wild in that way, I suppose. Something regal

50

about that ... in its own way." Mrs. Sudley smiled at Prudence and retreated into her cottage.

Prudence gazed back down the road. The Feral Boy caught her eye, then smiled. She smiled in return, but it quickly faded to a frown—she had spotted a figure behind him. Approaching fast.

A large horse was galloping toward the Feral Boy, and he seemed oblivious to it. Perhaps the nearby sound of the workers unloading barrels obscured the sound of thundering hooves. The horse was now only a few feet away with no intention of diverting.

Prudence's eyes widened in horror, and she prepared to scream a word of warning when the Feral Boy nonchalantly stepped to the side and allowed the horse to whisk past. Prudence gasped with relief, but her fists remained tightly clenched by her side.

The Feral Boy grinned playfully back at her, having known all along that the horse was there. He had felt the vibrations through the ground first, and then the sound. He could even tell it was moving directly toward him. But he was curious to see how the new girl from out of town would react. Was she always so stoic and stern? Apparently not all the time. He crossed the road and made toward a pile of discarded ceramic containers.

She turned away with a huff and made for the shack, keeping a wary eye on the Horseman who continued thundering toward her. She paused by the doorway.

The rider drew closer. It was General Pound, and he held something large in his left hand—a wooden chair. He brought his agitated steed to a sliding halt at the front of Efscott's shack, just a few feet from Prudence.

Efscott emerged, with a mix of trepidation and attentiveness. His eyes searched anxiously for the cause of the commotion and the whereabouts of his daughter. Upon finding Prudence, he placed his hand gently on her shoulder, then stepped apprehensively out to meet Pound.

Pound lifted the chair. "Is this your work, Carpenter?" he barked.

"Yes," replied Efscott, clearly nonplussed.

"Your King would like you to know that he appreciates your ability to capture delicate grace and majesty!" Pound casually tossed the chair aside, and it smashed on the ground near Efscott's feet, splintering into many pieces.

"Thank you," replied Efscott in a hollow voice.

Pound handed a palm-sized wooden tablet to Efscott.

"An invitation," said Pound. "The King requires your services. You will help him, or we will kill your family. And your friends. And then you."

Efscott took the wooden tablet and inspected it. The royal standard was carved within. Engraved below were the words: *You are hereby summoned. Do as I bid and ...*

Efscott was perplexed by the incoherent message that covered the entirety of the wooden tablet.

Pound offered the solution with a gruff order. "His Majesty likes to build tension. Turn it over."

Efscott did and discovered the rest of the King's engraved message on the back. ... *I will not kill you. Hope to see you soon!*

"I see," muttered Efscott, shifting uneasily on his feet.

Pound turned his horse and galloped away.

Efscott inspected the invitation again, but movement across the road drew his attention. It was the Feral Boy, kneeling beside a pile of discarded clay oil canisters, with his arm extended deep between them. He was dunking his tuft of straw into an oil puddle that had been created from the accumulated drops of discarded vessels. He stood and darted across the road, passing Efscott and Prudence, with whom he exchanged a brief, awkward glance.

"Hello again, friend," said Efscott. "I have some oil if you need it."

"No, I'm fine," replied the Feral Boy as he strode purposefully along the gap between Efscott's shack and the Sudleys'.

Sir Sudley was returning home and approached Efscott. They watched as the boy retreated into the shadows, picking up his pace to a run. "Some of the townspeople say he was born of the forest," mused Sir Sudley, "created by the woods themselves. Others say he was just a crippled orphan, thrown into the deadly woods by parents who were ashamed of him."

"One thing's for certain," replied Efscott, "he's a survivor."

"And perhaps even more than that," said Sir Sudley thoughtfully.

They watched as the Feral Boy passed the refuse bonfire and stopped. He dipped his torch of straw into its flames, and with a whoosh, it ignited. He retreated swiftly from the lights of town, toward the creek, becoming a black shape within the darkness, silhouetted by his own torch that flickered in the cold evening air as he ran.

* * *

The rope was old, but it did the job. The Feral Boy fastened it swiftly around a tree trunk, then looped it around the Mantrap's neck as Armageddon let out an occasional whimper.

"It's okay, it's okay," the Feral Boy said reassuringly as he pulled the rope hard, then tied a knot, locking the Mantrap against the tree trunk. He grabbed his torch of burning straw from where he had safely wedged it between the thick roots of a large tree, and he lifted it to within a few inches of the Mantrap's mouth. "Let him go!" growled the Feral Boy, glaring defiantly up at the massive green clam-shaped head of the Mantrap. Its lips trembled and snarled, and its head jerked violently back in a bid to pull away, but the Feral Boy's rope held it firmly in place.

He knew the plants were reasonably resilient to fire, hence the need to make a torch that combined straw, oil, and wood. The hardwoods like ash always burned long and slowly, providing an excellent lighting torch, but they didn't offer the fast heat or copious smoke that he needed now. He had learned some years ago that this usually enticed the Mantrap to open its mouth.

The Feral Boy pointed the burning tip down so that the flames ignited the entire tuft of straw with a whoosh. It burned quickly, emitting a gush of smoke and searing heat. His hand twitched in protest as the flames licked closer to his skin. Still, he kept a firm grip on the torch and lifted the burning tip toward the Mantrap's lips, which squeezed tightly together, then tighter still, trembling now. Finally, with a hiss and a growl, it opened its jaws and spat out the giant wolf, which toppled onto the Feral Boy in a gunky mess. They both hit the ground together. The Feral Boy scooted back quickly, anticipating Armageddon's attack. Instead, the giant, terrified wolf coughed and shook off the green slime that covered him. His battle armor flew off, along with a shower of gunk, which splattered all over the Feral Boy. "Arghh, gross!" he moaned. Still seated, he backed up a bit more and stopped, forever apprehensive about making any sudden moves. "Go on, boy," hushed the Feral Boy. "Go home!"

He motioned toward the twinkling lights of town beyond the tree line, but Armageddon held the Feral Boy's gaze and whimpered softly. The colossal animal stood and approached the Feral Boy with slow, deliberate steps. The Feral Boy tensed, ready to spring into a sprint if needed. Armageddon came to his side, stopped, and sat down beside him. The Feral Boy was perplexed and rose very slowly. Even when standing fully erect, he was not as tall as the giant wolf. Armageddon's atypical large eyes, short snout, and long fur made him look surprisingly friendly and cuddly.

Regardless, the Feral Boy retreated into the forest while keeping a wary eye on Armageddon, who stood up and followed him. The Feral Boy stopped, and Armageddon stopped. The Feral Boy smiled, and Armageddon gave an excited woof, then wagged his tail.

The Feral Boy wondered what it might be like to have such a magnificent beast as a pet. And again, his mind drifted to the tiny bird that had died under his charge. The truth of the bird's death was, in fact, more sinister than just bad luck, and he knew it.

The Feral Boy had been careless, lazy, and selfish. He was aware that the fragile bird needed regular feedings, but he had gotten caught up with trying to make friends in town—trying to play games with them so that he might be liked. He had forgotten about the small bird, and it died.

He buried it without shedding a tear. Then, two days later, he broke down in the middle of the day and sobbed uncontrollably. It caught him off guard—an overwhelming emotion out of the blue. He knew he couldn't turn back time. It was over. A silly thing, he knew, because he hunted animals regularly so he could eat. But it was sad to adopt something only to betray it.

The Feral Boy took a shaken breath and approached the giant wolf ever so cautiously, getting nearer, then stretching out his hand. It was now within inches of the wolf's mouth and its dangerously long fangs. The Feral Boy lowered his hand carefully behind Armageddon's shoulder and gave an awkward light pat, and then a stroke. The wolf lurched forward, which caused the Feral Boy to tense up in dread. Had he made a stupid mistake to trust this monster? As soon as he felt Armageddon's tongue licking the side of his face, he realized with a laugh that he was safe. And even more importantly, he realized he had found a friend.

CHAPTER SEVEN

Something Familiar

King Luxurous sat regally on his throne, polishing a gold rock with a pair of white fluffy mittens. Two small ears jutted out slightly on the back of one hand, and a short tail hung from the other. They were unmistakably made from soft, fluffy puppy's fur. The nugget he was rubbing with absolute reverence was the one he had drawn from the creek.

Head bowed, Efscott stood humbly before him, with two burly guards behind. The room was grand yet stark, with high ceilings and a somber mood. Two large fireplaces were set on either side of the throne, from which the crackling of burning wood emanated, resonating in the chasm of the vast room.

"My son must soon rule in my place," Luxurous said crisply. "I plan to leave this town under his rule by winter's end."

Luxurous noticed movement to the side. "Oh, there he is."

Prince Perfeyn leaned out from behind a distant pillar but ducked back again.

Luxurous called out, "Come out, Perfeyn. Meet our Carpenter."

Perfeyn poked his head out once more and hissed.

"Hmmm. He likes to pretend he's a snake sometimes," Luxurous added.

"Oh," replied Efscott.

"Kids, huh?"

Efscott smiled and nodded politely.

Luxurous gestured toward the pillars where Perfeyn was still hiding. "And you see, here is my problem."

"That he thinks he's a snake?"

"No, you idiot—that he's painfully shy."

"Oh. And quite young to rule a kingdom … perhaps?" offered Efscott as meekly as he could.

"Not at all! Don't be so insolent!"

"Sorry, Sire," said Efscott as he bowed his head lower.

"I ruled my first kingdom when I was seven! Sentenced my first man to death when I was eight." Luxurous gazed into space. "Ah yes," he reminisced with a sinister smile, then pulled himself back to matters at hand. "Anyway!"

Luxurous rose from his throne and approached Efscott.

"I want you to carve a statue of him! Capture his inner strength." Luxurous studied Efscott's reaction as he spoke.

Efscott was intrigued. "But, I'm not a Stonemason, Sire."

A figure shuffled over to him from behind. It was the Witch. "Not from stone," she croaked as she stepped into the warm light cast from the fires. "Wood! Ash wood! You will go deep into the Ash Forest and take your wood from there."

"But … I have heard that it is death to enter the Ash Forest."

Luxurous bristled. "Would you deny your King this request?"

Efscott stiffened, and Luxurous stepped closer. "You have a daughter, don't you, Carpenter?" the King asked, his voice cooling to a more menacing tone.

Efscott nodded, surrendering his resistance.

"Wouldn't want anything to happen to her now, would you?" added Luxurous.

"No, Sire. But won't the wood perish in the rain if it is outside, Sire?"

The serpent around the Witch's neck hissed at Efscott.

"We shall coat it in gold," said the Witch. "Man's gold. Indestructible!"

She leaned in, glaring at him. "What is your name, Carpenter?"

"Efscott. Efscott Borelle."

"Why do I know that name?"

"I'm not sure, ma'am. I am but a simple Carpenter."

"Yes, he is simple," interrupted Luxurous. "Leave him alone, Witch. Thank you, Carpenter. Go now, and begin work on the sculpture immediately! Or you know, blah blah blah, I will kill your family, blah blah!"

Efscott bowed and left, very much aware that the Witch was watching him closely, every step of the way.

***

Efscott trod across the drawbridge, forlorn and weary, returning to the sparkling torchlights of town, forever with the helpless look on his face of a person struggling to find a solution to a significant problem, with no success.

***

The tower's rooftop floor had no walls or crenellation and provided a stunning view of the town and the Ash Forest below. It stood eighty feet tall, which meant it stretched forty feet above the waterfall it enclosed. Six stone columns encircled the tower floor's perimeter, adding a sense of royal enclosure. They were twelve feet high with more height gained from the gold standards perched above them, serving as their capitals. Four large, gold candelabra were placed between the columns, each eight feet tall with a nine-foot-tall ceremonial spear in their center.

A vibrant light flickered from the fire that heated the giant, defense oil pot located between the two columns at the rear of the floor, placed there so its boiling contents could be tipped down onto any encroaching enemy entering the courtyard.

A stone feature sat in the center of the floor—the wishing well. It had four stone gargoyles perched on its rim, with water arcing from their mouths into the well. A ring of fire burned brightly at the base of its round, tapered walls. The Witch methodically stirred the bubbling waters of the well- cum-cauldron with her staff as a plume of steam continually rose around her, twisting skyward. The same plume of steam that Sir Sudley had noticed.

Luxurous plodded begrudgingly onto the rooftop level via the large opening in the floor that was accessed by a stone stairwell leading up from the throne room. It was the only entry point. He had been interrupted from his nighttime bath and was wearing his royal bathrobe.

He clearly did not enjoy the long climb to the rooftop and made it clear when he came to the Witch's side, sighing melodramatically.

"What is it?" he spluttered.

"More visions of wood. The forest here is strong. I do not like it!"

She turned and surveyed the Ash Forest below with a troubled gaze. From its perimeter on the embankment, the woods stretched up to a peak that was almost half the height of the castle. Beyond the peak, the woods descended, but it was impossible to tell how far; fog and low-hanging clouds obscured whatever lay beyond.

"Hush, devil woman. Just tell me what you see!"

She returned to the wishing well, and her eyes turned a glistening black, and she examined the waters more closely. "A child I see, with a toy in his hand, will conquer the King and … rule the land!"

Luxurous cast a discerning gaze over the town below. "Easily fixed!" he exclaimed. "Only my son shall have toys." He raised his eyebrows. "Problem solved!" and pointed to himself with both thumbs, declaring proudly, "And that's why *I'm* the king!"

The Witch's eyes returned to their normal color. She smiled politely, then rolled her eyes as he departed.

***

The chopping of an ax cutting into wood echoed through the forest. A large, thorn-ridden leafless tree fell from the forest into the clearing. It wriggled under supernatural forces and came to life, taking the shape of a hand, after which it morphed again, this time into the form of a giant snake. It reeled around and lunged at a nearby tree, biting it hard with a thunderous cracking noise.

The Feral Boy's eyes sprang open. A nightmare. He didn't get them often, but there was something very unsettling about this King and his entourage, and it was clearly having an effect on him.

He sat up and caught his breath as the sweat on his brow cooled and dried. The final imagery of the dream was quite peculiar, but dreams had a tendency to be like that anyway. More intriguing than this was that the trees also talked to him in this dream. They seemed pragmatic and positive when they spoke and had no intention of raising concern. Regardless, the Feral Boy still felt he needed to be cautious about any carpenters who approached him.

The clatter of galloping horses grabbed his attention and promptly sharpened his mind from the haze of sleep that still lingered. He peered through the brush toward town, squinting and trying to discern the shapes within the darkness—men upon horses, carrying burning torches.

***

It was Pound and the other three Generals at the front, with the army of four hundred behind them.

They brought their charging steeds to a rattling halt outside the Blacksmith's home, and Pound drew a scroll of parchment from his vest. He unrolled it grandly and bellowed with an air of formality as he read it.

"'From this day forward to the end of the world, toys are forbidden!'" he barked.

The Feral Boy had made his way to one of the side streets close to the Blacksmith's home, where he watched curiously from the dimness of his vantage point, with an empty bag in his hand.

One of the guards nailed a sign on the Blacksmith's wall, with just two words inscribed upon it: NO TOYS.

The four armies charged through the town with battering rams and baskets.

They infiltrated the cottages, ransacking them and seizing all toys, even wrenching them from the futile grips of children.

62

Wooden horses, boats, dolls. And a kitten! Meow! A real one! Meow! Understanding his mistake, the soldier returned the kitten to the dumbfounded girl and ripped the doll from her pocket. A moment of silence. And then her tears came flooding.

The Feral Boy made his way to the southern point of the village and could see Prudence and Efscott emerging from their shack. They watched perplexed as the guards shoved by, barged in, and lumbered out again with a bag of Prudence's hand-carved figurines.

The soldiers and guards brought all the acquired toys in a wagon to the south perimeter wall and dumped them onto a freshly built bonfire, sending up a whoosh of flames and embers.

The cries of children fused with the crackling of the inferno that engulfed the very objects they loved. Inanimate items, perhaps, but in the minds of these children, they were the things they intuitively wanted to protect and nurture. And today they could not.

Pound concluded his speech in the amber glow of the bonfire, under the gaze of a very attentive and intimidated group of townspeople. "Any person who breaks this law shall be executed! Both the person who giveth the toy and also the person who haveth the toy!"

Pound's expression was passive as he rolled up the parchment, looking across the sea of sad faces. But his gaze lingered for just a moment on a young boy, perhaps only seven, whose dirty cheeks were streaked with dried tears.

Pound seemed out of sorts as he shoved the parchment into his vest pocket and turned his horse back toward the castle, walking at a slow pace, with four of his men following.

The Feral Boy felt that he recognized Pound's expression. It was that of a person dealing with shame—a familiar feeling since he had stolen Efscott's shiny chisel. But life was cruel, he reminded himself, turning and making his way home. The Feral Boy adjusted the bag on his shoulder, which was filled with discarded beef bones acquired behind the Baker's kitchen and a warm, elk heart pie from his windowsill. *Perhaps madness had indeed arrived in their town,* the Feral Boy thought to himself as his eyes flitted over at the departing soldiers. But Armageddon would eat well tonight, and that was a pretty good consolation.

CHAPTER EIGHT

Into the Heart

The following morning, as the sun was rising, Efscott and Prudence ambled past the bonfire that was in its final stages of consuming the wooden toys. The flames were lower now, but there was more smoke. Efscott had a small, two-wheeled trolley strapped to his back. He looked apprehensively up the hill at the Ash Forest, and Prudence squeezed his hand.

"I should come with you," she said.

"No, definitely not." He paused at the creek bed, which was now only a quarter full. "Stay here, and promise me that you will come no farther." He fixed her with a stern yet loving glance. She nodded reluctantly, and Efscott feigned a smile. He turned and made his way across the shallow creek, then up the grassy hill, with Prudence watching all the way, intently.

*****

Panting slightly, Efscott stopped only three feet from the forest's perimeter and glanced over his shoulder at Prudence, who remained at the bottom of the hill. Far behind her, through the haze of the bonfire's heat, Efscott spotted a figure. It was motionless. Dressed perhaps in a royal cloak of some sort, and looking in his direction. A shroud of smoke wafted between them, and the figure was gone. Efscott waved to Prudence and turned to face the woods once more. He took a deep breath—and stepped into them.

Shards of light broke through the canopy, illuminating the fall leaves, mist-filled air, and moss-covered earth, and creating a kaleidoscope of brilliant colors. He stepped warily forward. A twig cracked beneath his foot.

"I wouldn't step there if I were you," came the disembodied voice of a boy. The words came from every direction, bouncing eerily off the trees as if they spoke on the boy's behalf.

Efscott froze and was unsure where to look. He could not see the person nor even determine where the voice was coming from. Furthermore, it looked as if Efscott was having trouble finding his own voice. He tried to talk but stammered. Then took a deep breath and tried again.

"Where would you suggest I step?" Efscott asked.

"Back from where you came would be wisest," replied the voice.

"I met a wizard once ... a great man ... he told me this day would come."

The eyes that watched him slid slyly between the trees. It was the Feral Boy making sure he remained out of view while sizing Efscott up. No one had been brave or foolhardy enough to enter the woods before, and he was intrigued.

"All the wizards are dead," replied the Feral Boy.

"Indeed. But magic is not. And before he died, he told me I would meet a boy of the forest, and if that boy walked with me, it would be the adventure of a lifetime. That he would grow higher than any tree. Indeed, he would forge magic itself."

"That sounds like a prophecy," replied the Feral Boy. "I don't have much time for prophecies. They're for dreamers and fools."

"I thought as much myself. But sometimes … people change."

The Feral Boy mulled over this, but he was also thinking about his recent nightmare. And now seemed like the perfect time to share it. "I had a dream last night. The trees talked to me and said that if I followed a carpenter, I, too, would be cut like a tree. Should I listen to that dream?" He eyed Efscott carefully, anticipating a defensive response or denial.

"Perhaps. For great trees can actually be built into great things."

The Feral Boy was surprised by Efscott's reply. But a nagging doubt buzzed around inside his head. "What do you want? To cut me down? To cut all my trees down?"

"No. I need a wise man by my side who knows these woods. To join me on a mission."

The Feral Boy's nagging doubt was giving way to curiosity. "What sort of mission?" he snapped.

"I suppose it starts with … today. Building something. For the people."

"You want to risk your life in these woods, for that?" asked the Feral Boy.

There was a growing fragility in the boy's voice, and Efscott's reaction suggested that he noticed it. It was understandably unexpected because the boy clearly knew these woods well, and therefore wielded an enviable power. But what

Efscott didn't fully appreciate was that these woods were the boy's only sanctuary, a place where no one would berate, belittle, or attack him. The boy allowing someone into these woods and guiding them through its hazards was the equivalent of jumping off a cliff and hoping it worked out for the best.

Indeed, the boy was poised on the precipice of such a decision, a moment of commitment and absolute vulnerability. But he had not been convinced by Efscott's argument. And so the Feral Boy turned, preparing to leave.

"I have no choice, I'm afraid," added Efscott. "For if I fail, they will kill my daughter."

There was silence for a moment, and then a gentle ripple of distant birds singing and the rustle of wind in the leaves. And then movement—directly in front of Efscott! And finally, the Feral Boy slid out from behind a tree. He was silhouetted at first, but the light reflecting off Efscott's ax shone onto his face. Efscott smiled upon recognizing him. The Feral Boy met Efscott's gaze and leaned calmly against a tree. He took a piece of bread from the stolen saddlebag and bit into it.

"Are you hungry?" asked the Feral Boy with a mischievous grin.

Efscott spotted the embossed royal standard on the bag and chuckled.

***

Deeper into the forest now, they had been talking for some time, walking side by side and chewing eagerly on bread. The air was alive with movement and color as butterflies fluttered vibrantly around them, some with iridescent blue wings and others with emerald green. Twigs and leaves crunched loudly under Efscott's every step, while the Feral Boy's stride was almost silent. He would occasionally lift his arm and point the way with his stick, and Efscott complied, walking exactly where he was directed.

"What else did the wizard tell you?" asked the Feral Boy.

"That when I met this child of the forest, he should go on a quest to find the most magic of blades in the land. Worthy of forging a courageous prince."

"What blade? Where?"

"Ah, well, that he didn't tell me."

"What's his name then? This child of the forest."

"He didn't tell me that either," replied Efscott. He examined the boy's face as he asked his next question. "Why do some of the townspeople call you Urdin?"

The Feral Boy frowned. "Because they're stupid and mean."

Efscott raised his eyebrows, still wanting an answer.

"It means 'rage' in our language. 'Fury'," said the Feral Boy.

"You? Rage and fury?" replied Efscott with surprise.

"Sometimes I hit the townspeople because they make fun of me. Because I look …" the Feral Boy's voice trailed off, "… different," he croaked while avoiding direct eye contact.

"People can be foolish," said Efscott as he pocketed the rest of his bread.

"Not hungry?" asked the boy.

"For my daughter. Prudence."

The Feral Boy gave Efscott the remainder of his own bread. "She's a bit skinny," he said shyly. "It gets cold here in winter. She should eat."

Efscott smiled. Suddenly the Feral Boy swung a stick at his head. "Duck!" yelled the boy.

Efscott did exactly that. And—whack! A giant Venus Mantrap lunged at Efscott's head, missing by an inch, just as the Feral Boy's stick swept past and connected with the area beneath the Mantrap's mouth with spot-on accuracy. It recoiled with a hiss. The incident was all over within a second. Blindingly fast.

"Thank you. Again," remarked the slightly shaken Efscott. This was the fifth time the Feral Boy had saved him, and he always did it with such incredible speed and ease.

"That's okay."

Efscott adjusted the trolley strung to his back, hoisting it a bit higher as his eyes darted around his surroundings. "Surely it would be safer for you in the town. Why do you stay here?"

"No one laughs at me here," replied the Feral Boy in a colorless voice. "I know the safe places to sleep. Besides, there are no snakes here."

"No snakes?"

"No. The giant spiders eat them all."

Efscott shuddered slightly. "Oh! And you don't like snakes?"

"No. They scare me."

"Oh. Yes. Well, they scare me too," said Efscott, looking more pallid than before.

The Feral Boy looked pensively ahead. "A wooden statue is strange! Why choose the wood from this forest?"

"I suspect his Witch knows about the magical properties of ash wood."

"Magic?"

"They say ash trees have the power to inspire great courage. I'd say the King is hoping that his son will find some. Or inspire some. The alchemy of emotions, perhaps."

The Feral Boy stopped, contemplating something. And Efscott stopped too.

"Then we should go to Grandastal!" declared the Feral Boy.

"Grandastal?"

"That's what I call her. She's in the middle. Where it's most dangerous. Where it's most safe." The Feral Boy pointed to higher ground. Denser woods. Darker shadows.

He walked onward, stepping over a tiny creek. Its babbling shallow waters were only an inch deep but crystal clear. Efscott followed, surveying the canopy and tree trunks in a futile way, searching for dangers that he knew would move faster than he could react.

***

They ventured farther still into the forest where the dark soil and light grey rocks were blanketed in patches of soft green moss. The air was alive now with the ethereal movement of fireflies instead of butterflies, tiny orange orbs that floated majestically one moment then darted away the next. The trees here were predominantly ash and yew. They were larger than those on the outer perimeter, and the canopy of leaves above was higher and even more brilliant in the colors of evergreen and fall.

Farther ahead, it seemed as if the bark of one tree moved. It was a giant spider, the size of an infant, creeping along the lower branch of a yew tree that Efscott and the Feral Boy approached. Engrossed in conversation, they were oblivious to it.

"I'm sure the Prince will thank you very much for all this," said Efscott.

"I have heard the prophecies," said the Feral Boy. "They say that one day, a boy who some called a snake would become king and unite the lands. He will free the people and join man and land together again. Maybe this is him … this Prince who pretends to be a snake." The Feral Boy spotted movement above. "Duck!"

71

Efscott did so, just as the giant spider sprang toward him with its two huge fangs bared.

Whack! The Feral Boy nonchalantly thumped it with his stick, and it toppled to the ground then scurried back into the brush.

"Thank you! Once again," declared Efscott with absolute sincerity while shivering at the sight of the monstrous arachnid as it disappeared behind a tree. He regarded the Feral Boy with a look of wonder.

The Feral Boy smiled unassumingly and kept walking. It always seemed odd to him that people did not have the same reflexes as he, nor the knowledge of where to hit the plants and spiders to stop them in their tracks. But obviously his life had been spent surrounded by these menacing creatures that tested him every day, and as a result, he had developed the speed, knowledge, and skills that helped him survive. He had no first memory, and he had no recollection of arriving here. Here was always home.

Efscott regained some of his composure and wiped his sweating brow with a handkerchief. "And ... tell me ... do you want the people of Ashville to be conquered by this King, by this Prince?" he asked.

"No. I want him to be a good prince. Perhaps this ash wood will make him brave. Make him good."

"And what would a good king do?" asked Efscott, studying the Feral Boy with intrigue.

"Not what he wants," said the boy as he stopped and met Efscott's gaze, "but what he should."

Efscott was caught off guard, not only by the profound comment itself but also by how casually it was expressed. The Feral Boy pointed ahead to the right, and Efscott's jaw dropped.

Beyond the brush, some thirty yards away, stood a giant tree, resplendent with orange and purple leaves. Its branches reached out wide and proud, like a giant crown of wood upon the earth. The sky pushed through the canopy and lit the air that was alive with the serene movement of precipitation and specks of pollen. It was a place where air, light, water, and earth came together as one.

"Grandastal," declared the Feral Boy.

Efscott was in absolute awe. "What a thing of beauty." He then spotted something else in the branches and cocked his head, squinting.

"My home," said the boy, pointing to the disheveled cubby house halfway up the tree. "You're the only one to ever see it."

No sooner had he finished speaking when a section of the wall fell off with a clatter and clunk. The Feral Boy shifted uncomfortably on his feet as his face flushed red. He hoped that Efscott wouldn't laugh; even though the Carpenter's home was relatively modest, it was a castle compared to his. And perhaps the Feral Boy was not supposed to refer to his cubby house as a home. He wasn't really sure what a home was anyway.

"I'll have a bigger house … one day," the boy said. "It's just for now."

"It's a fine home," said Efscott warmly. "Hard to build. Up there. You did very well."

The Feral Boy smiled and shrugged. They strolled toward the tree, over the dark soil that was scattered with fallen leaves. There was a stillness in this part of the forest unlike anywhere else in the woods. The birds here were fewer and larger. with formidable talons. Their song was surprisingly quiet and serene; more of a trill that resonated off the trunks and canopies of the mighty trees. Efscott and the Feral Boy treaded over a shallow stream that cascaded down three tiers before pooling in a deeper basin, where it ended. The water from this point flowed into a crevasse about one foot long, channeling into a series of natural underground aquifers.

Efscott gazed admiringly up at the great tree that now towered above them, examining the lines of the trunk and branches. An ominous growl prompted him to halt. He turned slowly to face a giant wolf, rising to its feet.

"It's okay. He's friendly," stated the Feral Boy, who patted Armageddon on the head.

The wolf responded with profound affection, burrowing the top of his head into the Feral Boy's chest. The boy was knocked slightly off balance and chuckled, then he emptied his food satchel in front of Armageddon, who wagged his tail, licked the boy's cheek with a loud slurp, and dove into devouring the food.

"What's his name?" asked Efscott.

The Feral Boy wiped his face with his sleeve and paused before giving the answer. He knew that Armageddon had no desire to return to the numerous beatings and absent affection awaiting him in Luxurous's army, so it seemed appropriate that he should mark the commencement of a new life with a new name. "Slipnor!" said the Feral Boy with a grin. "His name is Slipnor."

Armageddon, now Slipnor, gave a jubilant woof that implied his total approval.

CHAPTER NINE

My Name is Arakin

Efscott diligently surveyed the tree again.

"How do you choose?" asked the Feral Boy.

"Hopefully I can see the statue's shape within," said Efscott as he circled the tree, still in awe. "And it should be a piece that, once removed, will detract little from the health and beauty of this grand tree." He paused and ran his hand over the bark. "Interesting," he muttered. "She is an ash tree, no doubt about it. But her shape is similar to a yew tree."

Slipnor finished his meal and, with his tail wagging, came to the Feral Boy's side, towering over him until he gently lowered his giant fury forehead onto the boy's chest again. The boy gave him a gentle rub behind his ears, and Slipnor responded with a contented rumbling purr. The wolf then leaped back and lowered his chest to the ground while keeping his rear up high, his tail now wagging even more frenetically.

The Feral Boy knew that this meant he was keen to play, which was encouraging, given that the wolf had been very frail overnight after his release from the Mantrap. The boy grabbed a branch from the ground, and Slipnor immediately crouched in anticipation, like an arrow about to be shot from a bow. The boy flung the stick higher up the hill toward the stream and a shrub dotted with bright orange berries, and Slipnor burst into a sprint after it.

The Feral Boy had been using the game of fetch as a way of teaching Slipnor the safer paths around the forest. Even though he was planning to keep Slipnor with him at all times, he still wanted the giant wolf to be capable of finding water and food on his own, once he was more rested, in case he ever needed it. The Feral Boy would have to go into town occasionally anyway, which meant leaving Slipnor behind, as much as that pained him. The two were quickly developing a powerful bond.

Efscott continued his surveillance of the tree, scrutinizing one branch in particular. It was shorter and thicker than the others, and also the lowest. It curved downward from the trunk and then hooked up slightly. Efscott nodded approvingly. "Thank you," he whispered as he patted the branch. He ran his hand over the bark with reverence. "I promise I will make something worthy of you."

***

A soft wind blew as Efscott scaled the tree and treaded carefully along the branch he had selected. The Feral Boy circled the tree below and placed his hand on its trunk as if assuring a friend that everything would be okay.

Efscott lifted his ax, took careful aim, and chopped into the branch, making precise cuts with each blow.

Slipnor, with the stick proudly in his mouth, came dutifully to the Feral Boy's side and flopped down at his feet. The Feral Boy could see that Efscott would take some time, and so he kept himself entertained by hitting an acorn with his stick, ricocheting it off the tree trunks around him. The acorn hit the same three trees in the same spot each time before returning to him. He would then alternate from a forehand hit to a backhand swing, sending the acorn in the opposite direction. He did this with effortless grace and musical rhythm, blindingly fast, and with precision, born from a life of survival alone in the deadly forest. Even the games he had created for himself, such as this, bolstered the abilities he needed to survive. Hand-eye coordination, hearing, and focus. He managed to do all this while keeping an occasional eye on Efscott and the branch he was cutting into.

Efscott soon adopted the same rhythm in his chopping that the Feral Boy set with his acorn. "You've been very kind to me," said Efscott. "Are you always this kind to people?"

"No."

"Oh. And why so for me?"

"You have kind eyes. And ..." the Feral Boy thought for a moment, "... your daughter seems nice."

Efscott chuckled. The Feral Boy looked away shyly and snatched the acorn as it ricocheted back to him at high speed. He spotted movement in the distance and gazed with wonder at a beautiful leaf that floated gently down from the ash tree. Slowly it fell. He marveled at not only its beauty but also its mechanics. It was birdlike in the way it majestically caught the wind.

The Feral Boy added, "Kind eyes usually don't last long in this town though. So you should be careful."

Efscott cut through the final section of the branch, and it peeled away, falling to the ground with surprisingly little noise.

Efscott descended the tree, and on the ground again, he rubbed the thick branch, studying its shape. "Perfect," he declared softly. He chopped away some of the smaller, extraneous branches for easier transport of the large log.

"So tell me, are the townspeople really that bad? Do I need to be so careful?"

The Feral Boy deftly rolled the acorn along the edge of his paddle. "They make fun of me. But I'm better with the paddle than all of them."

"I'm sure you are."

"They hate being beaten by a cripple. And I hate them! I hate them all!" The Feral Boy eyed a leaf that fell from a branch some thirty yards away. He flicked the acorn up and, with brutal force, hit it with his paddle, sending it through the gaps of tree trunks and entanglement of branches, straight through the center of the falling leaf and deep into the bark of a distant tree with a thud. A display of incredible power and accuracy. Efscott regarded the Feral Boy's reaction with both compassion and concern.

***

Efscott hauled the hefty stump behind him on his small wooden trolley, with the Feral Boy walking beside him, occasionally darting ahead to move a branch that obstructed his path or assisting by hoisting the wheels over a large rock or root. They talked. They laughed. And sometimes they were quiet, just appreciating the majesty of the forest.

"Stunning," hushed Efscott. "I feel sometimes that I have stepped into a painting created by a true master ... so beautiful ... simply amazing. And then I realize that the only reason I survive in these woods is because of you, young man. These woods would devour me in an instant if I were alone. But I am so glad that I have been given the chance to appreciate it for all its beauty. Ahhh, and now I am rambling," said Efscott with a laugh. "I suppose I am overjoyed and relieved. What a day … what a day."

The Feral Boy smiled modestly and, with his foot, brushed a small rock away from the path of the trolley's wheels. He liked Efscott and was relieved to hear his genuine admiration of the forest. If Efscott had expressed a dislike for the woods instead, the boy would have definitely felt offended, as if someone had criticized a member of his family. This forest had protected him, after all, even though it challenged and sometimes fought with him. But in the end, that is what families sometimes did too. The Feral Boy had only ever heard people talk negatively about the forest because of its dangers. This made sense because they hadn't ever been inside and felt safe. Were they capable of appreciating its stunning beauty though? Efscott clearly was. And his comments were similar to someone complimenting the Feral Boy on how amazing his mother was. And they would be right; she was indeed all of that. And more.

Peering ahead, the Feral Boy could see the first glimpse of the sky through the distant curtain of trees and branches, and then a sight of cottage roofs. No doubt, Efscott would be feeling a sense of anticipation right now, and the look on his face confirmed this.

They stopped at the edge of the forest and could see Prudence, still standing where Efscott left her. She had not moved. She saw her father and burst into a sprint, dashing across the creek without even trying to keep her feet dry on the stepping stones.

Efscott turned back to the Feral Boy. "Well … I am so grateful to you, young man," he croaked with a warm smile.

"Arakin," the Feral Boy replied softly.

"Sorry?"

"Arakin. My name is Arakin … now."

Arakin watched Efscott closely, wondering if it met with his approval. He never had a name before because he never needed it. It seemed practical to have one now, though, because he had a friend. But he wasn't sure if he had done this right. How do you get a name if you do not have a parent or guardian who bestows it upon you? Was he making a fool of himself?

"A perfect name!" declared Efscott.

Arakin beamed.

"How did you come up with that?" asked Efscott.

Arakin shrugged. "It's the noise the forest makes when it wakes me up in the morning."

"Well, Arakin of the Ash Forest, thank you again. I am eternally grateful."

Arakin grinned at hearing the title, but something else was weighing on his mind. He reached into his leather bag and pulled out a small object wrapped in a cloth, which he unfurled. "I think this is yours. I found it." Slightly abashed, he handed it to Efscott. It was his chisel—the one Arakin had stolen earlier.

Efscott chuckled with immense relief and took it. "Ah, yes. Well, that was lucky. My favorite chisel. I really did miss it. Perhaps you have to lose something before you truly find it. Thank you, Arakin. Very kind of you."

Arakin felt his cheeks blush slightly and hoped that Efscott didn't notice. He wondered if the Carpenter knew that he had stolen it. Something in the Carpenter's grin and final remark suggested he did, and yet he wasn't the least bit angry. Arakin shoved his hand deep into the pocket of his pants and shifted his weight self-consciously on his feet.

Efscott nodded a final farewell to Arakin and was preparing to turn but stopped. "Tell me, what would you want," asked Efscott, "more than anything in the world?"

Although Arakin appeared stoic, he glanced away furtively, then met Efscott's gaze again. "Two arms," replied Arakin. Then he shrugged, smiled, and turned.

Efscott smiled sadly and nodded. He turned and stepped through the tree line of the forest and onto the grass that signified safety. Prudence sprinted up and hugged him with such gusto that it almost knocked him over.

Arakin watched them pensively through the dense scrub. *This is what family truly was*, he thought to himself. He was beginning to understand it better now.

***

The sun had set by the time Efscott and Prudence returned to their shack. Prudence was wolfing down some of the bread Efscott had given her, relishing every bite. She took the salted beef out from the satchel and wrapped it in cloth, then peered cautiously through the shutters of a window. "I still think it was a risk, taking stolen food from that boy." She placed the beef in a cold box and put the bread beside it.

"His name is Arakin," replied Efscott.

"Arakin," she repeated, reflecting on the name. "It was very kind of him though," she said as she closed the cold box and wiped her cheeks.

"It was indeed." Efscott's grin faded as his eyes settled on something in the distance. Through the narrow crack of the window shutter, he could see the smoldering bonfire of charred toys. He placed the shiny bronze chisel on his bench and stared thoughtfully at it, then took a deep breath and locked the shutters.

***

81

Efscott tapped earnestly on a small block of ash wood with the shiny chisel. He chipped, shaved, and peeled away at the hard timber with the finesse that only an extremely experienced carpenter possessed.

Efscott worked into the night, a picture of concentration, as the room became vibrant with the scent of ash wood. Prudence brought him a bowl of broth but frowned when she saw what Efscott was working on. It clearly worried her. He tried to reassure her with a look, but it did little to help. "You should sleep, darling girl."

"You should be careful, darling father," she replied anxiously, as she placed some bread down beside his broth.

CHAPTER TEN

A Dangerous Gift

As dawn pushed its ambient orange glow over the horizon, a lone figure draped in a purple-and-black cloak made its way down the main road. It was the same figure that Efscott had seen behind Prudence just before he entered the forest. The shape slid to the windows of each cottage and peered in. Perhaps hoping to find a secret of some sort.

It was Minus. He was mumbling to himself.

"Spy Chief ... no ... Spy Captain. Yes, yes, Spy Captain! That's a title with a ring to it. Prove special skills, earn a special title, well done Minus old boy ..." his voice trailed off, and he cocked his head, his attention now drawn to the faint sound of hammering coming from Efscott's shack.

Minus approached with stealth and peered curiously through a crack in Efscott's wall.

His eyes narrowed, his face twitched, then he spun on his heel and scurried back up the street, wheezing and grunting excitedly.

***

Efscott trudged up the hill to the edge of the forest, keeping one hand firmly on the flap of the tool bag that hung from his shoulder, his back laden with planks of timber strapped securely in place. Unlike his trek toward the forest yesterday, he was enthusiastic and jovial.

***

Efscott spent a good half of the day refurbishing Arakin's cubby house, repairing the broken wall and finishing up with some shingles on the hole-ridden roof that had previously been made of straw. It looked sturdy and cozy by the time he banged in the final nail.

Arakin watched intently from a higher branch, fascinated by the way Efscott worked—cutting, hammering, and shaping different objects into a cohesive, functional whole. It was a kind of magic in its own right.

"It's good," said Arakin with a huge smile.

"Fit for a king," said Efscott casually, as he descended the tree cautiously. Arakin, meanwhile, bounded down effortlessly.

At the bottom, Efscott pointed to his bag, "I have something else for you. A gift."

"A gift?" asked Arakin innocently. He understood the word, but it caught him off guard. No one had ever given him a gift before.

"A present," replied Efscott. "Something a person gives to another person without expecting anything in return—like when you gave me the food yesterday, or when you stopped the giant spiders from attacking me."

Arakin smiled modestly and shrugged.

Efscott's expression became more serious. "But I must point out that this gift is quite dangerous. To me. To you. And to my daughter. You must be very, very careful with it. Show it to no one. And never bring it out from the forest."

Arakin nodded earnestly, and Efscott reached into his bag.

"And maybe you are too old for it. The age of toys is perhaps behind you, though it is more than just a toy, I think. To give it life is an art in itself."

Efscott drew something out, and Arakin craned his neck, dying to see what it was. Efscott handed the intriguing beige-colored object to him.

It was a wooden puppet, twelve inches tall, carved in the shape of a grinning warrior adorned in elegant armor. He had a bow slung over his shoulder, a quiver of arrows upon his back, and a sheathed sword. Strings led from its joints to a crossbeam control-handle and five wooden rings.

Efscott had designed it so that it could be operated with one hand. More than a puppet, it was an extraordinary work of art. Arakin stared at it with absolute wonder.

Efscott gave a quick demonstration, and the puppet sprang to life. Arakin laughed with the utter joy of a true child, and Efscott quickly handed the controls to him. Arakin hurriedly slipped his fingers under the crossbeam and into the five rings, and the puppet immediately came alive to his touch.

"I have two arms after all!" Arakin yelled.

"Indeed. He doesn't have a name yet. What do you think?"

"Ash! His name is Ash!" declared Arakin.

"A good choice! He's like you. He's from the forest. A fighter. But he will need your wisdom to be guided," said Efscott thoughtfully. "And perhaps he is too courageous, too angry. He needs your help, Arakin."

Arakin guided Ash into a low squat and sent him into a leap, making Ash move with an incredibly lifelike quality. Arakin brought him to a pose with both fists on his hips and laughed, with Efscott joining in.

Efscott clearly relished seeing him behave like a boy. A happy boy.

Slipnor barked cheerfully at the puppet, then tilted his head slightly. He wasn't sure what to make of it.

Efscott stood up and slapped his thighs in that universal way that says, *it's time for me to leave*.

***

As Efscott exited the forest, the sun was sinking beyond the horizon behind him. He made down the hill toward home, searching for Prudence in twilight's fading light, but she was nowhere to be found. He quickened his pace, and as he drew nearer, he made out several figures surrounding his shack: horsemen. Seven in total.

Prudence sat on a stool at the front of their home, with her head bowed. The horsemen that towered over her seemed to be asking questions.

Efscott dropped his tools and ran straight toward Prudence, spotting the occasional movement of more burly horsemen inside the shack who were ransacking the place, hurling clothing, pots, and pans through the windows and front entrance.

General Pound was closest to Prudence, and upon spotting Efscott, he ordered his men to charge forward on their horses. Minus was also on horseback, and he followed Pound, who marched his horse up to the dumbfounded Carpenter.

Another Horseman followed them, drawing a tiny wagon upon which was a large steel cage. The wave of coordinated fury was quickly upon Efscott, and he was soon surrounded by the thumping clatter of angry hooves.

86

Minus pointed at him. "This man!" he declared.

The four horsemen surrounding Efscott leveled their spear tips at his head. Another two dismounted, grabbed his arms, dragged him to the cage, and hurled him in.

"What is this?" asked Efscott desperately.

He fell hard on the cage floor and was visibly shaken and stunned. Prudence, by now, was pushing her way between the horsemen but was stopped by Pound, who grabbed her. "Steady, lass," he said calmly.

No, please. I beg you," Prudence exclaimed.

Efscott was trying to get his bearings and spotted Prudence off to the side. The cage lurched forward as the horse broke into a trot, and Prudence watched helplessly as Efscott was ferried away.

Three horsemen led the charge to the town's center, with the Carriage-Horseman following, and three more horsemen close behind. All were in tight formation, moving swiftly and in harmony with each other.

"Papa! Papa!" screeched Prudence as they pulled away.

CHAPTER ELEVEN

Two Arms of Gold

Arakin sat cross-legged on a rock about thirty yards within the forest's perimeter, munching on the last of a yellow apple while Slipnor, close by his side, finished off some beef. Arakin was industriously attaching a piece of square cloth to the puppet's crossbeam handle with a length of finely woven twine. He had marveled at how falling leaves could float or fall based on their position and was convinced, like all young boys, that he should conduct some action experiments of his own. He did indeed love the ability to control Ash, but what he loved even more was the feeling of being able to set him free.

"Trust me, Ash," he said softly, "I'll catch you. Besides, you don't want me telling you what to do all the time, do you? This way, you're totally free. And you'll want to be free because the next few days especially are going to be filled with high adventure! Get ready!"

Arakin slid off the rock and brought Ash closer to his face. "Good luck, Sir Ash."

He leaped up and tossed him as high as he could, sending him hurtling into the sky. For a moment, Ash was weightless as he hit the apex of his climb, then whoosh, he plummeted back down to earth, spinning slightly off course. And as he fell, Arakin's concern rose.

He braced himself, ready to dive into the thorn bushes if necessary. Then with a whoop, the makeshift parachute Arakin had attached to the handle popped open and caught the air within. Ash floated gently down, straight into the outstretched hands of Arakin, who giggled with wide-eyed fascination and delight.

"Told you!"

The distant screams of a girl cut his laughter short. He inclined his neck and peered through the brush and over the rooftops of the village below. To his horror, he saw Prudence scrambling down the street, with the royal prison-carriage barreling ahead of her—and Efscott captive within. He stiffened in terror. "No!" he said in a hushed voice.

Rage overwhelmed him of the kind he had never experienced. He'd been angry before. But not like this.

He gritted his teeth and sprang over a rock, but something dawned on him, and he froze and then spun to face Slipnor, who was close behind. Arakin realized his loyal friend would follow him, which would only make things worse; the army would surely retake possession of him, and he would be back to a life of taking regular whippings from his handlers. "Stay! Stay!" he bellowed.

Slipnor whined but sat down dutifully, albeit with some shifting on his front paws. Arakin bolted through the thorn bushes ahead, over rock, ditch, and tree stump. Lightning fast!

He exploded out of the woods and bounded down the embankment as if his life depended on it. "No," he pleaded. "No!"

***

In the center of town, two guards drove a long wooden spike into the ground. A forlorn Efscott sat in his cage nearby as Minus prowled around it, glaring at the townspeople who were giggling. He was clearly flustered.

"Firstly, my job is very important!" he barked. "So don't laugh at my job title. Secondly, you better listen up, because it could be you next! General Pound, continue!"

A Guard nailed a sign onto the wooden pole, with the following words upon it: EXECUTION NOTICES— EFSCOTT BORELLE.

Pound unraveled a scroll of parchment and read in a booming voice, "'Carpenter Efscott Borelle, you are guilty of a crime against the King. You shall be sentenced to death on the third afternoon from this night, upon the midday.'"

There were murmurs and gasps from the crowd. An arrow in the butt was one thing, and so was being conquered by a pompous dictator, but executing someone was a whole new level of scary.

Pound continued reading. "For you are guilty of breaking the King's law, Efscott Borelle! You are guilty of making a toy!"

The King galloped in with Prince Perfeyn close behind, wearing a suit of absurdly ornate gold armor embossed with snakes and thorns.

Prudence pushed through the crowd toward Efscott, with tears streaming down her face. She burst through the front line, but the Blacksmith grabbed her and pulled her close. "There's nothing you can do, child," he said compassionately.

She stepped back, and he eased his grip on her, assuming it was safe to do so. But something was clearly weighing heavily on Prudence's mind. She took a deep breath. Her arms stiffened, and her hands curled into fists. She exhaled a heavy sigh, and her entire body began to tremble. Efscott met her gaze and grabbed the bars of his cage desperately, shaking his head furiously.

No, he mouthed.

No one else really noticed the exchange. It was perhaps just seen as a daughter holding back tears and a father telling her not to worry. Little did they know that something far more formidable was going on under the surface.

Prudence acquiesced and relaxed. Her fists unfolded. She nodded to her father. And she wept.

The Witch skulked around Efscott's cage, leering in at him.

***

Arakin could see the crowd milling around the cage as he continued his sprint across the creek that was now bone-dry. Though his legs were numb and starting to wobble slightly from the intensity of his effort and his lungs were screaming for air, he kept pushing. Confusion and rage bubbled like a storm inside him. Would he grab a rock and bludgeon the soldiers with it, or claw his way through them to get to Efscott? What was he thinking? He knew he couldn't overpower Luxurous's men, but he had to do something. He also needed to think more clearly and be more realistic. He needed to be smarter than this.

But why did they even arrest Efscott? What could he have done that was illegal? Was it because he made …? Arakin slid to a halt upon a horrifying realization. If it was because they suspected Efscott had made a toy, then Arakin was running straight to them with the evidence. He was still holding Ash, the puppet.

"Stupid!" muttered Arakin, berating himself.

He had to think fast. Retreating was not an option. He wasn't going to abandon the one person who was kind to him. Call it conscience or perhaps instinct, he didn't fully understand where the drive came from, but it was clearly commanding him to be there—with Efscott and Prudence. He wondered if he should drop the puppet now, though this came with the risk of someone finding it. And when he looked into the eyes of the small wooden knight, he was met with an expression that seemed to plead with him, *keep me close by*. Once again, it was as if the Ash Forest was talking to him, even if it was from just a small slice of one branch.

***

Leering through the bars of the cage, the Witch gazed deeply into Efscott's eyes, then slowly turned, looking menacingly over her shoulder, searching for something—for someone. And she spotted it through the crowd. Prudence. Her snake hissed.

"Yes. Interesting," croaked the Witch.

She waddled toward Prudence, who remained still. Terrified, yet also defiant. The Blacksmith took his hand off her shoulder and stepped aside. She was on her own.

The Witch studied Prudence carefully. "Something very interesting is hidden in your eyes, dear!" The Witch loomed over her, and the snake hissed louder. "I don't like her either, pet."

Whoosh! The snake lashed out, opening its jaws and bearing its fangs, straight toward Prudence's face.

Thunk. Out of nowhere, Arakin's arm blocked it.

The snake bit deeply into his forearm, leaving large puncture wounds in his sleeve. Arakin tripped, hitting his head hard on a rock, but he tried to stand immediately. His vision dimmed, and his legs weakened. He stared up into Prudence's eyes, then blacked out and collapsed onto the earth.

Prudence and the townspeople stiffened in terror with mouths agape. The Witch lingered over Arakin's seemingly dead body, then looked back at Prudence with growing curiosity. The King noticed this and brought his horse closer. "What is it?" he asked, with a hint of anxiety creeping into his voice.

"I thought I saw magic in her eyes. But I think now … it was just luck, masquerading as such." She eyed Prudence coldly. "Today, he dies for you. Your lucky day." The Witch glanced down at Arakin. "Him … not so much."

Luxurous looked Prudence up and down carefully. "Is she the one in your vision?"

"No." replied the Witch, calmly.

"Perhaps we should kill her anyway, to be safe," suggested the King dispassionately.

"The snake is docile, and so we will wait a while," the Witch replied.

"Please, just in normal English!" snapped Luxurous.

The Witch, growing impatient, snapped back, "If you place faith in the black arts, then you must kill only those who are in the vision! But do not force the snake to kill willy-nilly, or it upsets the balance and—"

"All right, all right!" blurted Luxurous. "A simple 'no' would suffice. Goodness me!"

The townspeople were awkwardly silent, like children watching their parents fight. Luxurous eyed Arakin's motionless body. "Are you certain it was a warrior child with *two* arms who would try to destroy me?"

"Yes! Two arms! A boy with *two* arms of gold! I told you!"

It dawned on everyone in the village that there was indeed a young boy nearby with two arms of gold. All eyes settled on Prince Perfeyn, sitting high in his saddle, dressed in—gold armor.

As if raised from a deep sleep, Perfeyn gazed dopily back at his father and the Witch and asked, "What?"

"Ooooh, that's awkward," mumbled the Fishmonger.

Luxurous weighed this all up and waved a dismissive hand. "Pfft!" He turned his horse and made for the castle, at which time the penny finally dropped with Perfeyn. He was immediately indignant that his father had so readily dismissed him as being totally incapable of usurping him.

"What's that supposed to mean?" whined Perfeyn as he turned his horse to follow Luxurous. "I might overthrow you. I could be extremely naughty—"

"Quiet!" barked Luxurous.

"Sorry, Father," replied Perfeyn in a chastened tone. His downcast glance darted self-consciously over the crowd parting before him, and he noticed a young girl close by, about seven years old, staring fixedly up him. Perfeyn clearly didn't appreciate the look on her face and kicked his foot out, hitting her squarely in the shoulder, which sent her tumbling into the mud. "Sorry," he snarled sarcastically. "Old war injury. Foot's got a mind of its own. I just can't seem to control those royal reflexes."

Pound followed Perfeyn, and the guards followed suit with Efscott's cage-wagon pulling into line behind them. The show was over, and the townspeople slowly dispersed. Prudence

watched Efscott disappearing down the road and then cast her
mournful glance down at the lifeless form of Arakin at her feet.

95

CHAPTER TWELVE

From Ash, Courage Rises

The Blacksmith pushed a wooden wheelbarrow with Arakin's lifeless body within, as Prudence walked beside him, still in shock, her head bowed. The wheelbarrow creaked and rattled softly over the gravel strip. The faint crackling from cottage fireplaces could be heard on the otherwise quiet road as dusk's orange glow gave way to evening's cold light, and a shroud of smoke wafted in from low-set chimneys farther ahead.

"We should throw his body into the fire straight away," suggested the Blacksmith.

"I want to clean his face and wrap him in our best cloth first," insisted Prudence.

People rarely disagreed with the Blacksmith, given his position as Chief of the village and his formidable muscular physique. The expression on his face clearly showed he was annoyed.

"Suit yourself," he grunted. "I wouldn't advise it, but if it makes you feel better … I suppose your father's been sentenced to death and all that."

At Prudence's shack, the Blacksmith guided the wheelbarrow through the main door, then nonchalantly flicked Arakin's body out of it, knocking some pots and pans over in the process. Prudence stared incredulously up at him.

The Blacksmith shrugged, "He's all yours."

***

Prudence closed the front door, then collected some bottles of various oils from a small wooden box in the corner and set them on a table. Arakin lay motionless on his back in the center of the room. Suddenly his eyes sprang open, and he sat bolt upright.

Prudence shrieked and dropped a clay bowl with a crash. Arakin, also genuinely startled, screamed out. His eyes darted around the room in a bid to get his bearings, but an odd fluttering movement under his sleeve grabbed his attention, and Prudence's.

They both became silent and stared fixedly at it. Arakin bit into the shirt sleeve and pulled it up, revealing a scarf wrapped firmly around his forearm. It flickered and convulsed with movement underneath the surface. Something was trying to push its way out.

Suddenly, Ash, the puppet, ripped through the scarf. He, too, sat bolt upright, wide-eyed and fully alive.

Arakin screamed. Prudence screamed. Ash looked at both of them—and also screamed. Arakin began shaking his arm wildly, in a bid to flick Ash off.

"Woah-woah-woah!" wailed Ash.

Arakin pulled himself up and scuttled backward, falling over a stool and back into more pots and pans.

Ash tore away the fabric of Arakin's scarf, freed himself, and jumped away from Arakin's arm. High and fast, he leaped toward the roof. His parachute opened, and he floated down, landing softly on the floor between them.

"Now you have to admit," declared Ash as he put his hands on his hips, "that despite all the distractions from your screaming and clattering, this was a pretty amazing landing."

Arakin rose from the kitchen rubble on wobbling legs with an inverted pot of daffodils sitting on his head. They all eyed each other in trepidation and disbelief.

Prudence spoke first, pointing at Arakin. "You were dead! The Witch's snake bit you. No human can survive such venom."

Ash, in the center of the room, patted the air with both hands in that universal gesture of *calm down, everyone*. Arakin noticed something odd on Ash's chest, and his eyes widened. Ash, upon seeing Arakin's reaction, looked at his chest as well. Two large holes stared back at him, like dark eyes: bite marks from the snake. Ash jumped back in shock. "Woah! That thing practically drilled through me!"

A bewildered Prudence shot a querying glance to Arakin.

"I had to hide Ash," he explained, "so I wrapped my scarf around him. The snake bit into him instead of my arm."

Arakin anxiously examined his arm, but it bore no puncture wounds. He then noticed a single drop of bright green liquid running down his wrist, ice cold and viscous.

"Venom!" exclaimed Prudence.

The stray green droplet fell off his arm and hit the floor, but it did not splatter as water normally would. Instead, it held together firmly, small as it was, then shook momentarily as if a force was acting upon it. Suddenly it shot across the floor toward Ash.

He frowned and leaped to the side to avoid it. But it shot up in the air and collided with his foot with a splat. It soaked quickly into the pores of his timber body, and his foot began to pound the floor uncontrollably, faster and faster.

"Yikes," Ash proclaimed, then he squatted down and shot upward like a spring, but the expression on his face made it clear that these were not actions he controlled. He smacked the roof hard with a thump, then floated down gently as his parachute once again caught the air. "I had to hit the one wooden beam in a shack with a cloth roof! It's okay, people, I'm finding a new way to relax, it's called a concussion."

"It was drawn to you," declared Arakin.

"The venom of the Witch's snake is inside you, giving you life," hushed Prudence.

Ash replied somewhat defensively, "Hey, let's just agree that the venom gave me movement. But Ash timber—that's what gives me life." He tapped his fist twice on his chest.

"I won't argue with that," said Prudence.

Ash landed on the floor and pulled in his parachute as Arakin tottered toward him. "Either way, you're talking, you're alive. Who are you? What are you?" asked Arakin as he knelt down for a closer look, now more fascinated than afraid.

"Who am I?" replied Ash, slightly taken aback. "We're brothers, Arakin. Brothers from the Ash Forest!"

Arakin smiled and nodded. "Brothers from the Ash Forest. Yes, we are."

Ash smiled, "And I'm glad you took me with you. Let's be honest. It's better that I got bitten by that snake than you."

"Thank you, Ash," said Arakin, smiling as he considered this. And the rest of the day caught up with him too. His eyes flashed to Prudence. "Where's Efscott?"

At the window, they all peered through a crack in the shutters.

"The Tower of Luxurous," she croaked.

"We can't let them do this," proclaimed Ash, as he tied his crossbeams to his back. With the parachute now firmly wrapped around them, they formed an X-shape behind his shoulders, like swords. He looked ready to fight. And that's what concerned Arakin.

Prudence pulled away from the window. "I know this is a foolish thought, but would the townspeople help us? Would someone speak on his behalf?"

"No," said Arakin in a hollow voice.

"Why not?"

"Because they're stupid, mean, and selfish." replied Arakin.

"Good points," added Ash. "Let's just storm the castle! Bust him outta there!"

"No, Ash," lamented Prudence. "We have to try reasoning with the townspeople. It's our only chance. The greatest of the wizards once said that *words* were the strongest of all powers. And not those that cast by spells, but those that forged the hearts of mankind."

Arakin regarded Prudence with a curious gaze. "I never heard that one."

"He told me this himself," said Prudence.

Arakin was more intrigued. But he also realized they had a problem to solve. He shook his head. "The townspeople won't listen to you."

Ash nodded at both of them with a serious look on his face. "I hear what you're both saying, and I can read between the lines. You want me to talk to them, right?"

"No!" shrieked Arakin and Prudence at the same time.

Prudence looked to Arakin. "Perhaps you could talk to them? I don't speak your language well."

"Are you kidding? They throw rocks at me even when I'm quiet," grumbled Arakin as he leaned his back against the wall, exasperated and dejected.

Prudence walked to the door, forlorn and desperate.

Arakin called out after her, "Trying to convince them to help you will also be considered insurrection. And you'll be executed too. This is not the best option to save your father."

She stopped at the door and looked back at him. "I know it's not the best option. But it's the only one I have." She pulled the door open and stepped out.

Arakin watched helplessly. "Wait!" he yelled.

Prudence turned, and Arakin stood up from the wall. He nodded at her. A bond of solidarity exchanged in that simple glance.

Ash held himself slightly taller and grinned. "Just a thought before we confront these aggressive, ale-swilling town's folk: you might want to take the daffodils off your head, little buddy."

Arakin blushed slightly as he yanked the inverted flowerpot from his head, but his embarrassment was quickly overcome by resolve. "Let's go," he added.

CHAPTER THIRTEEN

Upon Deaf Ears

They liked their ale in Ashville, and the town tavern was, therefore, their largest establishment, accommodating up to two hundred people, with enough room still for dancing between the tables. Tonight, though, the bar was filled with four hundred, crammed in tightly. The mood was somber, and the air was pungent with the sweet smell of pipe smoke, ale, and burning olive oil that fueled the lanterns. No one was dancing. This was more than a gathering; it was a town meeting. Plus, there had been much gasping over the last couple days, which had left their throats very parched. A refreshing ale was undoubtedly going to be appreciated.

All eyes were upon the Blacksmith, who stood in the center of the room. "And so maybe the creek is now dry," he confessed, "but King Luxurous offers us work, mining the black stones."

"What did they call that strange stone again?" asked the Baker.

"Lead," replied the Blacksmith.

The Baker let the letter *L* roll slowly off his tongue as he repeated it. "L-L-Lead. Hmm. It's a very pretty name, isn't it? Must be good for us with a pretty name like that."

The townspeople nodded amongst themselves. Sir Sudley, however, did not. He stood nervously, and all eyes turned to him. He cleared his throat. "I know of this King. He comes from the same lands as I. The Oracles claimed that his hunger for gold would result in the enslavement of all mankind and the destruction of the land itself. They had a name for him: The Killer of all Worlds."

There was a moment of silence until Driyetta, the Baker's wife, declared with a tone of revelation, "Lead! It is such a pretty name, isn't it?"

Again the townspeople nodded eagerly over their agreement about lead, oblivious to Sir Sudley's retort. Sir Sudley sighed and sat back down despondently. If the townspeople weren't going to listen, what else could he do? He took a big gulp of his ale.

The front doors opened to a loud clunk, and all heads turned to see the silhouette of a boy framed in the doorway, street torchlights burning brightly behind him. He entered. They gasped upon realizing that it was Arakin. Prudence followed behind him, and Arakin treaded warily to the center of the room.

Jirrabenna, the Fish Monger's wife shrieked, "The boy was dead! What witchery is this? Is he a witch?"

"Very boyish witch!" grumbled the Baker as he hiccupped.

"I was not dead! I just bumped my head." declared Arakin.

"He even rhymes like the witch!" hollered the Shoemaker.

"I was not rhyming, and I was not dying," Arakin assured.

"Another rhyme!" shrieked Driyetta. "A witch! A witch!"

The townspeople all murmured anxiously among themselves.

Arakin held up his arm. "I had a wooden splint on my arm. The snake bit into that. I am alive and well. I am not a witch!"

"Because we burn witches!" growled the Fishmonger. There was a rumble of agreement behind him.

Arakin defiantly met their gaze. "You didn't seem to be in a hurry to burn the King's Witch." They fell silent.

"She is a Black Witch," blurted out the Fish Monger, "and a member of the King's court!"

"I see," added Arakin. "Or are you just scared because the bully is a bit stronger than you?"

The Blacksmith stepped toward Arakin. "Watch your mouth, boy, or we will kick you back into the Ash Forest, where you belong."

"We're not here to bicker. I promise," said Arakin calmly, trying to bring his own temper under control. "We're here to reason with you." Arakin stepped to the side and nodded to Prudence. She took a deep breath, but as she looked over the leering faces of the townspeople, she trembled, her eyes widened, and her body tightened.

"I ..." It seemed she could say no more. The room was unnervingly quiet, punctuated soon by some coughs, mumbles, and chuckles. Prudence looked helplessly to Arakin and shook her head, an admission of surrender and a plea for help. She could not find her voice. She could not find the words.

Arakin felt a cold chill sweep over him. He wasn't sure how he could help, but seeing Prudence so helpless was like a stabbing pain erupting in his chest. He stepped forward, and all eyes turned to him instead. He could feel his whole body grow tighter and his legs weaker.

"We are here to lead a campaign that will reshape this kingdom!" he announced. "For united, we are indestructible. And it all starts with freeing Efscott Borelle, Carpenter and … nice person!"

The room fell totally silent, then erupted in laughter, some of the townspeople even slapping the tabletops repeatedly as if this was the funniest thing they had ever heard, and they just couldn't control themselves. All except for Sir Sudley. He was quietly eyeing Arakin with great earnestness.

The Blacksmith, who had stopped laughing, sauntered up to Arakin, towering over him, his expression turning dark. "The sentence for insurrection is death, boy. Who are you to ask us to follow you?"

Prudence edged up beside Arakin, glaring at the Blacksmith and speaking with a tone that was void of any self-consciousness. "He is the only one smart and brave enough to walk the entirety of the Ash Forest, from north to south, east to west. He treads where you dare not step one foot. He masters that which you dare not even touch!" Her crisp words permeated the room with gusto, resonating with peculiar power.

Arakin was astonished by her apparent fluency in their language. She actually proved to be an excellent orator after all.

Murmurs of discontent quickly rippled through the room, but there was someone who remained transfixed by her declaration: Sir Sudley. It was as if a great realization had hit him.

The Blacksmith lumbered ominously up to Prudence, but Arakin stepped in and blocked his path, and the Blacksmith eyed Arakin imperiously. "I wonder what the King will say when I tell him of your plans? You have no followers here. You have no friends."

Arakin and Prudence backed away toward the front door, and upon reaching it, a volley of jeers and food scraps were hurled at them.

***

They stumbled out of the bar and onto the main road. In the corner of his eye, Arakin detected a projectile ricocheting off the door and spinning toward Prudence. It was large and flying fast. It felt more like a reflex move to Arakin as he sidestepped in front of it, without even realizing what it was, using his back like a shield. With a splat, the thrown lettuce heart smacked him in the head and exploded into tiny pieces, to the uproarious laughter of the townspeople. *Lucky it was something soft,* he thought to himself. Arakin shut the door fast, muffling the bar noise behind them and swallowing them into the stillness of the empty street.

Prudence clasped her chest and turned apologetically to Arakin, "I'm so sorry. I was wrong to drag you into this."

"No. It's not your fault. We're in this together."

She smiled warmly back at him, then looked anxiously up and down the main road. It was quiet— for now.

"I know a place we can hide," said Arakin. "Somewhere they wouldn't dare enter."

Prudence nodded, understanding his suggestion. "When we pick up Ash from home, I'll take some supplies."

They hastily made their retreat toward the south side of town, moving through the back streets to avoid the Royal Guards.

***

106

In the castle's throne room, Luxurous was reclining leisurely upon his throne, with one of his legs swung over the arm, while eating some grapes. Minus stood dutifully before him.

"And what's wrong with your job title?" blurted Luxurous.

"Well, Sire. The townspeople laugh at me," sniveled Minus. "Plus, it's hard to impress the ladies with the current one. Perhaps we could change it to Treasurer and Chief Engineer of Essential Infrastructure Plumbing?"

"Don't be ridiculous, it's too long," barked Luxurous. "You're the Treasurer and Manager of Poo. Enough!"

Minus winced but nodded in acquiescence, muttering through gritted teeth, "Of course, Sire."

Two guards wheeled Efscott's cage into the room and parked it in front of the King. The Witch ambled in behind them.

"Good evening," said Luxurous in a surprisingly chirpy tone as he waved to Efscott.

"Good evening, Sire," replied a forlorn Efscott.

"My Witch would like to have a little chat with you."

The Witch stepped closer. "Efscott Borelle. I remember your name now," she snarled. "And I wonder, do you remember the name Nobellius of the North?"

The Witch's eyes turned to a glistening black, and Efscott bowed his head.

"Yes," he replied, "he was my teacher."

Luxurous set his grapes down. His eyes narrowed.

"Look at me!" barked the Witch, and Efscott raised his head. The Witch studied his eyes carefully. "And why does a simple Carpenter receive lessons from the greatest wizard who ever lived?" she demanded.

Efscott shrugged, "Just lucky, I suppose."

She hit his cage with her staff, and Efscott tensed. She moved slowly around him like a vulture, her eyes never leaving him. "Insolence! Luck indeed! Lucky to learn what? Wizardry? Sorcery?"

"No, ma'am. Sculpting. He said that one day, I might need to create a great sculpture. A thing of majesty. For he who would be king."

Luxurous inclined his head. "What king? Who?"

"King of all the lands," replied Efscott. "To unite all mankind. So that they may be free."

Luxurous rose and directed his question at the Witch. "Well?"

Her eyes returned to their normal color. "He is telling the truth," she replied.

Luxurous stroked his beard as he weighed this all up, then straightened himself and relaxed as a thought occurred to him. "Of course. It makes sense now," he declared. "The statue of my son! *This* was his prophecy." He stroked his beard again. "Not so sure about that bit on all the people being free though. But we can work on that."

"Indeed, Sire," said Efscott. "And this is why I say that I am lucky. Because I am lucky to have such an honor as this."

"Kill him," said the Witch crisply.

"What?" asked a confused Luxurous.

"What?" blurted a horrified Efscott.

"Kill him!" she reaffirmed, this time louder.

***

Back in the village, Arakin and Prudence approached the front door of Prudence's shack. Arakin craned his neck, eyeing the Ash Forest, and whistled a bird-like tune. A large, pale, lithe figure slid out from the tree line and shot down the hill toward them, moving with remarkable speed.

"What on earth is that?" asked Prudence.

"A friend. A big one."

***

Back in the castle, a very perplexed Luxurous turned to the Witch. "Kill him? But I thought you said he was telling the truth."

"He was. But it's what else I see in his eyes."

Luxurous leaned in. "Ah, yes, there's an eyelash!"

"No!" she yelled. "Danger! Great danger!"

"Are you sure? You are getting a bit old, you know. Maybe a tad shortsighted."

"Great. Danger!" she exclaimed, louder and more deliberately than before.

Luxurous sighed and grunted, "Oh, all right, yes, I suppose we have to be safe. Safety first, safety first." He turned and shrugged indifferently at Efscott, whose jaw dropped in disbelief.

Luxurous nodded to the two guards. "Take him back to the cell for execution."

The guards trundled in and yanked Efscott's cage away, drawing it out through the vast doorway. Luxurous turned to the Witch and muttered with a huff, "He did have an eyelash in his eye though."

She rolled her eyes but made sure he wasn't looking.

No sooner had Efscott's cage exited the throne room when the large timber doors swung open again. Pound strode purposefully in through the yawning entrance, with the Blacksmith close behind, shuffling quickly to keep up while glancing nervously at Luxurous.

"General Pound, what is it?" asked Luxurous.

"Sire, something of great importance!"

109

Luxurous didn't seem too worried about the news. "Are the toilets blocked again? Just get Minus onto it."

Minus still stood to the side and winced.

Pound and the Blacksmith stopped before Luxurous.

"No, Sire. Even more important than that. An attempted rebellion!" declared Pound.

CHAPTER FOURTEEN

The Quest

Inside Prudence's shack, Arakin stepped to the window and peered through a gap in the shutters. Ash stood on a narrow cabinet beneath the window, lifting himself up to his toes but failing to raise his eyes high enough to reach the window.

A noise behind them caused them all to turn, and Prudence froze with her mouth agape upon seeing a giant wolf staring at her, inches from her face. It filled the entire doorway. Slipnor.

"It's okay. He's with us," said Arakin with a proud grin.

Ash stared in wonder. "Woah! That thing is a freak of nature. And coming from me, that's saying something."

Slipnor wagged his tail at Prudence, and she smiled. Her posture eased.

But when Slipnor saw Ash, he cocked his head curiously and growled.

"Hey, relax, Fluffy," said Ash. "And just so you know, I'm not going to play fetch with you. You'll probably think I'm the stick!"

Slipnor growled again. Prudence continued to bustle around the shack, collecting a variety of herbs, including some bright blue leaves.

"What's that for?" inquired Arakin.

She self-consciously shoved them into a bag. "Just food. Medicines."

Prudence darted across the floor again, grabbing from a shelf a small clay bottle that she uncorked and tipped into her hand. A rusty key fell from it into her palm, and she made quickly toward a wooden box in the corner, which was the only item in their shack that had a lock upon it. She promptly unfastened it with the key and whipped open the lid. There was only one item inside, a thin rope with a small, glistening, silver grapple hook at its end, about the size of a fist. Prudence took it out and handed it to Arakin.

"The last of the great wizards gave me this," she revealed. "He said I would know who I should give it to."

Arakin took it reverently. "Is it magic?" he whispered.

"No. It's just a rope ... with a hook," Prudence replied dryly, then shrugged.

Ash nodded in approval. "Well, at least it's shiny."

Thump thump thump! A banging on the front door caused them to freeze. The following short moment of silence felt like an eternity to Arakin, and they turned to each other, terrified. Arakin grabbed Ash and placed him into his carry bag. The tiny wooden knight was about to object, but Arakin pressed his index finger to his lips to advise silence, and Ash complied. Arakin gave a reassuring nod to Prudence, who gingerly opened the door.

It was Sir Sudley who stood outside. And they all breathed a heavy sigh of relief.

"We must be quick, young ones," cautioned Sir Sudley, "for danger comes this way."

He met Arakin's gaze with a particular wonder. "Tell me, child, can you truly travel through the Ash Forest? From end to end?"

"Yes," replied Arakin indifferently.

Sir Sudley directed his next question at Prudence. "How fast is your horse?"

"Not very."

"Mine can run like the wind," declared Arakin.

Sir Sudley raised an eyebrow. "You have a horse?"

Arakin nodded and pointed to the corner. Sir Sudley followed his finger and leaned around the door-jam, coming face to face with Slipnor, who filled the entire area from roof to floor while seated. Sir Sudley gulped. "He's not really a horse."

"He likes to pretend he's a horse," said Arakin.

Slipnor stayed seated and woofed good-naturedly.

"Well, I won't argue with that," replied Sir Sudley.

Mrs. Sudley stepped in behind him and placed a gentle hand on his shoulder, regarding the children with nurturing eyes. "Hurry, young ones. To our house!"

***

Inside the Sudleys' shack, Mrs. Sudley stood guard by the window, on the lookout for the imminent attack of the Royal Guards. Sir Sudley drew an old paper scroll from an ornate wooden chest and hastily unrolled it on the table in the center of the room. "The last of the Northern Knights told me of an ancient prophecy: The age when the golden sword Gun Ronin would be found was the same age when a king would travel to these lands. A king who was capable of destroying all before

113

him. But a boy would lead a quest of salvation to unite man and land."

Sir Sudley pointed to a drawing on the scroll of a tree stump into which a beautiful sword was driven, as if mounted perfectly in the tree stump's center, a vertical line of metal rising straight up from the wooden base. It was elegant in design, and the blade's slightly convex shape bore some similarities to a spearhead.

"Gun Ronin. The King Maker!" said Sir Sudley in awe. "The blade that cuts the darkness. The edge that heals the land."

"But the King already has Gun Ronin," contested Arakin.

Sir Sudley shook his head. "Many kings have claimed this. I was … unconscious at the time." He blushed. "I kind of … fainted … at the gates. Tell me, was his sword huge with lots of jewels in it?"

"Yes," affirmed Prudence.

Sir Sudley snorted. "They always do that. But that is not Gun Ronin. The truth is, the last Knight who searched for this sword was certain it would be found on the peak of Mount Drass."

Arakin looked skeptical. "I'm not sure a sword is what I need," he mumbled. "There's a reason you don't find many one-armed swordsmen. Feel like I'd be pushing my luck."

Prudence wasn't deterred by Arakin's deflection. On the contrary, she stepped closer, clearly intrigued by what Sir Sudley had to say. "Mount Drass. I've heard of this mountain," she declared. "It's surrounded by liquid fire. Even the base cannot be reached."

"Indeed," said Sir Sudley. "But the Oracles spoke of a bridge. It was accessible only through a forest that no one dared enter. A forest feared by all, but for one warrior."

Sir Sudley met Arakin's gaze.

"The Ash Forest," said Arakin calmly.

Sir Sudley nodded. "And while I failed terribly as a soldier, I know I shall fulfill my role as a messenger." He straightened himself and lifted his chin. "For I am that Knight's grandson. He told me I should wait the rest of my days here, that I would know when the time was right. Arakin, that time is now. That warrior … is you."

***

Ten horsemen charged out of the castle, led by Pound. These were not men on a crusade to unblock toilets, but men on a campaign of bloody vengeance. The drawbridge trembled under the quick step of their battle horses, the last of which drew a carriage with an empty prison-cage upon it.

***

At the window, Mrs. Sudley tensed. "They're coming!"

Sir Sudley rolled up the scroll.

"Why didn't the Knight just burn the forest down?" asked Arakin, regarding Sir Sudley judiciously, not feeling entirely sure if he should believe this prophecy. "It's the easy way. It's what most people would do."

Sir Sudley answered the boy's query. "The Oracles prophesied that the righteous must not burn any forest on this quest." This struck a deep chord with Arakin. Sir Sudley could see that his words were resonating, and he continued. "For if they were to find the sword known as the King Maker, the path itself would maketh the king."

***

Pound led the horsemen through the center of town in a high-speed wave of clattering hooves, eliciting yelps from the townspeople, who darted out of their way.

The horsemen reached Efscott's shack, and Pound leaped off his horse as it was still sliding to a halt. He was at Efscott's door entrance in a few heartbeats, kicking the door in and entering without a moment's hesitation. Empty! He stormed toward the Sudleys' house.

***

Pound kicked in the door of the Sudleys' cottage, ripping it off the hinges. But only Mrs. Sudley sat inside. She looked innocently up at him while stirring a pot.

"Ohh," she said, slightly startled. "Hungry?" she asked politely while offering a spoon of her turnip soup.

Pound grimaced and stepped back.

"Lord, to the west!" roared the first Horseman, pointing to a group who were making their way up the hill toward the Ash Forest. It was Arakin, Prudence, Ash, Slipnor, and Sir Sudley.

Pound spun, grunted, and leaped onto his horse.

***

Climbing the embankment, Sir Sudley passed the scroll to Prudence, and she placed it in her bag.

"The Oracles said that this sword would always find its way to the hand of he who should wield it," added Sir Sudley. "The most magic of blades in the land. Worthy of forging a courageous prince—or king."

Arakin was struck with a profound idea. He turned to Prudence, declaring with a sense of hushed revelation, "Forging

116

a prince! Prudence, I know how we can save your father. We need this sword!"

Sir Sudley grinned.

Ash raised his head from inside Prudence's bag, jumped onto Arakin's left sleeve, nimbly ascended, and was now hoisting himself onto Arakin's shoulder. From here, Ash could see Pound and his men approaching fast.

"Wow," declared Ash. "They look so angry!"

"Hurry, children," urged Sir Sudley.

Arakin leaped onto Slipnor and helped Prudence up behind him. Slipnor reared onto his hind legs with an enthusiastic bark, with Arakin holding on tightly.

"Charr!" howled Arakin.

Slipnor bolted into action, sprinting up the hill for the Ash Forest, with Pound and his horsemen close behind. They thundered past Sir Sudley and began gaining on Slipnor.

"Go, boy!" yelled Arakin.

Slipnor accelerated, sending up a spray of dust and grass.

The horsemen drew their swords in unison, while the second Horseman drew his bow. He aimed and fired, missing Arakin but almost decapitating Ash, who ducked just in time. It whizzed past, missing him by a whisker.

"Yikes!" bellowed Ash. "Well, it's official: we're now enemies of the state. Tick that one off the bucket list!"

Slipnor bolted into the green, wall-like perimeter of the Ash Forest, disappearing immediately. A Venus Mantrap lunged at them from the right but couldn't reach, snapping, hissing, and groaning as it stretched to its limits. Arakin knew the woods well and held a steady course. He knew it would be a fatal mistake to swerve reactively to the left, where slippery, moss-covered ground lay beneath some even faster Mantraps.

Pound and his men pulled their horses up to an awkward and aggressive halt, and another huge Mantrap lunged out from the forest, snapping just inches from Pound's face. He backed away quickly, as did the other horsemen. The second Horseman swung his sword at the Mantrap but missed. Another fired an arrow but also missed. Too slow. The Mantrap retreated behind the curtain of brush and branches.

***

Slipnor bolted onward, guided by Arakin, who let go of his fur and steered now by applying pressure with his legs. Arakin surveyed the forest swiftly yet methodically. He found what he needed, then reached out and grabbed a branch from one of the trees. He was going to need it. The quickest way through the Ash Forest was straight ahead. It was the shortest and flattest path, but it was also fraught with far more dangers: multiple Mantraps that were lightning-fast and even other predators he dare not mention to Prudence. But the safer paths would take them an extra quarter of a day, and this was time they most probably did not have.

A growl came from ahead as a giant Venus Mantrap slid its head between two trees, preparing to strike from the right. Arakin saw it and guided Slipnor to the left with a squeeze of his right leg. But another Mantrap appeared to the left of them, which meant they were outflanked if they continued forward. Ash grabbed his bow. "I've got the one on the left!" he shouted.

"Aim for the green nuggets on their bottom lip!" yelled Arakin. "That's their soft spot!"

"Roger that. Aim for the nuggets!" Ash loaded an arrow and took aim, the taut string of his bow creaking louder as he drew it back to its extremes.

Both Mantraps lunged at them with jaws wide and fangs bared. Arakin smacked the one on the right, and Ash shot his arrow at the one on the left. Despite its small size, the arrow launched with incredible speed, cracking the air with a whiplike slash, and then hit one of the bulbous green extrusions under the Mantrap's bottom lip with a loud thunk. Both plants swiftly recoiled with a surly hiss.

***

Pound and his men struggled to bring their flighty horses under control. The frustrated General maintained his resolve, though, and with a nod of his head, gestured for them to enter and take chase. "Go!" he hollered.

"But Sire, it's death!" replied the first Horseman. It was Grub, the wolf-keeper who had whipped Slipnor moments before he was swallowed by one of the Venus Mantraps. "It even ate our battle wolf, Armageddon."

"Really? Well, that's odd because that looked a lot like Armageddon they were riding, did it not?"

"But ... it's really scary, General!" croaked another Horseman.

Pound rode closer to them. "Go or face the King! All of you!"

They steadied their horses and dug their heels in hard with a battle cry, "Yarr!"

And all eight horsemen charged in, fading quickly behind the brush and disappearing into the shadows.

Pound watched and listened attentively from his safer vantage point.

The silence was soon broken by a loud series of thunking noises, followed by eight horses whinnying as they came bolting back out of the forest in wide-eyed terror and without riders upon them.

They galloped past Pound, who steadied his terrified stallion. A daunting scraping noise approaching from the woods caused him to frown and stiffen. Creak, creak, creak. He placed his hand on the grip of his broadsword, ready to fight.

He could see movement in the grass within the forest, something coming toward him. It took form as it got nearer— the helmets of the eight horsemen. They emerged from the woods and rolled closer, coming to a halt before his jittery steed.

"Bah!" grunted Pound, then turned and galloped down the embankment, cutting a straight line to Sir Sudley. He brought his horse up close, scowling down at him. "Old man, what business did you have with those children?"

"They were asking for directions," replied Sir Sudley innocently.

"To where?" barked Pound.

"Freedom," said Sir Sudley as he stared pensively up at the Ash Forest.

CHAPTER FIFTEEN

What Lurks in the Woods

Cutting through the forest under shards of the full moon's pale light, Arakin spotted a large blue circle of mud ahead, circumventing the base of a grey-blue tree. They were approaching it at high speed. Arakin knew how dangerous these were and immediately steered Slipnor away by squeezing his legs so that his weapon-wielding hand remained free.

A spider leaped at them from a branch ahead, and Arakin promptly swiped it away with his stick. From the side, another Mantrap struck. Ash fired an arrow—a direct hit—and it recoiled.

But no one saw the spider poised for an attack on the branches behind, its mottled-brown carapace camouflaging it perfectly in the tree. The spider was about the size of a man, a different species to the others they had encountered, with more hair, more power, and more like something from your worst nightmare.

It launched itself with deadly accuracy and landed on Slipnor's hindquarters. Before the giant wolf had time to turn, the spider grabbed Prudence with its front four legs, shot a stream of its web up to a branch behind them, and began pulling itself away, with Prudence screaming in its clutches. The pedipalps on its head wrapped around Prudence's face and mouth, thus muting her cries.

Arakin had already turned though. He had felt the rush of air the spider had created from its attack and landing, albeit soft. He had felt the light tap on Slipnor's hindquarters vibrate toward him, barely noticeable over the thumping of their gallop, but noted nonetheless. He had already squeezed his legs tightly around Slipnor's ribs and could see Prudence being pulled away from him in his peripheral vision with his head partially turned. He dropped the stick, and his hand shot out. Prudence took it. They fastened upon one another.

Arakin was yanked back hard. He couldn't hold on tightly enough with his legs and slipped straight off Slipnor, who turned and skidded to a halt. The spider lost its upward flight and descended to the ground; two human bodies were just too heavy. But it was determined to eat on the run. It bared its fangs and lunged at Prudence, who was now pinned to the ground under its front four legs. All the while, the spider kept its furry pedipalps pressed against Prudence's face and mouth. She couldn't talk or breathe.

Ash tumbled off Arakin's shoulder, hitting the earth, but swiftly rose to his knee and shot an arrow into one of the spider's eight eyes. It reeled from the pain and screamed with the shrill tone of a wild boar. But it wasn't over. The spider pulled the tiny arrow out with its front legs and prepared to lunge again.

Slipnor bolted in, and Arakin pointed to the side while yelling, "Left side! Left!"

Arakin locked his knees around Prudence's ankle to keep her pinned to the ground. He grabbed another branch, a heavier one, and he quickly analyzed his surroundings. He was well aware that they were only six feet from the glistening blue mud that surrounded the pale blue tree to the right of them. And this was dangerous. But it also provided a possible solution. Slipnor lunged in and fixed his jaws around the guileful spider's front leg and tugged ferociously.

Arakin smacked his branch hard against the ground just as the spider lunged again at Prudence, who gulped for air. With a whipping noise, a massive tentacle-like root shot up from the blue mud toward Arakin's stick. Arakin timed it perfectly, pulling the branch across the ground toward the spider's mouth and its two huge fangs that now glistened with saliva from the anticipation of its meal. Arakin jammed the stick up as the spider lunged down to bite, driving the wood hard into its mouth. Not fatal in any way. Just the first move. A gambit.

The tentacle-root from the blue sludge whipped around Arakin's branch, and he flicked his wrist, hooking the sinewy vine around the left fang of the spider. The tentacle-root pulled hard, but the spider dug its rear feet firmly down and jerked its head away with a growl, and the tentacle-root slipped off. This was a fatal mistake for the spider, for as Arakin knew, the first tentacle-root was just the feeler, nimble and fast but with no significant power. The prey always panicked upon being initially grabbed and gave away their position more clearly with heavy footfalls. Several thicker tentacle-roots shot up from the blue mud and wrapped around the spider's rear legs, then hauled it back toward the blue quicksand. But the spider kept a firm grip on Prudence, who was being pulled along with it.

Arakin was ready for this, though, and in one deft move, he whipped his dagger out from its holster and flung it at the spider. Although the bronze blade had been broken in the grove from prying open nuts, there was still enough metal above the handle to serve a purpose. The sharp, jagged tip sunk into the spider's largest eye, where it remained firmly lodged. The spider howled in rage and pain, letting go of Prudence in a reflex action as it shook its head and clawed at its eyes. But the spider was still trapped in the vice-like grip of the tentacle-root that dragged it swiftly across the soil. With a splash, it was pulled down into the deep blue mud, where it thrashed wildly. It disappeared quickly into the mire, invisible now to the rest of the world but serving the purpose as fertilizer for the big blue tree.

"Thanks," croaked Prudence, catching her breath and looking over at Arakin.

"Don't mention it," said Ash, assuming the compliment was for him, as he brushed some dust off his arm. "And by the way, how cool was that! Right? I mean, world's biggest spider or what?"

***

Back on Slipnor, they bolted through the last fifty yards of the forest. Slipnor leaped over a giant, fallen ash tree as if it were nothing, going airborne and landing with incredible grace, without missing a step.

Arakin could see thicker beams of moonlight ahead through pockets of the less dense canopy. But the lower foliage of thorn bushes and thick shrubbery made it hard to see through. Beyond it, though, Arakin spotted the movement of another light source—fireflies perhaps, drifting gracefully upward.

"We're almost there. Go, boy!"

Slipnor quickened his pace and jumped over the thorny shrubs, bursting through the dense layer of leafy foliage. They exploded out of the western edge of the forest and finally had a clear sight of everything in front of them. But it wasn't good.

Slipnor locked his legs and tried to dig his paws into the earth. He was sliding fast to the edge of what looked like a cliff. A puff of dust coiled up from under his grip as they came to a stop, and a flurry of tiny rocks was sent rolling over the edge of the steep ravine. Their rigid bodies soon loosened, and shock gave way to wonder. "It's true!" marveled Arakin.

The ravine they stood above was five hundred yards deep. Its steep embankments were covered with white dust and pale stones, and dotted with trees. Their bark was crusty white, and their branches were resplendent with a smattering of semitransparent red leaves. These glowed partially from the moonlight but more from a source below, a glowing red river of molten lava more than one hundred yards wide, coursing through the base of the gorge.

Arakin was intrigued by the eerie white dust that thermal forces lifted up from the lower banks of the ravine. Hot orange embers also drifted upward, at times coming close to their faces. This was what Arakin had mistakenly thought were fireflies. Ash puffed them away irritably.

"At times like this, I get worried when people call me Ash."

Low clouds obscured whatever lay in the far distance on the opposite side. Fifty yards to the left, they could see a steeper camber where the ravine became a legitimate cliff face. Water gushed from a few large holes about a third of the way down, fed by the natural aquifers under the forest. The streams of water plunged down to the lava river. Most of the downpour turned to steam before it even reached the red-hot surface. The rest sizzled upward upon impact with the lava and created hissing, billowing plumes of steam.

"Look!" exclaimed Arakin. He pointed to the right. Barely visible through the haze of heat and dust was a bridge of white stone. They moved toward it, keeping well away from the perilous edge.

Upon reaching the mouth of the bridge, they carefully dismounted. Arakin eyed the moon perched well above the tree line of the Ash Forest and frowned.

"Not far from midnight," he said softly. "Two days and a half from now is when they plan to ..." his voice trailed off. He couldn't say it.

"Execute my father," croaked Prudence.

"Let's not waste any time."

Arakin examined the fragile stone bridge with trepidation.

"Single file might be best."

"Good idea," agreed Ash, "and fat dogs at the back, I say."

Slipnor growled as Ash strolled past him, onto the bridge, and merrily onward with barely a moment's hesitation. Arakin, Prudence, and Slipnor gingerly followed.

They were a quarter of the way across when Arakin suddenly stopped.

"What is it?" whispered Prudence.

Arakin pointed ahead to the bridge's center, where it was thinnest. "Is that ... a crack?"

A dark line traversed about half of the surface. The wavering heat haze and rising dust obscured the finer details of what lay before them and evoked an unnerving sense that everything ahead was a vacillating half-reality. The hot air stung their eyes and lungs, even from this distance.

"Will the bridge hold all of us?" asked Prudence.

"I'm the lightest. Let me go!" insisted Ash.

Arakin nodded. "Okay. Be careful, Ash."

Ash nodded with an expression of good humor. "Hey, I'm made of wood. What could possibly go wrong over a river of lava and floating embers?" Arakin managed a weak smile as Ash walked onward.

He made his way carefully to the bridge's center, closing in on what looked like the thick crack, and stopped just a few feet from it. He paused and laughed, then turned and yelled, "It's not a crack! It's a snake!"

But the hissing and groaning of the lava flow made it hard to hear. "What? We can't hear you," hollered Arakin.

"It's a snake!" yelled Ash, louder than before, launching himself on to his tiptoes as if that might assist with projecting his voice. He could tell by their response that they were still befuddled. So without a moment's hesitation, Ash spun, approached the sleeping snake, and picked it up by the midriff. He held it above his head with one hand and pointed to it with the other.

"Snake!" he bellowed once more.

Like all snakes, it had no eyelids, yet it was clear that it had been awoken from its slumber when its eyes flickered menacingly around and its tongue darted out. It did not seem happy, hissing in protest and pulling itself free from Ash's grasp. Whipping around, it recoiled and launched an attack. Ash swiftly drew his sword and dodged, then parried. The snake's head was about half the size of Ash's whole body. Ash backed away, encroaching on the very edge of the bridge.

Arakin tensed. He understood what it was now. "Ash! Be careful!" he screamed. He bolted across the bridge toward Ash, with Prudence joining him.

The snake struck again at Ash with full force, jaws wide open and teeth bared. Ash sidestepped, and the snake's own momentum carried it over the edge, down into the lava. It disappeared in a puff of ember and smoke. Ash peered over the edge. "Yikes. Sorry—kind of."

Arakin and Prudence breathed a sigh of relief and relaxed back into a light-footed walk.

Ash quickly tightened the strings of his crossbeam that had shaken loose during the short battle. "You go," he said and waved them on.

Arakin, Prudence, and Slipnor caught up and passed Ash, who followed while continuing to adjust his strings. "Good job, Ash," affirmed Arakin. "Glad you're still with us."

***

Arakin and Prudence reached the end and breathed a sigh of relief as they alighted the bridge, their footfalls now reaching solid ground.

Ash was close behind, still tightening his strings, but a sudden wind caught the partially opened parachute on his back, filling a few pockets and causing it to unravel. The cloth yawned wide as the wind filled it fully. Arakin took a rigid step forward, wanting to yell, but it was as if the moment was in slow motion. Ash braced himself, realizing the horrible ramifications. With a whoosh, the parachute caught the breeze and dragged him swiftly back to the middle of the bridge again.

Arakin screamed out in horror as Ash flew sideways toward the bridge's edge. Closer. And then over. Down. Out of sight.

Arakin screamed louder and ran back onto the bridge. And then he detected a flash of movement beneath the bridge, to the side, rising.

"Woah!" screamed Ash as he came flying back up from the rising force of the thermals. He pulled on the strings and clumsily steered back to the bridge. Closer and closer. And with

128

a smack, he landed face-first on the white stone. With his head still face-planted, he raised a fist and gave a thumbs-up to Arakin. Ash got to his feet in a flash and quickly pulled the parachute in. "All good!" he declared. "Don't know what all the fuss was about."

Arakin waved back, but his relief was soon replaced with concern when a deep, rumbling moan emanated from the bridge. Ash started walking toward them but picked up his pace while tightening the parachute crossbeam down to his back again with rapid, deliberate tugs.

"Hurry, Ash. I don't like the sound of this."

The bridge trembled slightly, and Ash stopped midstride, standing perfectly still, his feet wide apart and his arms held high as if for balance. He was now in the very center of the bridge. Eternally cavalier, he waved a dismissive hand back at Arakin. "Nah, I think we're good!" said Ash. "It feels pretty solid." He stomped his foot down firmly on the stone surface three times. "They knew how to build 'em good in those days!" he yelled.

Ash heard a crisp snap, prompting him to stiffen in fear. He looked down. A small crack had appeared under his heel. With a tremor and bang, it grew longer, moving at high speed toward the opposite side of the ravine behind him. It zigzagged its way across the entire rear half of the bridge.

"Ash! Run! Run!" yelled Arakin.

Ash broke into a sprint, but the crack followed him, zigzagging with serpentine-like malice.

"Faster, Ash, faster!" hollered Prudence.

"Five-inch legs don't go much faster than this!" he cried out.

A tremendous roar shook both the ground and the air as the section of the bridge behind Ash fell away in a billowing cloud of smoke and dust. The rest of the bridge promptly followed suit.

Now it was not just a crack following Ash, but clear air itself, as the entire bridge behind him plummeted into the river of lava far below. Ash looked over his shoulder, and his eyes widened. "Oh, you mean *faster*!" he bellowed. His tiny arms and legs pumped even more furiously, and his pace quickened. But he wasn't going to make it. The threshold of the tumbling bridge was now dangerously close to his heels.

Arakin screamed another helpless vote of encouragement, but he knew it wasn't helping. He ran back to Slipnor and grabbed the grapple rope from his bag.

Even as he looked up, though, he saw the ground fall away beneath Ash's feet—and Ash fell with it—down to the lava flow. To death. Prudence gasped. Arakin had no time to wind up a swing or aim. He threw with pure force and instinct, letting the rope unfurl within his hand as the hook hurtled toward Ash.

Ash stretched down for it but couldn't reach as the grapple hook and rope sailed past beneath him.

Arakin yanked back on it hard in a whip-like motion, reeling the hook back faster than it flew out. The grapple hook caught Ash around the torso and brought him careering back toward them.

"Catch meeeeeeeee!" With a smack, he landed firmly in Arakin's hand. They regarded each other with a relief that changed quickly to humor. "Good catch," croaked Ash.

They all gazed in disbelief at the yawning space where the bridge once stood. The opposite side of the ravine now looked so far away. They peered down at the rubble of earth and stone that filled the entire breadth of the lava river. Even some of the settling dust ignited in the air as it drew closer to the liquid fire, turning to short-lived micro embers.

Ash grimaced. "Oops. Sorry."

"It's not your fault, Ash," assured Arakin.

Prudence pointed to some of the stones on the outer edge of the rubble. "They're burning." The others saw it now too; the rocks closest to the lava dissolved into nothing, and the amber river encroached further over the rubble, eating into it.

"If we cross it now, we can make it back home," advised Arakin. "It's burning fast, but we have time."

Prudence nodded, and Arakin met her gaze. They knew this was a moment of truth—a big decision—with little time to consider options.

Arakin strode up to Slipnor and jumped onto his back.

"But I think we should keep going," he declared with calm resolve. "It's the only plan we have, and we should make sure we at least have something worth returning for." He smiled warmly at Prudence, and she beamed back at him.

Ash patted her reassuringly on the back of the leg as he trod past. She looked thoughtfully back at the west bank of the Ash Forest and the burning lava bridge below, then turned her back on them and joined Arakin, Ash, and Slipnor.

CHAPTER SIXTEEN

Into the Wasteland

Slipnor charged up the short embankment of soft dust with Arakin, Prudence, and Ash aboard, the lava river now hissing and gurgling behind them. Upon stopping at the top, they were met with the haunting view of what lay ahead.

Stretched before them for miles was foreboding white desert dotted with pale, leafless trees that looked eerily like gaunt hands reaching out from the earth. Vines of white thorns spiraled around their haggard, stout trunks and gnarly branches.

"Not your first choice for a holiday destination, is it?" said Ash.

A brisk headwind drove swirls of dust toward them and caused the nearby trees to sway menacingly with an ominous creak, their branches stretching wider apart as if to reach out and grab them. Slipnor whined and backed away, but Arakin patted him reassuringly.

"Easy, boy. Just the wind."

The trees eased back with a groan. Prudence took the parchment out and read it. "'Beyond the liquid fire, you're in the hands of fate. Don't turn left and don't turn right, charge forward always straight.'"

"Going straight in a desert is a bit hard, though, isn't it?" said Ash. "It's not like there's a road."

Arakin surveyed the mountain ranges to the left and right of the desert, their snowcapped peaks gleaming under the light of the full moon, jutting up over the horizon just enough to be seen.

"The desert is flanked by two mountain ranges. I've heard people call them the Twin Ranges because the ones northwest of Ashville are the same height as the ones that run southwest. People think they're identical. Not that anyone has ever climbed them. Too steep. Too dangerous."

"So what does that mean?" asked Ash.

"We keep both ranges visible, same height above their horizons. I guess that's about the best we can do." He looked to Prudence, who nodded.

Arakin gave two gentle taps on Slipnor's shoulder. The giant wolf understood the command and trotted into the desolate moonlit wasteland.

It was now that Arakin was struck with a realization and a sinking feeling in his stomach: he had never been farther than a thousand yards from his beloved Ash Forest. It had not only been his home, it had also been his shield. A river of lava now separated them, and he was running even farther away into a desert. In an attempt to combat the cold feeling of fear that was stiffening his shoulders, he reminded himself of what was at stake—Efscott, and saving him wasn't going to be achieved through convenient measures. Arakin gave a gentle tap of his heels against Slipnor's ribs, who enthusiastically quickened his pace, cutting their way through the desert that looked like it rolled on for eternity.

***

"Now I know why this place seems so familiar," said Prudence, breaking what felt like a long spell of silence.

"You used to live here?" said Ash with mock enthusiasm. "Cheery place on the corner block, maybe?"

"No."

"Please don't tell me you came here for vacation."

"No, Ash. The White Wastelands in the heart of the Twin Ranges," said Prudence in a sorrowful tone as she surveyed the terrain around them. "They say that King Luxurous's great-great-grandfather mined these lands. King Jaraxus. These plains were once great forests, filled with life. But he, too, sought for nothing but gold."

Arakin nodded thoughtfully, eying the bleak, unchanging terrain. He couldn't comprehend how the pursuit of gold could satisfy anyone, given the cost of destroying something as beautiful as a forest. But clearly, gold could buy things he didn't understand or care about. And clearly, some people in the world were very different from him.

"How did King Jaraxus get to these lands?" asked Arakin.

"Dragons," said Prudence. "Apparently, when the dragons fulfilled their purpose of transporting him and all their gold out, they were killed."

"Tell us more about this wizard you met," said Arakin enthusiastically as he glanced over his shoulder at Prudence. "Who was he?"

Prudence took a moment to answer. "He would say he was a drifter and a messenger. The wizards before him called him the greatest of their kind. He was the last wizard on this earth."

"Did he ride a dragon?" asked Ash excitedly, still seated on Arakin's shoulder but swiveling around to face Prudence directly.

"I'm not sure. He passed quickly through our town."

"Why?" asked Arakin. "Was he running from someone?"

"Yes," replied Prudence. "Luxurous's father was determined to execute all the wizards that survived the Dragon Wars."

"This wizard—what was his name?" asked Arakin.

"Nobellius," replied Prudence. "Nobellius of the North"

Arakin noticed a breach in the eternal flatness of the horizon ahead, causing his heart to quicken and eyes to widen. Just visible through the dust and haze, shapes were emerging under the silvery moonlight: three mountains. The peak of the most distant one, in the center, disappeared into a blanket of clouds.

"Look!" cried Arakin, pointing ahead.

Prudence took Sir Sudley's scroll out of the bag and read, "'You cannot see it for the peak is tall. And those that see it are bound to fall. Bound you must be to reach this blade. When one is many, then light is made.'"

Ash frowned and shook his head, swiveling around again to face forward. "Oracles and riddles! Why can't they just give us simple directions? Turn left, turn right. Yep, it's under the apple tree. Simple!"

Prudence grinned. "Prophecies are like a lock, Ash. And only the right people become the key to unlock them."

"So which one is Mount Drass?" inquired Ash.

Arakin and Prudence answered at the same time. "The middle one."

"You cannot see it, for the peak is tall," said Arakin, reflecting on the words from the scroll.

"I like it," snorted Ash with a grin. "It's the toughest one to climb. Probably impossible for most. And definitely the farthest away."

"And that's why we need to run," insisted Arakin with a tone of conviction.

Slipnor woofed, and Arakin gave a firm tap of his heels against the wolf's sides, sending him onward at a speedy gallop.

***

They charged ahead into deeper darkness, as the moon rose above the cloud line and their only source of light diminished with it. They were charging ahead now into an inky black.

"I can't see the mountains anymore," said Prudence anxiously.

Arakin felt a bolt of anxiety run through him. They needed to keep a straight path, or they would end up running in circles. He peered over his shoulder and surveyed the Twin Ranges behind them on both sides, and immediately felt a wave of relief rush through him.

"It's okay," he said, trying to sound calm. "The moon is still lighting behind us. We just need to keep the ranges even on the horizon."

Slipnor continued to nimbly dodge, duck, and bound beyond the reach of the zombie-like trees that continually swayed, swiped, and grabbed.

"Wow, how does he even see those coming for us?" exclaimed Ash.

"Great ears, nose, and eyes," said Arakin, equally impressed.

Onward they ran into what felt like a deepening cold, with Arakin continually checking behind them to gain his bearings and keep them on a straight course.

***

The horizon behind them soon gained an amber glow, heralding the imminent sunrise, welcome not only for its light but also its warmth.

They cut through the windswept badlands and into the new day, with Mount Drass forever discernible once more in the distance, yet never seeming to draw any closer. Despite this, Arakin felt a new glimmer of hope; there was a unique bond forming between them all. He once overheard one of the Generals say that their strength as an army lay in their conviction multiplied by their numbers. Arakin had always lived a solitary life and had wondered what it felt like to be a part of something—a cause, a team. And now he had these. They were a pack with a mission.

But then the seed of doubt crawled cunningly back in. He dearly wished that his quest had been less daunting than finding a mythical sword, and the stakes less ominous than someone close to him being executed by a maniacal king. The brisk westerly winds felt colder suddenly, hitting him in the face and

137

torso and driving deep into his bones. *Was he really worthy of leading this campaign*, he wondered as he began to shiver. *Was he really capable of saving Efscott?*

Ash's out-of-the-blue comment broke the silence. "Are we there yet?"

"No, Ash," replied Arakin curtly but with a grin, appreciating Ash's humor and its timing.

And within a few breaths, Ash asked again, "Are we there yet?"

"No, Ash," replied Prudence.

On and on they ran.

The sun sank behind Mount Drass, and the cold chill of night returned as the moon rose behind them.

***

Speckles of vegetation over the white earth heralded the approach of different terrain. The first two mountains took surprisingly little time to pass. They were tall, narrow things of dark grey rock and sparse foliage, towering over them and adjacent to each other as if they were enormous sentries at a gate. Arakin guided Slipnor onward through the gap between while surveying the mountains thoughtfully.

"What is it?" asked Prudence.

"Nothing … I just … I've never seen mountains like this before. They're almost alive."

"I know what you mean," said Prudence. "Like statues that were never finished."

"We'll make sure your father finishes his," said Arakin reassuringly.

In the distance, he could see the stark, pale flatlands give way to the foreboding steep incline of Mount Drass's eastern face. *At last, they were emerging from the desert*, Arakin thought to himself. His hand was so cold and numb that he found it difficult to move his fingers, his throat was dry and parched, and his stomach rumbled for food. He couldn't imagine how tired and sore Slipnor must be, and yet his giant companion gave absolutely no sign of objection or weariness.

Slipnor breached the last line of dead trees and quickened his pace. The dust under his feet soon turned to dark soil, and this soon yielded to a blanket of grass and moss.

At the base of the mountain, Arakin pulled back gently on Slipnor's shoulder fur, and they came to a halt, surveying the stunning accent ahead and catching their breaths. Arakin put his hand into his bag and took out their rations. He handed some bread to Prudence, along with the water canister.

"You're not too cold?" he asked.

She shook her head. "Your body blocks most of it. You must be frozen though. Let me ride the front for a while."

"No. I'm fine. We'll move slower up the hill anyway. I'll warm up."

She nodded with an air of reluctance, drank the water, and gave it back to Arakin. He dismounted and poured more into his hand for Slipnor to drink. The wolf lapped it up zealously and quickly devoured the beef and dried blackberries that Arakin offered.

"Arakin, you haven't drunk or eaten. You need—"

"I'll be fine, it's okay," he insisted as he jumped back onto Slipnor.

He flicked his heels, and Slipnor charged up the steep climb. Prudence gave a slight start and impulsively wrapped her arms around Arakin's waist to avoid sliding off, and Arakin felt his heart leap and his stomach somersault. Suddenly his hunger and pain were all but forgotten. He could feel the warmth of her body on his back, and although the front of his body still took the brunt of the cold winds, he no longer seemed to notice the discomfort.

They climbed higher and higher and were soon ensconced within fog and cloud, so dense they could see no farther than twenty feet ahead.

And then only three feet.

"We need to stop!" Arakin called out, pulling up on Slipnor, then alighting him. Arakin reached into their bag for the wizard's rope, then chose his old cord instead merely because the knot around the old, rusty grapple hook was much easier to untie. It was a decision he would soon regret though. Arakin took his old, weathered rope and hastily fastened it around the giant wolf's chest and back.

"What are you doing?" asked Prudence.

"The Oracles' poem!" he said and recited from memory, "'And those that see it are bound to fall. Bound you must be to reach this blade.'" He looked to Prudence. "That's us! I'll walk ahead. It's safer."

"But," said Prudence as if launching a protest, then realizing the logic to Arakin's argument.

Arakin detached the old grapple hook from the rope's end, placed it back in their bag, and fastened the rope around his waist. Then he grabbed Ash from his shoulder and set him on Slipnor's head.

"Hey!" said Ash objectionably.

"It's safer this way, Ash," said Arakin as he stepped forward. But an ominous groan emanated up ahead, causing them all to freeze.

"What was that?" whispered Prudence.

"Whatever it is, it's taller than me," replied Ash. "Not that that's saying much."

"We'll be fine," Arakin assured them, and he recommenced his climb, stepping purposefully onward. He quickly disappeared into the white fog, with Slipnor following at the same pace. And while they were visually disconnected from each other, they were still bonded via the rope.

Again the deep groan issued from the dimness ahead. Louder this time.

Arakin faltered, then continued. He slipped on dew-covered rocks that slashed into his pants and legs. The stones also cut partially into the rope around his waist. But of this, he was unaware. He doggedly picked himself up with each stumble, sweating and puffing from the exertion, and continued without complaint.

CHAPTER SEVENTEEN

Reaching Out

Onward Arakin pushed in the hollow of cold blue fog, where he seemed totally alone. But he knew his friends were close behind. The darkness was slowly receding now; the sun was creeping toward the eastern horizon behind them. And while this meant that they were gaining the comfort of light, it also meant that they were losing something else. "We're running out of time," exclaimed Arakin. "It will take us at least a day to return."

He pushed on with a higher purpose. His heart pounded harder in his chest, his lungs burned hotter, and his body dripped from a heavier cold sweat. The ground had changed from soil to smooth stone—damp, cold, slippery, and harder to get a grip on. He stumbled more often but pushed on with greater determination each time, knees bloodied and fingers red-raw from clawing at the rocks.

***

The sun broke over the horizon behind them, and the fog around them illuminated, becoming ethereal yet dangerous because of its density and blinding brightness. And then … the ground leveled out, becoming flat.

"You should let me lead, Arakin. I'm lighter," yelled Ash.

"Your legs are too short, Ash," came Arakin's reply.

"Sure, pick on the short guy. I'm here if you need me, though, buddy!"

Again a deep, rumbling groan permeated the frosty silence, much louder than before, and this time the earth trembled with it. But something else grabbed Prudence's attention. She inclined her neck, turning her head as if listening for something. She frowned. "Arakin, I think you need to stop."

"No. I'm okaaaaaay …" Arakin felt his stomach lurch upward before he even realized that he was falling. The rope tethering him to Slipnor violently yanked tight, and Slipnor, despite his size, was dragged forward over the slippery stone and dew-laden moss.

"Arakin?" Prudence screamed.

Slipnor dug his paws down hard and found traction, coming to a halt. Prudence and Ash bounded off just as a soft breeze rolled in, blowing the fog away. It unfurled in a spiraling dance as cold winds and thermals collided. The mist was gone, and now they could see where they were and what had happened.

They stood upon the very peak of Mount Drass. The northern clifftop. The rope tied around Slipnor drew a tight line, traversing the edge of the sheer drop—where Arakin now hung. Or did he?

Prudence and Ash bolted forward and peered over the edge. Arakin dangled ten feet below, staring up at them with panic-struck eyes.

There was a flat, dense blanket of cloud ten feet above them and another ten feet below, spreading out for miles, a visually striking artificial floor and roof of the heavens.

The taut rope dug into the rock and soil, sending chunks of dirt down, showering Arakin and punching holes through the clouds beneath that rippled outward. The valleys could be seen through them—very far below.

Arakin looked down and gulped. "Oh boy, that's not good!"

A solitary tree was perched on the edge of the cliff above Arakin, some ten feet to the right. It was a tired-looking old thing with only a few leaves. Most of its roots dangled over the cliff; only a couple were embedded in the mountain itself. A strong gust of wind caught the tree and caused it to sway. Its roots pulled upward on the soil. Wood and earth groaned loudly, and Arakin recognized it as the same noise they had heard during their climb.

The tree swayed more violently now, back and forward, leaning over the cliff like a death-defying diver hovering on indecision. But finally, its mind was made up, and it tipped forward one final time and toppled over the cliff's edge, ripping out of the earth, roots and all, plummeting now through the clouds.

The ground trembled from the force, and so did the rope. Arakin held on tightly for dear life, but with an audible rip, the damaged portion of the line above the knot on his waist broke, and down he fell. With lightning-fast reflexes, he shot his hand up and grabbed the rope higher up. Safe—for the moment.

Slipnor stepped gingerly back to hoist him up, but as the rope drew across the moss and rock, it collected dewdrops that ran down the line, straight to Arakin's hand. His grip loosened, and he slid helplessly down the rope. He squeezed hard and gained purchase on the final two inches, bringing him to a stop.

But he knew he wouldn't be able to hold on for much longer. His fist trembled, and the rope swayed. He looked up desperately to Prudence. Was this his final moment?

Suddenly Prudence's eyes changed color, turning to a bright, glaring white.

Her voice resonated as loud as thunder and as clear as light. "Exodus moord entrus tie! Twine and limb shall be with thy!"

Arakin slipped again, this time off the last inch of rope and into thin air, falling now through space, toward imminent death.

Prudence flicked her hands, and the rope around Arakin's waist flew off and flipped up around his wrist, then tied its other end to the main line. Arakin was caught in the firm grip of the rope, ending his descent.

Prudence's white eyes returned to their normal color, and she spun to Slipnor. "Go, boy! Go!"

Ash joined in with the same enthusiastic command while gesturing with his hand, and the giant wolf treaded backward carefully, dragging Arakin up and up and over the edge—to safety.

Arakin wheezed with relief and collapsed, relieved to be back on solid ground. Ash raced in and placed a comforting hand on his back, patting him affectionately.

Arakin looked to Prudence in disbelief, still catching his breath, and lifted himself up to a seated position. "You're a witch!" he whispered.

"Only an apprentice," she replied. "From the White Witch Order. And without a teacher."

"No teacher?" asked Ash.

It dawned on Arakin why. "Because there are none left," he muttered.

Prudence nodded sadly.

Arakin spoke to Ash, recalling the history. "Luxurous hunted them all down. Only Black Witches were spared. Because they'd work for him."

Prudence nodded again.

Arakin was perplexed about something though. "But witches can detect the presence of another witch. Why couldn't the Black Witch detect you?"

"I haven't made my vows and embraced my destiny. Until then, I will always be an apprentice and only have a fraction of the power I could ever have."

"So why don't you do it?" asked Ash. "That sounds cool."

"When I make my vows, I become a part of nature. And a true witch. No longer human. And then I will be found by, and attacked by …" her voice trailed off.

"Every Black Witch in the land," finished Arakin, softly.

Prudence nodded.

Ash sighed. "Just wish everyone could get along," he said with a shake of his head.

Arakin cocked his head, looking inquisitively at Prudence. "The wizard—Nobellius of the North—he taught you, didn't he?"

Prudence nodded again. "Both of us," she added.

"Both of you?"

"My father too. For every day that Nobellius spent teaching me spells I might one day use, he spent two days teaching my father."

"Teaching him what?"

"Sculpting with magic."

"Wow," exclaimed Ash, "that's a wizard who really appreciates the fine arts! I guess he was more fun to hang out with than the wizard who taught the magic of math."

"Why sculpting with magic?" asked Arakin, equally perplexed.

"I'm not really sure. All he said was that the times were changing and that magic was being hunted out of existence by Luxurous's family. Nobellius said that the body was always both a vessel and an ocean, and in some way, this would soon come together—like a lock and key—and magic would find a way to be free once more."

"So why didn't you take your vows when they arrested your father?" asked Ash rather innocently. "Maybe you could have saved him."

Tears welled in Prudence's eyes, and she hung her head. "I'm not strong enough," she confessed, "but I wanted to. Perhaps I should have—but I knew the time was not right."

"What's the right time?" asked Ash.

"The exact moment my heart is truly broken. Torn to nothing. Not a moment before. Nor after."

"Humans—wow—you're so complex!" said Ash with a shake of his head.

"Your secret is safe with us," assured Arakin. "I promise."

And it was at that precise moment that a gold light flashed across Arakin's face. A reflection. Arakin turned to the direction that it came from, beyond the cliff, through the layer of dissipating clouds up high.

Arakin smiled with elation. And Ash spotted it too.

"Well. You don't see that every day," chirped the wooden knight.

An eight-foot-wide chunk of earth, similar in shape to an inverted pyramid, hung in space about eighty yards from the cliff's edge and some fifteen feet above them. Roots dangled from the soil, swaying in the breeze. Its surface was a soft blanket of grass and moss, and in its center was a tree stump, about three feet high.

And in the center of it, a gold sword was driven.

The sun rose higher behind them, traversing the bottom layer of cloud and sending a glistening flash of reflections across its blade, which hummed ethereally.

They marveled at Gun Ronin's beauty as it hovered mystically and motionless in space before them, like an emperor of nature on a throne within the heavens. They had found that which had alluded all before them. It was real.

But despite being so near, it was still unattainable. How could they reach it?

Arakin's mind drifted to Efscott, wondering how he was holding up and ruminating over the issue of time that was quickly running out. He felt his heartbeat quicken and his chest tighten from the sense of urgency that swelled within him.

They had to get Gun Ronin—and quickly.

CHAPTER EIGHTEEN

Reflections

Back in Ashville, the Blacksmith was sliding a thin plate of metal into his kiln, when he saw something that caused him to pause: the fire within was much lower than usual. He craned his neck to examine the wooden pole behind. It ran from the paddle wheel outside, through the wall, and into the rear of the kiln. It would usually be turned at a speed strong enough to operate a fan, which was essential for providing a constant force of moving air. This would maintain the heat of the furnace so it could soften the metals he would forge. Without this, he could not work. The wooden pole was utterly still but not broken, which left him perplexed and concerned.

He made his way outside and approached the rear of the cottage. It was the still figure of someone through the afternoon haze that caught his eye first though. The Baker. He was standing by the edge of the creek, gazing vaguely down, with an empty bucket in each hand.

The Blacksmith eyed the creek, and his jaw dropped in disbelief. It was bone dry. No longer did it supply the crucial water for the farmers or a current to push the Blacksmith's paddlewheel or that of the grain mill. The stream of life that ran through their village had been cleanly severed by Luxurous's wishing well. The Baker turned and met his gaze with a sad, helpless expression.

The clatter of hooves and steel prompted the Blacksmith to turn. General Pound led a brigade of several tarp-covered carriages, coming to a halt in the town's center. The Blacksmith approached, eyeing the wagons warily.

Pound pulled the tarp off the nearest carriage, revealing a pile of earthmoving tools—picks, spades, and buckets. "I've got a wee job for you and your townspeople," he said in a gruff tone.

The Blacksmith eyed the tools with a bemused expression. Pound leaned down from his horse. "You'll get no money, but your bellies will get food and water, and that'll do ya."

The Blacksmith looked indignantly up at him. "But we're not miners."

"You are now," croaked Pound with a mischievous grin.

***

There were no windows in Efscott's cold dungeon cell beneath the castle, so it was impossible to tell the time of day. He had received no meals, only a single cup of water. He had drunk very little but had spent a lot of time staring into it and at the faint reflection of his own silhouette within. His worrying gave way to sleep for just two minutes, and he awoke with a gasp as if prodded hard by reality's fist.

A clanging noise permeated the silence. Efscott's eyes struggled to focus. Five figures were standing before him, outside the cell, leering down. They came closer. One was carrying a large set of keys—it was the Dungeon Master. Behind him were four Royal Guards brandishing spears.

"Get up!" barked the Dungeon Master. "It's showtime."

150

Efscott was stunned. The time had passed quickly. He blinked against the flames of their torchlights, which seemed so blindingly bright given the relative darkness he had become accustomed to. The Dungeon Master gave Efscott's foot a firm kick. "Get up!" he snarled.

***

Efscott shuffled up the stairs, with his wrists bound in iron cuffs behind him and his ankles tied together by a short chain. There were two guards behind him, two in front, and the Dungeon Master leading the way. "Crocodile-lunch walking!" bellowed the Dungeon Master, then chuckled at his own joke. He yelled it out again. "Crocodile-lunch walking!" This time Efscott heard a familiar laugh in the distance. It was Prince Perfeyn. Efscott had arrived at the top of the dungeon stairwell, so they were close to the throne room. They turned into a corridor, intended no doubt to keep scruffy prisoners away from the decorum of the royal lounge. But Prince Perfeyn yelled out, "Bring him here! I want to see him!"

The Dungeon Master motioned to the guards, who took Efscott by the shoulders and guided him to a nearby doorway. It fed into the throne room.

Prince Perfeyn was lying back on a comfortable couch, with two servants dutifully massaging his neck and feet. Perfeyn cackled upon seeing Efscott limping and shuffling in. "He is a crocodile-lunch walking, isn't he? Yum yum, pig's bum!"

The Dungeon Master bowed to Perfeyn, then led Efscott and the guards away, to a door at the very end of the hall. It slowly opened, and sunlight billowed in, and Efscott squinted as his eyes welled with tears. The silhouetted figure awaiting him at the door was the Executioner, a hulk of a man who could be easily mistaken for a gorilla at first glance.

151

Efscott's knees buckled beneath him. The moment of truth was closing in. "How did it come to this?" he hushed to himself. The guards behind grabbed him under the armpits to keep him upright.

"He doesn't look very tasty though!" yelled Prince Perfeyn as they shuffled away from him. Efscott flinched as something struck him on the back of his head. It was a tomato hurled by Prince Perfeyn, who threw another that hit him on the back with a splat. And yet another that connected with his leg. "That will make you much tastier, Carpenter. A bit less woody. A little tomato sauce goes a long way."

Efscott was guided through the door, at which point the Executioner took over, taking him by the shoulders and pushing him ahead, down a narrow ledge toward a cage that stood at its end. The cage was tall enough to fit one person and tight enough to stop him from crouching or sitting. It had an iron eyelet on the top through which a long piece of rope ran, leading up to a large, wooden beam overhead, about twenty feet long. As Efscott shuffled toward the cage, he peered over the narrow ledge to the moat forty feet below.

As soon as Efscott reached the cage, the Executioner shoved him into it and slammed the door shut. The Executioner placed his large, wart-covered hands on a small, metal wheel pinned to the castle wall and turned it around. The rope running through the eyelet overhead drew taut, pulling the cage up a few inches from the ledge and forward, over the very end. The stone shelf disappeared from under Efscott, and the moat came into sight— as well as the crocodiles. Efscott took a shaken breath and stiffened. His rigidity was contrasted by the crocodiles that sprang into action, swimming frantically to the spot directly beneath his cage as it came to a halt.

The rope and the wooden beam groaned under the weight, as the cage swung back and forward slightly.

Efscott nervously surveyed the iron mesh floor and the hinges on one side of it. It was a trapdoor. No doubt it would soon open when the Executioner pulled the locking pin, and he would fall into the crocodile-infested moat below. Efscott anxiously looked up at the sky.

The Executioner gave a sinister chuckle. "Nah. It's not midday yet," he called out casually, just loud enough so Efscott would hear him over the slight wind and distance. "Not far off it though."

Efscott glanced back down at the moat.

"Yeah," hollered the Executioner, referring to the agitated crocodiles, "I just like to whet their appetite with a glance at what's on the menu. Gets 'em excited. Adds to the spectacle of it all. Consider myself a bit of an artist, really. It's a bit like being a comedian. All about the timing."

He placed a locking pin into the wheel on the wall, securing it and the cage into place, then wiped his hand on his legs and turned to leave. He paused and looked back at Efscott.

"I've got a couple of errands to run," said the Executioner. "So don't go anywhere, all right?"

Efscott stared at him with a bemused expression. The Executioner laughed out loud, slapping both hands against his thighs, clearly very proud of his joke, then turned and lumbered away, along the narrow ledge.

***

Time passed, and Efscott remained perfectly still in the tight cage for fear that the slightest movement might activate the trapdoor beneath him. This and the exposure to the cold, biting winds had taken their toll on him—he looked exhausted.

Efscott could not see where the sun was from his vantage point because the castle blocked his view. But the sun was not overhead, which meant that midday and his execution were still some time away.

He could see the townspeople far below, disheveled and despondent, working in chain gangs as they heaved buckets of soil and lead through the dark, muddy fields. Some of them gazed up and froze upon seeing him, but they always hurried back to work and quickened their pace. Efscott's current position was a warning to all about the ramifications of breaking the King's law. Judging by their renewed vigor, it clearly worked.

Beyond the rooftops of the village, Efscott could see a distant shape that looked like the Executioner trudging into a field at the center of which was another lone figure, frozen to the spot. A scarecrow. Its clothes were torn and tattered from the years of exposure to the wind and rain. Efscott could also make out his carriage. His home. But it seemed broken now.

The crocodiles had begun swimming in a circular formation directly beneath him. In the center of that circle, Efscott could see his own reflection, a dot amid the muddy waters. Soon he would fall, and his reflection and he would meet, and it would all be over. Despite his sorrowful position, his mind was clearly on someone other than himself.

"My dear Prudence," he whispered softly.

A gentle breeze blew, and his cage swung back and forward, causing the wooden beam and suspension rope to creak and groan under the load. The breeze subsided, and he was soon still once more, dangling in space, against an eternal stark blue sky.

CHAPTER NINETEEN

The Power that Eludes Us

Arakin scrutinized the chunk of earth that held Gun Ronin in its center, hovering in space before them. Only twenty feet separated them, but miles lay in the drop below. It seemed so close yet so far away. He dove his hand into his bag, which was still tied to Slipnor's back, and drew out the wizard's immaculately polished, steel grapple hook—the gift from Prudence. He wasted no time, moving closer to the edge of the cliff and winding up a mighty swing. He released the hook while keeping the rope's end firmly between his thumb and index finger. The hook flew out on a perfect course toward the sword. But at the halfway mark, a strong wind suddenly rose and blew it backward. It spun in the air and dropped once it got within a few feet of them. Arakin retrieved it while biting his lip, deep in thought.

"Let me try something," said Ash. He stepped confidently forward, aimed, and shot an arrow with a string tied to its end. It was a perfect shot, and it soared on a direct course toward the tree stump, but again a mysterious wind blew it back.

"The force against us is supernatural," said Prudence. "Perhaps a supernatural force from our direction will help." She stepped forward and eyed the sword intently, her eyes once again glowing a brilliant, bright white.

Her words cut through the air like a blade. "Terrance et nimbus ground of thee. Come through space, come to me!"

But nothing happened.

"Well, that was definitely the biggest anticlimax from the three of us," said Ash with a chuckle. "Have to admit, I was almost expecting lightning bolts or something." He now seemed to be restraining an outburst of laughter.

Prudence spared him a sideways glance and a slight smirk, not wrangling at the barb; instead, she just shook her head while gazing back earnestly at Gun Ronin. "The scroll was right. Whatever we throw to it will always be thrown back."

"And they say no individual can ever claim it," added Arakin. "Wait a minute. The rest of the Oracles' poem: 'when one is many, and light is made.'"

"Are you sure that it really means something?" asked Ash. "It could be that the Oracles just wanted it to rhyme so it would sound good, so they added that extra bit."

"No, Ash!" said Arakin excitedly. "One is many! It means … we have to work as a team. Together. As one!"

"What light, though? Sunlight?" asked Ash.

Arakin bent down, took a small handful of grass, and sprinkled it over the edge of the cliff. It fell gently, then suddenly floated back up.

"No!" declared Arakin with the revelation hitting him." Light, as in weight … thermals … hot air. Heat rises! We approach it from behind. Outflank it. And we throw the rope back to ourselves!"

Arakin and Ash looked sideways to each other and grinned. A shared eureka moment.

****

Arakin quickly relayed the plan to Prudence while Ash nodded enthusiastically, enacting the proposed action with grand gesticulations. Prudence was horrified at first but soon agreed that it was a viable solution and did indeed address the Oracles' poem in terms of teamwork, if that was what the intended subtext was.

All three of them nodded to each other in agreement, and Arakin bent down and tied the end of the wizard's rope around his ankle. He grabbed the grapple hook and held it parallel to the ground, just an inch above it. Ash leaped onto the shaft, straddling it like a saddle, and hooked his legs under the bottom two claws. Then he wrapped his arms tightly around the top two, pressing his chest firmly into the curve.

"Oh my," hushed Prudence.

"It's even more uncomfortable than it looks, but the ride will be worth it," said Ash with a smile.

Arakin looked skyward. "I'm starting to have doubts, Ash."

"Come on," coaxed Ash. "Who else is going to fit in this grapple hook? You?"

"My throw won't get you that far," confessed Arakin, becoming increasingly concerned.

"I can give the extra push. But I'm not sure how strong that wind can get," said Prudence with fading confidence.

"It's fine," Ash reassured them. "Look at me—what could possibly go wrong?"

He looked even more contorted and uncomfortable within the grapple hook than before. Prudence and Arakin both feigned smiles.

"Ash, we're a long way above that valley," said Arakin. "Those are birds way down there. Big, high-altitude birds," he added, pointing to several white dots far beneath them.

"I'll be fine. Let's do this!" declared Ash. He pulled the cloth-covered crossbeam into his chest, then wrapped his arms once more around the two top claws and braced himself. He nodded to Arakin, who sighed and then turned and nodded to Prudence.

"This is going be one wild curveball. Out to the far left!" said Arakin.

"Yeah! Aim for the hippies!" yelled Ash.

Arakin spun the hook, and Ash kept himself wedged tightly within, gritting his teeth as the world blurred around him, faster and faster.

Arakin flung the rope out, and Ash dove forward out of the hook, like an arrow, staying streamlined and moving fast.

Ash soared up to the left of the earth chunk, keeping clear of its supernatural winds. He reached the apex of his climb and began to descend.

Prudence had been watching closely and flicked her hands outward. "Ash from ash, your courage sings, this verse of words now gives you wings!" A wind suddenly pushed Ash up and forward, past the floating earth chunk.

"Now, Ash. Now!" yelled Arakin.

Ash threw the crossbeams above his head, and with a whoosh, his parachute unfolded and grabbed the air. The thermals immediately took him higher, but the supernatural winds still had some reach, and Ash frantically fought them as they pushed him farther to the left.

"He isn't being pushed back," said Arakin excitedly. "That's a good sign."

Ash moved higher and higher, gradually beyond the reach of the supernatural winds, then clumsily steered himself around and down toward the handle of Gun Ronin from behind.

"That's it, Ash! You got this!" yelled Arakin.

Ash maintained his line, descending gradually and moving straight toward Gun Ronin.

"Oh yeah, I got this in the bag, baby! Come to papa!" affirmed Ash with a cheeky grin.

Closer and closer he flew. Then suddenly faster.

"Whoa!" yelled Ash, realizing he was losing control. Bang! Ash slammed face-first into the handle of the majestic sword. Arakin winced in sympathy while Prudence cheered. A breeze yanked the descending parachute forward again, and Ash's face slammed into the handle once more, leaving him with a very dazed expression. He hung on to the sword's grip with one hand, then groggily raised his other and gave the thumbs-up signal. The crooked smile on his face made it clear that despite his hard landing, he was all right.

"Yes!" yelled Arakin, "And … owwww!"

CHAPTER TWENTY

Drawn Together

Arakin knelt down where the recently fallen tree once stood. He pushed his hand into the upturned earth and withdrew a thick, broken section of its root that was a bit shorter than his arm.

"Time to see if our plan worked," he said as he stood.

Ash, now kneeling on the hilt of the broadsword, aimed an arrow at the empty space just two feet away from Arakin's left side and fired. The arrow followed the intended trajectory, pulling a long piece of string with it that Ash had attached behind the quiver. The other end of the string was fastened around Gun Ronin's grip and handguard.

A gust of wind arose and forced the arrow off target, much farther to Arakin's left, just as they suspected it might. Arakin was prepared for this moment, and he broke into a sprint. He dove, hit the ground, and slid toward the edge of the cliff. He could hear an anxious bark from Slipnor and a cry from Prudence as he dug his feet into the earth to brake, just in time, as his torso pushed over the edge. Arakin came to a halt, then stretched his arm farther out, with the root fragment still held firmly in his hand. And with a thunk, the arrow hit it dead center.

"Nice catch!" hollered Ash.

Arakin cautiously picked himself up, and Slipnor gave a woof, then shook his head with a series of snorts that were more of an expression of joy and relief than actual sneezes, all the while shifting excitedly on his paws.

Arakin yanked Ash's arrow out of the wood and gently reeled in the slack. He paused at the moment the string became taut, forming a straight line. And with great care—he pulled it in.

With a resonating groan, the chunk of earth moved toward them, gliding through space and gently descending to their level.

"It's working!" exclaimed Ash with a whoop.

Forty yards away now, and the detail of the sword was clearer and brilliant. But so was the detail of the soil beneath.

"Why are those roots moving?" asked Arakin.

Prudence had noticed it too. "They're not all roots. They're …" her voice trailed off.

"Snakes!" Arakin croaked.

The soil was rife with them—various shades of brown, black, and green slithering slowly through holes in the bottom section of earth. All equally terrifying, especially to Arakin, who stiffened in terror.

His fingers became lax, and the string connected to Gun Ronin slipped from his grasp.

Prudence stepped closer. "Arakin?"

"What's up?" yelled Ash.

Arakin backed away, and the earth chunk slowed, coming to a stop, still suspended in space.

"It's all right," said Prudence softly. "I can bring it in." She picked up the string and pulled in the earth chunk, occasionally casting a concerned glance over at Arakin.

He remained frozen to the spot, watching with a sense of horrified detachment, becoming a passenger in the events of his own life instead of the driver.

Ash kept calling out to him but was unanswered.

"He'll be okay, Ash!" said Prudence, reassuringly.

Just ten feet away now, and Prudence's eyes narrowed upon seeing something of greater interest dangling from the lower section of soil, in between the writhing snakes: a thin-leafed, gold-colored herb. Her eyes widened.

Now just three feet away, she let go of the string. The earth chunk continued under its own momentum as if the cliff face had a magnetic effect on it. Prudence knelt down and reached out, fearlessly pushing her hands between three snakes that weaved in and out of holes within the mound.

Arakin flinched in dread, then stepped forward but stopped again.

Prudence grabbed the gold herb and pulled hard, but it wouldn't budge. It was deceptively robust and was also anchored firmly in place. She refused to give up, though, and pulled even harder while placing her other hand higher up on the earth chunk to gain greater leverage. The jagged rocks on the lower section now threatened to crush her arm and were becoming a more significant threat than the writhing snakes.

"Prudence! What are you doing? It's not stopping!" cried Arakin.

He bolted forward and dropped to his knees beside her, thrusting his hand onto the mound and stretching himself over the shrinking two-foot gap. He pushed hard, keeping a wary eye on the snakes that moved perilously close, but the earth chunk continued its advance without slowing. It groaned even louder as it drew closer to the cliff, forcing Arakin across the slippery moss and stone on his knees. His feet struggled frantically for purchase, without success.

"Prudence … I can't hold it," he stammered.

Still empty-handed, Prudence pulled her arm up, much to the relief of Arakin and Ash. But she promptly reached into the left pocket of her top, withdrew a blue herb, and thrust her hand back into the narrowing gap once more.

Arakin groaned in horror, then dove sideways, grabbing a large rock and jamming it into the gap. But with a creak and a deafening crack, the encroaching chunk of earth crushed the rock, shattering it into pieces, sending some of the exploding fragments up into their faces.

Prudence refused to budge.

The earth chunk was now only five inches from crushing her arm. Prudence frantically rubbed the blue leaves over the base of the gold herbs, and her eyes turned a radiant white. "Take this herb for we're in need, blue herb set this gold herb free," she whispered anxiously with her brow beading heavily with sweat.

The gold herb glowed momentarily as the blue herb dissolved around it. Prudence pulled with all her might upon it, and the gold herb popped out.

But as she tried to withdraw her arm, her sleeve caught a root a quarter way up, trapping her. Her arm was now just an inch from being crushed. "Oh no," she muttered helplessly, frantically struggling.

With a mix of terror and conviction, Arakin held his breath, plunged his arm down into the closing jaws of the gorge, and grabbed her sleeve.

Ash winced. "Oh, this is not pretty!" he cried as he jumped off the sword handle, onto the tree stump's edge, and crouched as if preparing to leap over to them. "Let me help. I'll dive in there and … well, I'm small but—"

"No, Ash, wait!" yelled Arakin desperately. His wild, steely glance was enough to make Ash pause.

Arakin continued to thrash wildly, pulling up without success and soon losing the ability to flex his elbow as the chunk of earth pushed in closer. His strategy wasn't working, and he knew he had to rethink it—and quickly. He adjusted his position, pushed down with his hand instead of pulling up, then twisted and yanked, unhooking Prudence's arm and bringing it out of the encroaching bone-crushing gap. Just in time.

The chunk of earth pressed against the cliff like a giant jigsaw piece with a rumble and a ground-shaking clunk, and the snakes disappeared from sight with it. Prudence sat back, exhausted and relieved. "Thank you—" she said in a hoarse voice.

But Arakin's shriek cut her off. He had sprung up and begun prancing on his feet like someone standing on burning ground. "Errrr yuck, I touched one!" he blurted out, referring to the snakes. He shook his hand hysterically in disgust. "That is so gross!"

"Well," announced Ash, leaping up to the sword's handguard and untying the string, "you were this close to being the no-armed boy!" He held up his hand with a small gap between his index finger and thumb.

Arakin calmed down considerably and sat on his haunches with a heavy exhale of air while clutching his stomach as if controlling extreme nausea. "I guess you really do like your herbs!" he croaked.

"I guess you really do hate snakes."

"Did you notice?" he said with a faint smile.

Arakin noticed that Prudence gazed at him with a hawk-like curiosity, perhaps searching his eyes for hidden truths that were afforded to her because of her powers.

"They say that White Witches can see glimpses of the future. Do you see this?" asked Arakin.

"Sometimes ..." her voice trailed off, then she snapped out of her pensive gaze. She gestured to the gold herb in her hand. "It's the only plant in the world that can dissolve magical vegetation. Good for fighting Black Witches. Very rare."

"Hah, so is his arm!" said Ash as he jumped from the stump to the earth and made toward them. Arakin stared curiously at the crack in the ground as Ash passed over it. It moaned loudly, and Ash quickened his pace. "You don't think that stump's about to turn into a giant spider, do you?" he asked rather casually.

"No, Ash, it's the earth. It's healing," said Prudence. Arakin nodded in agreement. He had no knowledge of such matters, but it made sense.

The moan subsided as the line between the cliff face and earth chunk disappeared.

Ash sidled up to Arakin and Prudence as they rose to their feet. They all marveled at Gun Ronin, still nobly upright in the center of the tree stump.

From a hole in the rear portion of the stump, there was movement. Arakin squinted. "Is that—?"

"What?" asked Prudence.

From out of the wooden stump rose a bright purple snake, much bigger than the other ones they had seen—over two inches thick.

"A gigantic snake," declared Arakin painfully.

CHAPTER TWENTY-ONE

The Wizard's Guard

Prudence and Ash could clearly not see the large, slithering snake that Arakin fretfully referred to. They looked to each other blankly, then back at Arakin.

"What does it look like?" asked Prudence.

"Big!"

"What color though?"

"Purple. A deadly, I-have-the-most-toxic-poison-in-the-world kind of purple."

"A Wizard's Guard," said Prudence in a hushed voice.

"A what?"

"Sometimes a wizard will place a guard on a divine weapon to protect it."

"Is it real?"

"Yes and no. The serpent is only real … and deadly to those who see it."

"Oh great," groaned Arakin sarcastically. "So why doesn't everyone see it?"

"Only those who are truly determined to *wield* the divine weapon can see the serpent."

The snake coiled closely around the blade without ever touching it, rising majestically to the handguard, where it finally rested its neck, keeping its head directed up at the grip.

"You've got to be kidding me!" hissed Arakin. He felt his body once again grow taut from fear.

"It's okay," assured Prudence, "I can get it. I can't see it, so it can't hurt me. Besides, I sometimes work with snakes anyway," she shrugged. "Part of the trade, I guess."

Arakin looked at her helplessly. He felt a sense of shame for not being able to help, but this feeling was far outweighed by the terror of approaching the purple serpent. He gave her an unenthusiastic nod.

***

Arakin took the rope that was tethered to Slipnor and handed it to Prudence.

"Just in case," said Arakin softly.

She wound it around her waist, and Arakin tied it off with a firm knot.

"Good idea," said Prudence.

Arakin took hold of the section of rope between Slipnor and Prudence, taking up some of the slack. She turned and nodded to him, and he nodded back. Then she took a deep breath and stepped forward toward the join-line where cliff and earth mound came together. And then over it, toward Gun Ronin.

The rope ran through Arakin's hands as he watched her every step with unfaltering attention, never breathing, his heart pounding faster in his chest.

Prudence pulled hard, but the sword didn't budge. She tugged again, more firmly, but still without success.

"Ahhh, girls," grumbled Ash. "They just can't do manual labor."

"I'm not really in a position to agree with you, Ash," mumbled Arakin.

"Hmm. Guess I'm not either," added Ash in a chastened tone.

Prudence kept trying, now with both hands, but the sword stood resolutely in its place, joined to the tree and earth as if it were one and the same.

By the time she took her hands off the grip and stepped back, her palms were red raw from her efforts. She looked back at Arakin, panting heavily, her face flushed and sweaty.

"It's no use," she confessed. "We're so close. This isn't fair!" she cried in frustration. She took a deep breath and stepped toward Gun Ronin again.

"Wait!" yelled Arakin.

***

Prudence, now back on solid ground, wrapped the rope around Arakin's waist. She held it in place while he completed the knot. Slipnor, becoming skittish, whined and licked his face.

"It's okay, boy," Arakin assured the giant wolf with a gentle pat.

Arakin fixed his gaze on Gun Ronin, which remained ensconced within the coils of the purple serpent. It slithered upward slightly again, raising its head even higher, placing it gently upon the lower side of the sword's grip. Arakin groaned. He looked over to Prudence and lifted his eyebrows in a well-here-goes-nothing expression.

"So, you really don't see that snake, do you?" asked Arakin. "It's just so ... real," he added. Prudence and Ash shook their heads.

"Only two kinds of people see the serpent," said Prudence, "those who are worthy of wielding the weapon ... and those who are not."

"And no one has ever drawn Gun Ronin before, have they?"

Prudence shook her head. "Only those who should wield it can draw it. Only those who should wield it will avoid the deathly bite from the wizard's serpent."

"How do I know which one I am?"

She paused for a moment. "You don't have to do this," she said.

"Yes, I do. And time's running out," said Arakin, feigning a smile.

Bracing himself, Arakin checked the tension on his knot one last time and warily approached Gun Ronin, stepping onto the newly joined chunk of earth. The serpent's body remained tranquil and static, but its head began to sway slightly from side to side.

"Don't be afraid! Snakes smell fear!" hollered Ash.

Arakin tightened.

"Snakes don't smell fear. It's okay," reassured Prudence.

"I think maybe the imaginary ones do."

"No, they don't. You'll be fine."

"She's probably right," declared Ash. "Sorry, buddy. Just trying to help. I think I get nervous watching you put yourself in death-defying danger."

Arakin tightened up even more. It felt like his stomach had done a somersault.

Ash winced. "I probably shouldn't have said that. Sorry, buddy. Just ignore me."

Arakin eyed the snake with abject terror, took a deep breath, closed his eyes, and placed his hand on the grip of Gun Ronin. The snake raised its head and flicked its tongue against his fingers. He flinched but maintained a firm grip on the sword. He pulled. It didn't budge. He tried again with all his might, but it still didn't move. He looked back at Prudence, perplexed and concerned, a reflection of her own expression.

A thought occurred to him, and he stepped back and looked with resignation at the rope around his waist. It was a wild hunch, but he was sure he had to try it. A soft breeze picked up, and the caw of a blackbird echoed in the distance, far below. He untied the tether that kept him safely connected to Slipnor on the solid earth behind.

"What are you doing?" blurted Prudence anxiously.

Arakin took the rope off his waist and tossed it back to Prudence, landing it near her feet.

He pondered the Oracles' words again. "'When one is many!'" he called out in a voice that wavered. "If we are going to be one, I guess we need to trust each other, don't we. All of us. Man—sword—earth."

Slipnor whined, and Prudence patted him reassuringly. He cocked his head and barked while shifting from one paw to the other in an unusual combination of anxiety and joy.

"You've got this, buddy!" yelled Ash to Arakin.

Arakin stepped toward Gun Ronin again, eyeing his own image that slid across the polished blade. His mind flashed back to the times he had caught his reflection in the creek back home, thrilled at first by the novelty of seeing himself so clearly but confronted soon after with the reminder of who he was. A boy with one arm. A boy no one loved.

He trembled for a moment as a cold wave of self-doubt rushed through him, leaving every part of him feeling heavy and numb. Who was he to draw this sword? What right did he have to claim this thing born of magic that had eluded so many? He stiffened as his mind flashed back to Efscott, the first person who really cared for him, now so desperately alone and powerless. And suddenly, Arakin's self-doubt was replaced with a surge of purpose and determination that felt like a fire in his chest. He would pull so hard on this sword, he would be prepared to lose his only arm. Nothing would stop him.

Steely-eyed, he reached down and wrapped his hand around its grip once more. The wind blew stronger, sending dust and grass spiraling into the air. The snake's head swayed above the handguard again, its tongue darting out, grazing Arakin's thumb. The sunlight reflected off the pommel, shining directly into his eyes, a blinding, bright gold light. Never before was he so aware that he was in the presence of something special. Something magical.

"I promise to be worthy of you," whispered Arakin.

He closed his eyes, then opened them. And pulled.

The earth rumbled as he drew Gun Ronin smoothly from the stump. A metallic ring vibrated the very air around them, which resonated into a deafening crack of thunder from a sky void of dark clouds. Prudence, Slipnor, and Ash all ducked instinctively.

The purple serpent hissed, bared its fangs, and lunged to bite, but it was sliced immediately into four pieces by Arakin's deft upward flick of the blade. The sections of its head and body tumbled over the cliff and plunged down through the dense clouds below.

Arakin followed through with the motion of lifting Gun Ronin in one smooth move, raising the gold sword high above his head, where he admired it. It felt to him that Gun Ronin had almost launched itself upward, as if giving itself to him. The sun glistened off it, and the blade hummed. The grip vibrated for a moment within his hand. It was indeed as if the sword was alive. Arakin found he was charged with overwhelming energy and a realization he had never had before: more than ever, he had a purpose.

Each of them stared silently in awe, appreciating Gun Ronin for its beauty while also understanding the profoundness of the moment; for they who had discovered the sword would share a bond forever. Neither of them expressed this joy with words. They did not need to. Arakin met Prudence's gaze. Both their faces glowed with the same expression of euphoria.

CHAPTER TWENTY-TWO

To the River with no Bridge

Slipnor bolted down the hill, with the group hanging on tightly upon his back, making their charge back to Ashville.

And faster still through the White Desert into the night, nimble and quick, the full moon rising before them.

The wind swiftly changed direction on them, though, coming now from the east. A headwind— constant, bitingly cold, and stronger than before—created a sand storm that lashed at their eyes and skin. Trees lunged from the dense shroud of whipping dust, and their branches clawed malevolently at them.

Arakin felt it was as if the desert was determined to stop them. Slipnor ducked, leaped, and weaved. Although he was forced to slow somewhat, he clearly refused to surrender to fatigue, receiving the constant praise and reassurance of Arakin.

***

The sun rose, blindingly bright before them, and onward they charged. It was now that Arakin revealed his plan on how he would use Gun Ronin to rescue Efscott. Prudence and Ash seemed dumbfounded and remained silent. Arakin knew that the idea would be the last thing they expected to hear, and he anticipated that they may raise an argument, but they did not.

As they rode on, Arakin mulled over other ways he could somehow save Efscott, but he kept coming back to this same plan.

"I know it's a risk," he admitted.

"It's brilliant," replied Prudence, putting his mind somewhat as ease.

Ash, still poised on Arakin's shoulder, stared fixedly ahead through the howling dust storm. There was clearly another subject on his mind.

"So, we're heading back to the river of deadly, fiery lava, right?" asked Ash.

"Yes," replied Arakin.

"So, what's the plan for that?"

"I haven't got one!" he confessed.

"Great! Improvisation! That's my favorite!" barked Ash with genuine enthusiasm.

Arakin couldn't help but smile.

***

The winds had died now, and the expanse of vast desert lay behind them as the familiar glow of orange embers grew more brilliant beyond the next rise. Slipnor charged up the small embankment to the top of the ravine, the threshold where the white desert ended and the lava-river gorge began. Arakin pulled on Slipnor's shoulder fur, bringing them to a halt.

They all eyed the Ash Forest on the opposite side with a desperate yearning. Nothing remained of the lava bridge—it had completely disintegrated. What they faced now was a seemingly insurmountable channel of liquid fire, one hundred yards wide.

"It's almost midday. They will soon feed father to the crocodiles," Prudence croaked.

"There has to be a way over," muttered Arakin. He watched as a few small stones in front of Slipnor's paws rolled over the edge and tumbled down the ravine. They hit more rocks on the loose surface, which also slid. A large, ten-foot-square section of white dust slid down with it, some two inches deep. Loose topsoil. From just a few small stones. A thought occurred to Arakin, and his eyes flashed up and down the ravine, scrutinizing its surface, desperately searching for something. And then he found it. He tapped Slipnor's shoulder just once, urging him on, and guided him along the ravine's edge to their left at a brisk trot.

"What is it?" asked Prudence.

"It's a long shot. But it might work"

Arakin brought Slipnor to a sliding halt and jumped off. He drew Gun Ronin out of Prudence's bag and unveiled it from her shawl, in which it was wrapped.

"We'll see if Gun Ronin truly can join the land," Arakin declared.

"How?" asked Prudence as she dismounted Slipnor.

He met her gaze. "By cutting it."

With Gun Ronin in hand, Arakin bounded over the edge and slid down the ravine to an area laden with large white boulders, through the center of which grew a large lava tree.

He climbed over the glistening igneous rocks and regarded the pale tree before him with admiration, then patted the trunk affectionately.

"Thank you, old great one," Arakin whispered. He stepped nimbly over the massive tree roots that extended over and between the mounds of stone. Arakin spotted one root that reached through a large gap lower down. It acted as a support strap for two huge boulders at the base of the mound. Arakin traversed the rocks and brought himself to the very front, where he now looked up the steep ravine at the large tree, towering mast-like before him. He studied the lower foundations carefully as Ash came to his right side.

"Not that side, Ash."

Ash nodded and sprinted to Arakin's left side.

Arakin raised Gun Ronin above his head and cleaved down hard at the root before him.

It cut through cleanly with a reverberating chime, slicing a fine line through portions of rock as well. The root, now detached from its own anchorage, popped up, and a loud groan ensued as a boulder on the right side rolled ever so slightly forward. It began to move faster, down the ravine, collecting topsoil and more boulders with it. What began as one rock quickly became an avalanche.

Arakin bounded onto a section of stones that remained steadfast, slicing the roots that traversed them with smooth strokes. Down the stones tumbled, taking out even more boulders, soil, and trees, pushing the earth down—but also pulling. The ground beneath Arakin's and Ash's feet trembled and shifted slightly.

Arakin and Ash ducked and dodged five boulders that came rolling down toward them.

The avalanche rumbled down the five-hundred-yard ravine.

From above, Prudence clapped her hands and cheered with unbridled joy.

Ash looked sideways at Arakin. "I love it when we make her happy," he said with a smile. "Not so much when I'm slamming my face into swords though. Those cheers, I can do without."

With a loud, reverberating splash, the avalanche made contact with the lava river, sending up waves of the orange liquid rock. Boulders, trees, and soil now stretched across the entire lava river, forming a natural bridge.

"Yes!" exclaimed Ash with delight.

Arakin studied the avalanche bridge and the lava around it. At first glance, it looked promising. But he quickly became troubled. The bridge was, unfortunately, acting like a dam. This meant that the lava on the right side of the bridge was now rising higher.

"We need to be quick!" advised Arakin. He fixed his stance, tightened his grip on Gun Ronin, and leaped forward. He picked up speed quickly down the ravine and elegantly zigzagged across the surface like a skier on snowy slopes. With a flick of his hand, he beckoned the others to follow. "Just zigzag!" he yelled. "It's easy!"

"Wow!" declared Ash to Prudence. "He's so graceful. He's like a ... dancing angel."

And at that precise point, Arakin's foot clipped a rock, and he nosedived then somersaulted down the steep hill, limbs flailing in every direction.

"Orrrrr, maybe not," muttered Ash.

Prudence and Ash winced as Arakin rolled uncontrollably toward the lava river. Down he tumbled, hitting with a crack a small lava tree at the ravine's base. It spun him around like a top but also slowed him down marginally. He came to a stop just inches from the lava flow. Safe.

Gun Ronin had been knocked from his hand, though, and was sailing through the air. It hurtled back down to earth—toward Arakin's head. With a thunk, the blade stabbed the earth just an inch from his face.

Arakin rose groggily to his feet and beckoned them to follow. "It's safe! Maybe just take it slower than me." He collected Gun Ronin and dug it into the earth at the mouth of the avalanche bridge.

"To be honest," hollered Ash, "you're not really selling it to me. But I love your style!" Ash looked up at Slipnor. "Come on, Fluffy." Ash sprang forward from the rock he was perched upon and slid down the ravine, with Slipnor's excited barks drifting away behind him.

Slipnor anxiously pranced back and forward, barked again, and jumped over the edge of the ravine, soon catching up to Ash. Both of them tripped over rocks at the same time and tumbled down with limbs flying awkwardly around them, thumping into broken lava trees and each other.

Arakin raced up the ravine in a bid to intercept their descent, knowing he'd be knocked clean off his feet but hoping to slow them down in the process.

They collided into him and slowed, coming to a stop a few feet from the lava, all splayed across the white soil. Ash lifted his head and declared in a reproachful tone, "I think I lost my concentration somewhere—oh that's right, it might have been when the wolf the size of a house came bearing down on top of me!"

Arakin rose wearily to his feet and waved to Prudence, who remained at the top, looking terrified. "It's okay!" he yelled. "We can catch you!"

She took a deep breath, nodded, and jumped over the edge of the ravine.

Fast, fast, fast, she glided with incredible grace and speed across the soft, white dust and between the precarious tree trunks and rocks. Down, down, down, she approached the base at rocket speed. Arakin tensed, preparing to catch her, but when she got within twenty feet, she turned adeptly, skidded sideways, and came to a graceful stop. Even the dust that flew up from her feet danced in circles with supernatural grace.

Arakin, Ash, and Slipnor stared at her, dumbfounded.

She chuckled, then added modestly, "I think the trick is to bend the knees."

"I think I loosened it for you. The soil, that is. Helped a bit, yeah?" said Ash dryly.

"Of course," she replied with a grin.

Arakin smiled and nodded mechanically beneath a layer of dust and bruises. "That was ... pretty smooth," he croaked.

CHAPTER TWENTY-THREE

Running on Fire

Arakin turned his attention to the avalanche bridge, surveying its gaps and structural flaws. Lava spat up between the cracks in some sections at the center, creating a particularly dangerous obstacle. On the side facing the lava flow, numerous rocks ignited and dissolved into ash and embers. The bridge's foundations were swiftly being penetrated and devoured amid the roar and hiss of liquid fire.

"Time's running out. It's burning quicker than I thought. Now or never!" Arakin announced. He returned Gun Ronin to Prudence's bag and bounded onto Slipnor's back, with Prudence and Ash quickly joining him.

With a mix of trepidation and conviction, Arakin eyed the bridge once more and flicked his heels against Slipnor's ribs. "Go, boy!"

Slipnor bounded ahead, first up the steep embankment to the mouth of the avalanche bridge and then traversing its narrow line across the lava river, his acute sense of hearing affording him the ability to detect the slightest howl of air as the lava raced up the gaps below. As each plume shot violently up through the cracks beneath them, Slipnor dodged out of its reach with lightning-fast reflexes.

But upon passing the halfway point, they watched with dismay as the entire section ahead burned and disintegrated into nothing. The safe path forward was now gone.

Slipnor slid to a halt, and Arakin looked frantically over his shoulder, only to discover that the fifty-yard section of bridge behind them had also disintegrated. They were now stuck on a tiny island—stranded thirty yards from the edge of the riverbank.

"Oh no," whispered Prudence.

Suddenly they all lurched forward violently as the rock beneath them fell two feet down, caused by the disintegration of its foundations. They now stood on the final remaining boulder, which kept them several feet above the lava, but the power of the current pushed the molten liquid up the sides, lapping threateningly just a few feet away.

"Look!" yelled Arakin, pointing to a robust lava tree just forty yards up the steep ravine ahead. One of its thick branches stretched out over the lava river.

Arakin took his grapple hook rope, swung furiously, and launched it. It sailed through the air on a direct course toward the tree. Closer and closer. With a dull, distant thunk, it hooked itself cleanly onto one of its branches. But Ash's and Prudence's cheers trailed off when they saw Arakin shaking his head.

"I should have aimed farther back. This part of the branch is too thin."

"Are you sure?" asked Prudence.

Arakin dismounted and pulled back on the rope, leaning into it. With a crack, the branch snapped halfway through, almost falling but remaining connected via the branch's sinewy, flexible fibers. The hook remained in place.

"Can you pull the rope back in?" asked Ash.

"Maybe. But there's a good chance it will fall into the lava river. Wait a minute!" He looked at Ash. "Thermals!"

"What?" replied Ash.

"Heat rises. Remember? You can ride the thermals all the way!"

"Are you sure?" Ash casually pulled the crossbeam off his back, and with a whoosh, he took off into the air, with his legs flicking wildly, his eyes wide in shock.

"Heyyy, you're right!" He hollered as he flailed wildly to gain control.

"Goodness!" exclaimed Prudence.

"Grab the grapple hook and wrap it around the trunk!" yelled Arakin.

He and Prudence lurched forward again as their island of stone sank deeper into the lava river. The edges were disintegrating even faster now, bringing them just two feet away from the lava. "Quickly, Ash!"

Ash soared up fast, struggling to control the mighty thermal winds. He veered off course, slightly to the left, and elevated higher than he needed to be. He pulled hard on his parachute strings and regained control, heading now for the sizable, rugged lava tree. Ash grinned proudly and nodded to himself in admiration of his newly acquired skills. "Make it look easy, don't I?" he hollered. Suddenly his pace quickened, and he accelerated toward the tree. "Argh, not this again!" Ash took his right hand off the parachute strings to protect his head, but a sudden breeze spun him around, and forward, fast, and with a bang, he slammed into the thickest branch—face first, on his left side.

"Yay!" Prudence cried with joy from far below. "He does that so well, slowing down with his face so he can catch things."

Arakin winced. "Not sure that's intentional."

Ash groaned. "Seriously? Is there a warning for this in anyone's flight manual?" He peeled himself away from the bark.

"Hurry, Ash!" yelled Arakin.

"I'm on it!" he wheezed.

The boulder beneath Prudence, Arakin, and Slipnor was sinking faster now. They were only one foot above the lava that splashed up the side of their sanctuary. Slipnor whimpered anxiously. He paced back and forward as the surface grew hotter under his paws.

"Arakin, how will we get Slipnor over?" Prudence asked, her voice faltering as she gently patted the giant wolf.

Arakin looked back at her, his face fixed with worry. "I've been asking myself the same question." He eyed the lava and the embankment anxiously. "There has to be a way. There's always a way," he said resolutely.

On the tree overhead, Ash heaved himself to his feet and hobbled along the branch, reaching out desperately for the grapple hook when getting just inches from it. But with a crack, the broken limb peeled away even more, and Ash fell with it. He threw himself back, teetered for a moment with his arms circling wildly, and regained his balance. He knelt down, reached out again, grabbed the hook, and carefully lifted it while stepping back.

Below him, the island of stone sank another ten inches. The lava breached the top edge of the boulder and made its way over the plateau-like surface upon which Arakin, Prudence, and

Slipnor stood, four feet away, now three feet away. They huddled closer together.

Arakin was gazing trance-like into space, considering options for escape, refusing to believe that all hope was lost. His eyes flashed to Prudence's.

"Can you make me stronger?" he asked desperately.

"No," she replied helplessly.

"Can you make Slipnor stronger?"

"No." But then an idea struck her. "But I can make him lighter."

"Perfect!"

"But it will only last for ten heartbeats."

"Then we'll spend it well," Arakin declared as he frantically tied a hitch twenty yards from the end of the rope using his teeth and only hand.

"But a spell like this will also make him equally heavier for the same amount of time at the end of the spell," added Prudence. "Nature always demands a balance."

"Then we'll make balance work for us. We're going to make it! And we're going to save your father. I promise!"

Higher up, Ash tripped on the wobbling branch and fell on his face with a dull slap, dropping the grapple hook. His hand flung out instinctively for it, and he grabbed it just in time.

"Quickly, Ash!" hollered Arakin.

Ash bounded up and sprinted to the trunk, with the grapple hook held tightly to his chest.

The lava was now just two feet away from the trio below and closing.

One foot away now. Slipnor paced on the spot more frantically as the stones got hotter. Arakin, drenched with sweat, red-faced, and also feeling the heat searing through the soles of his shoes, frantically looped his end of the rope around Slipnor's chest and lower stomach, creating a harness of sorts.

"Get on!"

Prudence jumped onto Slipnor, and Arakin bounded on behind her. He fed the rope's end through the hitch higher up.

The section of rope that once hung in the air was drawing tighter now, thanks to Ash. He had successfully carried it up the branch and was now throwing the grapple hook around the trunk, hooking it quickly back onto its own line, thus anchoring it to the tree.

Arakin gripped his end tightly and pulled it taut through the hitch, then braced himself. They were ready.

"Okay, Prudence!" Arakin called out hoarsely over the top of the hissing, splashing lava that was becoming increasingly louder. Arakin could feel his skin starting to prickle uncomfortably from the heat. Even breathing was becoming increasingly difficult with air that seared his throat and lungs.

Prudence took a deep breath, and her eyes turned bright white. "Bound up high for bound we be, so light you are to set us free!"

Arakin could feel the very air around them tremble and cool as the spell manifested itself into the tangible, born of words, born of thought, born of hope.

"Now, Slipnor! Jump, boy!" he yelled.

Slipnor barked and leaped forward, with Arakin and Prudence clinging on for dear life. He went airborne, moving higher than ever before, his lighter body effectively adding four times more spring to his jump.

Arakin and Prudence pulled back hard on the rope, again and again, taking up the slack as quickly as possible. Arakin tied a quick knot to lock off the hitch just as Slipnor descended from the apex of his leap. The rope snapped tautly—and held.

They swung smoothly forward, but also down toward the lava river.

Slipnor's paws grazed dangerously close to the searing lava at the bottom of their swing, and he strained to lift them higher still while whimpering slightly. They gradually swung up toward the safety of the embankment, and Slipnor began running in midair in anticipation.

But they didn't reach it. They swung back, and it was clear they were also sinking deeper into the swing. Slipnor was getting heavier again.

"The spell is wearing off!" said Prudence, her voice shaking slightly.

They continued their backward swing toward the boulder in the middle of the stream, only to see the last few inches of it disintegrate beneath them, leaving nothing under them now but hot lava.

Ash watched anxiously from the trunk where the grapple hook was lodged. "Come on, you can do it!" he muttered with his jaw and fists clenched tightly. Slipnor's weight increased even more though, and the tree trunk behind Ash bent and creaked where the grapple hook was fastened. Ash's eyes flashed back at the tree trunk, and he pointed at it. "Don't give up on me!" he pleaded. "Timber to timber!"

"Lean into it!" called Arakin, and Prudence joined in, pulling back hard on the rope with all their might as they approached the end of their swing. "Slipnor, tail up!" he yelled, and the giant wolf lifted his hind legs high behind and dipped his head. Arakin and Prudence had to lean back hard to avoid slipping down over his head. They squeezed their legs and hung on tightly. For a moment, they were all frozen in space at the peak of their backward swing. Woosh, they swung forward. Slipnor lowered his rear, and they hurtled forward even faster.

They swept across the lava, lower than before, with Slipnor's full weight now bearing down on the rope but also giving them greater momentum. Slipnor lifted his paws as high as they could go, and they sailed an inch above the flame-crested liquid, fast approaching the river's edge, then up, up, and over to the safety of the embankment.

Arakin yanked the end of the rope, thus releasing the knot, and they fell to the ground with a resounding thud, toppling over to the side. Arakin landed safely, but Prudence spun around and teetered over the edge, just inches from the lava. She began to fall and Arakin dove out with his hand outstretched, managing to pull her back, but he lost his own balance in the process. They both hit the dirt face first. Covered in dust. But safe.

"Yes!" screamed Ash. He spun on his heel and hugged the tree trunk. "Let's hug this out, you sterling chunk of timber!"

Arakin, now dangerously close to the lava flow, lifted his head and turned to see if Prudence was all right. She raised her face to meet his and their eyes locked.

"Arakin, you're on fire!" she croaked in a husky tone.

"Thanks," replied Arakin, assuming it was a compliment. "I was pretty quick, wasn't I?"

"No, I mean, you're really on fire!" she announced anxiously. "Your hair is burning!"

Sure enough, Arakin's hair was on fire. Smoke at first, then flames. And lots of them. Arakin sprang to his feet, shrieking while patting his head furiously. The blaze increased, though, fanned now by his hand movement. Prudence grabbed a handful of white dirt, jumped up, and dowsed it over his head, smothering the flames in an explosive cloud of smoke and dust.

"Thanks," whispered Arakin, now totally covered in fine white powder.

Ash slid down toward them, bringing the grapple hook with him. "That's an interesting look," he said.

A cloud formation overhead drifted past the sun, thus revealing its position—near the center of the sky. Arakin shot a worried look back at Prudence. "We don't have long. It's almost midday."

CHAPTER TWENTY-FOUR

The Race Against Noon

Slipnor made short work of bolting up the steep embankment with Arakin, Prudence, and Ash back on board. It was like traversing a wall, for it was much steeper than it first looked. But Slipnor's paws were perfectly adept at permeating the soft surface, finding traction while also keeping speed.

He bounded over the precipice of the ravine and dove through the dense tree line of the Ash Forest. Ash was poised on Arakin's right shoulder, his bow at the ready, and Arakin grabbed the first branch available as a thwacking bat.

They charged through the woods with a mix of desperation and unyielding focus, navigating the treacherous environment with ease.

***

They burst out the other end of the Ash Forest, continuing down the slope toward the castle. They could see the fields on the eastern side over the rooftops, in which the townspeople worked in various chain gangs.

"I didn't think that so many of the townspeople would have volunteered to work in the King's mines," said Ash with surprise.

"No choice," replied Prudence. "Their crops perished."

She pointed farther eastward, to the fields of dead harvest. The soil was blackened from lead and covered with white, thorn-ridden vines strangling all the crops.

"The Ghost Thorns of Death and Pain!" gasped Prudence.

"I'm guessing you can't cook that up with potatoes," said Ash dryly.

"The wastewater from the mining creates them. The water kills everything. And it feeds these thorns." Prudence pointed to the eastern section of the castle's moat. It was fed a constant stream of black, inky water from the gargoyles' mouths, perched near the tower's rooftop. A spillway located on the eastern side released the overflow of water from the moat. From here, it ran down an embankment and onto the crop fields, then spread farther across the flatlands to a small hill where the townspeople toiled in their chain gangs within the sludge and mire.

The primary lead deposits had been found in a belt of ore within the small hill. It was a broken hill now, cleaved through its center with picks and spades. The chunks of ore were hauled out and passed to others, who smashed them into smaller stones amid the chatter and crack of sledgehammers. These were collected in wire baskets and carried away to the castle's rooftop in a long, snaking line of subjugation and misery.

"Nothing can stop it now, except what started it," said Prudence solemnly. "A wish granted by a Black Witch."

Their anxious gazes drifted higher, along the castle walls to the tower.

*****

On the rooftop of the castle, the King and Witch stood by the wishing well. The chain gang of townspeople trudged in, and one by one, they lowered their wire cages into the well, paused briefly, then heaved them out— except now the lead was gold, glistening brilliantly in the midday sun.

From here, the townspeople plodded down the long, winding stairwell with their hefty loads, depositing them finally in the King's treasury, after which they returned to the fields with their empty wire cages to collect yet another load.

Arakin saw something else even more alarming and pointed. "Look!"

They could see Efscott locked in a small iron cage on the castle's ledge. It dangled beneath the wooden beam that was fixed to the western wall, fifty feet above the moat and the albino crocodiles swimming within and occasionally sniffing and snapping in the air with anticipation of Efscott being delivered as their next meal.

The Executioner walked to Efscott's cage, wearing his traditional black mask and carrying a scarecrow with a pumpkin head. Its arms were splayed out high to the side, at shoulder height. The Executioner reached for a lever of some sort on the castle wall, and Arakin felt his heart pound furiously and his whole body tense.

"No," Prudence cried.

But they quickly discovered with immense relief that it was a pulley wheel the Executioner reached for, which he now turned to retrieve Efscott's cage. Upon bringing it in, the Executioner pulled Efscott out and hooked his wrist bindings to

191

a clasp on the wall. He shoved the scarecrow into the narrow, empty pen, but it would not fit. In fact, it barely got a quarter of the way in due to its long arms splaying out so wide. Not being the brightest of people, the Executioner assumed that if he shoved a bit harder, the problem would resolve itself. But it did not. The scarecrow would still not fit in the cage, which clattered and swung back and forward from his efforts. The Executioner pondered this dilemma earnestly with his chin resting firmly on his fist. An idea came to him, and with glee he reached out, snapped both of the scarecrow's arms at the shoulders, and shoved it into the cage. This time it fit.

Efscott gulped as the Executioner grinned at him and slammed the cage shut. He turned the tiny pulley wheel beneath the wooden beam to send the pen off the ledge again, away from the castle wall and to the end of the wooden shaft, where it resumed its position dangling precariously over the center of the moat. The scarecrow's haunting dead eyes gazed through the bars and across the field below at the fast-approaching Arakin, Prudence, Ash, and Slipnor.

The Executioner yanked down on a lever beneath the wooden beam, and the floor of the cage gave way with a sharp clank. The scarecrow fell, and before it even hit the water, it was broken in half by the jaws of the first crocodile that sprang upward. The rotund pumpkin head was shattered into a hundred pieces from a bite by the second crocodile.

***

Arakin's eyes narrowed with loathing in witness to the spectacle as they continued their rapid approach, and he could feel Prudence shudder in terror.

"An albino crocodile execution practice session!" said Ash. Boy! Don't you hate those?"

192

Arakin had steered Slipnor down into the dry creek bed to avoid detection from the guards who patrolled the town. Although exhausted, Slipnor quickened his pace, sensing the urgency of their race against time.

***

The Executioner drew the cage back in and grinned once more at Efscott. He was genuinely proud of his work. "Finest engineering, that cage," grunted the Executioner. "Always works a treat."

He shoved Efscott back into the narrow prison, locked it, and turned the pulley wheel, sending him out to the end of the beam once more. Efscott stared helplessly through the floor of the swaying cage at the moat of growling crocodiles below that now seemed more agitated than ever. The scarecrow test had not only provided a mechanical rehearsal for the Executioner but probably also served the desired effect of doing nothing to satisfy their hunger, and everything to infuriate them.

***

Arakin pulled back on Slipnor's shoulder fur, bringing them to a halt. They were at the northern end of the village, where the last of the cottages and patches of shrubbery provided them cover. Arakin dismounted, looking warily around, with occasional anxious glances up at Efscott in the distance.

"Are you sure you want to stick with this plan?" asked Ash.

"I thought you didn't mind it," said Arakin.

"Well, I didn't say anything because ... I was kind of hoping you'd come up with something better."

"Well, I didn't."

"I've got an idea!" declared Ash.

"What's that?" asked Arakin.

"Let me go in. I'll take them down one by—"

"No!" said Arakin and Prudence firmly at the same time.

"But you risk losing—" Ash was cut off again by Arakin.

"Sometimes you have to lose something before you truly find it," said Arakin softly, reflecting on what Efscott told him that day at the edge of the Ash Forest when Arakin returned his prized chisel to him.

Prudence alighted from Slipnor, and Arakin turned in protest, but she held up her hand.

"I'm coming too."

"Prudence, it's too dangerous."

"I'm coming too! I think your idea is brilliant. And it's just given me an idea as well."

Arakin nodded and smiled, then took a deep breath and turned to Ash, who was standing high on Slipnor's neck.

"Remember, Ash," said Arakin, "keep to the banks of the East Born Creek—"

Ash cut him off, "I know, where it's safe." He gestured to Slipnor. "I'll keep the fluff ball out of trouble. Just call if you need us."

"Slipnor will need food and water. There's a bag of dried beef and berries under the black rock at the—"

"At the base of the Dwarf Oak. I know," said Ash with a warm smile. "And the best place for water is the stream thirty yards to the right. We've got this. You drilled all that into us. Not that I'm a fan of the word *drill*, but anyway. Just make sure you call us if you need reinforcements."

Arakin nodded, smiled, and turned on his heel.

Ash and Slipnor stood rigidly as Arakin and Prudence walked away.

"I'm made of solid timber, Fluffy," said Ash, "but tell me, why does my stomach feel like it's filled with knots and my chest feel so empty?"

Slipnor whined. And Ash patted him.

"I know. I don't like it either. But we take our orders, and that's what good soldiers do. But I tell you this: if that King hurts any of them, they'll have us to deal with. Right?"

Slipnor growled. Ash patted him and steered him away, back to the Ash Forest.

CHAPTER TWENTY-FIVE

Arresting Developments

The absence of ceremony around Efscott's cage was definitely promising, signifying they still had time before the execution. Regardless, they ran as fast as they could toward the castle, slowing finally to a frantic walk as they got closer. Royal Guards did not look favorably upon anyone racing toward them. It was usually met with an arrow to the chest, and that was considered the warning shot.

Arakin and Prudence scampered toward the drawbridge, disheveled and exhausted, with steps that hiccupped in their harried gait.

The two burly guards in front of the main entrance stepped forward menacingly and pointed their spears at face height. Arakin and Prudence froze.

"I have something your King needs!" declared Arakin proudly.

"What—a sense of humor?" grunted the first Guard, who chuckled at his own joke.

"Ummm. No. It is of much greater importance."

"A better-looking witch, perhaps?" chuckled the second Guard.

The first Guard leaned in closer. "Here, hang on a minute! You're that runt they're looking for!"

Arakin stood tall, terrified, but defiant. "We bring a gift for the King. For we are adventurers, returned from a noble quest!" declared Arakin.

"You're nicked, is what you are."

Both guards reached out and yanked Arakin off his feet.

****

In the center of the throne room, Arakin stood in leg irons with an absurdly large, wooden stock perched on his shoulders, locking his neck and wrist, his head bowed. Prudence was beside him, and the two guards from the main entrance stood behind them. Luxurous, Minus, and the Witch regarded Arakin with contempt and wariness.

Arakin spoke softly. "And I'm sure that if you check my exact words, Sire, you will find there has been a misunderstanding."

Luxurous read from the unrolled parchment he was holding.

"You then said to the townspeople, 'and I am here to lead a campaign that will reshape this kingdom,' correct?" Luxurous raised his eyebrows in a how-do-you-explain-that? manner.

By tilting his head in the stocks, Arakin was able to meet Luxurous's gaze. "Exactly, Sire. You see, the campaign I spoke of was to find a chisel worthy of carving the statue of your son, the Prince. We reshape the wood, and we shape the love the people have for him."

Luxurous studied his scroll again. "And then you said, 'and it all starts with freeing Efscott Borelle, Carpenter and … very nice person.'"

The Witch rolled her eyes. Minus snorted and added sarcastically, "Pffft, great speech."

"Yes, Sire," affirmed Arakin. "And by bringing this magic chisel, worthy of such a job, I thought you might release Efscott, the great Carpenter of Ashville."

Minus stepped forward, fidgeting and snarling. "I saw that man carving a toy!"

Arakin maintained his friendly tone and addressed Luxurous. "Actually, Sire, that was a practice version of the Prince's statue."

Minus narrowed his eyes, not totally convinced.

Luxurous, however, nodded thoughtfully, weighing it all up. "And you know all this because …?"

"We are his loyal servants, Sire," answered Arakin.

He could hear the shuffling of feet as the Witch drew nearer, then felt the rotund end of her wooden staff under his chin. She pulled it upward, lifting his gaze, and Arakin knew why. She was checking to see if he was lying.

Arakin thought about his next words carefully, knowing that he needed to connect a more truthful element to his story. He reflected on the Oracles' claims regarding Gun Ronin's power and destiny, and its other name of King Maker. He raised his head even higher so the Witch could see his eyes clearly if she wanted.

Her eyes turned jet black, and she studied Arakin carefully.

"We went on this quest," said Arakin evenly, "to find the most magic of blades in the land. And I am certain, Sire, that this blade is worthy of forging a courageous prince, of shaping the future king. And for this, we needed a blade worthy of a king."

The Witch pulled her staff slowly away from Arakin's chin. "He is indeed telling the truth," she stated crisply, with slight surprise.

Luxurous regarded the object at Arakin's feet with greater curiosity. It was wrapped in Prudence's shawl, which was now quite tattered due to tears created by the constant rubbing of Gun Ronin's tip and edge against it during their long journey.

"Not the most expensive wrapping, is it?" grumbled Luxurous. "Let's hope your chisel is more impressive than what's around it."

Luxurous nodded to one of the guards, who picked up Gun Ronin and brought it to him. Luxurous unfolded the shawl and frowned upon seeing Gun Ronin fully revealed. "Very big for a chisel! Looks a lot like a sword." He eyed Arakin dubiously, and Arakin smiled innocently back with a shrug that was mostly subdued by the heavy stocks on his shoulders.

"It is nice though," added Luxurous. "And shiny, I'll say that!"

Arakin tensed as the Witch approached, bringing with her the snake that was eternally draped around her neck. His fear was evident. She smirked upon seeing this and examined the sword again. "It has magic," she croaked. "Without a doubt." She eyed Arakin suspiciously. "Where did you get this?"

"I prayed for a chisel that could forge a sculpture of our mighty Prince, and it fell from the heavens and cut my arm off, as you can see."

Luxurous suddenly became more intrigued. "Oh! Really?"

The Witch shook her head, keeping a stern eye on Arakin, who shook his head in acquiescence, adopting a humble demeanor.

"Umm, no, Sire. Just joking, sorry. The guards said you might find that funny."

Luxurous pondered this and chuckled. "Hmmm. Yes, very good. I do enjoy laughing at cripples, it is true." He looked back at Gun Ronin. "So, where did you get it?"

"Pulled it out of a tree stump, Sire. Found it at the top of a mountain, beyond the Ash Forest."

The Witch studied Arakin carefully and nodded to Luxurous; he was telling the truth. Luxurous contemplated this and peered down the hall. He could see the doorway at the end that opened out onto the western ledge where the Executioner stood. Efscott still dangled in his cage at the end of the beam.

Arakin glanced across at Efscott, too, but lost his balance from the weight of the stocks. He tried to regain stability, but with his feet bound as well, he fell and landed flat on his face.

Luxurous stared down at him bemused, then sideways at the guards. "A bit much with the stocks and ankle bindings, isn't it? He's not exactly dangerous."

The first Guard picked Arakin up. "Yes, Sire. We just thought it looked funny, Sire."

Luxurous chuckled. "Hmm. Yes. Very good, very good." Luxurous stared thoughtfully out at Efscott again. "Executioner!"

The giant childlike Executioner ducked his head around the doorway. "Yes, Sire?"

"Bring him in!"

"Into the crocodiles, Sire?" The Executioner pointed to the moat and placed his other hand on the execution lever, preparing to pull it, thus sending Efscott to his death. Efscott's eyes widened. Arakin's heart thundered in his chest.

"No, you idiot!" barked Luxurous. "In here!"

***

Efscott was still bound at the wrist and ankles as the Executioner carried him in, holding him under his armpits. He set Efscott down between Arakin and Prudence.

"Well," mused Luxurous, "you're not getting executed now, so ... that's nice for you. Isn't it?"

"Yes, Sire," replied Efscott with genuine relief.

"So, let's make a statue!"

"Yes, Sire. But I will need the log of ash wood from my home."

No sooner had he finished speaking when a stocky Guard slapped the large ash log down in front of him with a thump, the same log Efscott had cut from Grandastal in the forest. And with a clank, another Guard dropped Efscott's toolbox down beside it and unlocked the Carpenter from his bindings.

Luxurous gestured to the log. "I took the liberty of raiding your carriage-shack ... thing. My guards probably bumped a few little items. Just so you know."

And indeed they had; Efscott's shack had been ransacked, smashed, and decimated. The four soldiers that searched it had made a bet with each other over who could create the most damage by just headbutting everything— purely to entertain themselves. And as it turned out, their heads were all as thick as mallets.

Efscott assumed the worst and nodded dutifully. "Yes, Sire. Of course, Sire."

Luxurous inclined his neck, peering toward the western corridor, and yelled to his son at the top of his lungs, "Perfeyn!"

"What?"

Luxurous jumped in surprise and spun. Perfeyn had been standing behind him, just inches away, eating a chicken drumstick.

Luxurous clutched his chest with one hand. "Argh! Boy, you'll be the death of me." He drew a long breath and pointed at the window on the northern wall, between the throne and corridor entrance.

"Stand there. The light is nice."

Perfeyn sighed. "I don't like standing. It's too hard!"

Luxurous sighed melodramatically and nodded to one of the guards.

The first Guard slid a comfortable Grecian couch in front of the window, upon which Perfeyn indignantly flopped himself. Continuing his sulking, he swung his feet up and reclined, leaning back into the arm. "And when the statue is finished," said Perfeyn, "do I get to rule the town then?"

"Yes, yes, soon after," replied Luxurous.

"And is that when I get the wishing well too? I've never had my own wishing well."

"Yes, yes, of course. Very soon," groaned Luxurous with a sigh.

"But I won't be able to wish for gold in it, will I?"

"Of course not. Only I can do that."

"I won't be able to wish for anything with it, really, will I?"

"No," said Luxurous pointedly.

"So, can I turn it into a whirlpool bath?"

"A what?" snapped Luxurous.

"A whirlpool bath! Lashings of fun. They're apparently very popular up North. Gosh, Father. You're so out of touch sometimes."

Luxurous sighed again and returned his attention to Efscott, beckoning him to hurry up toward him with a frustrated flutter of his hand.

Another Guard placed a fruit tray beside Perfeyn, who took an apple and examined its smooth, red skin. "I once ate a whole apple in just six bites," he declared.

"I've done it in four, Sire!" replied Arakin with jovial enthusiasm. But even as the words escaped his mouth, Arakin realized it was a mistake. Upstaging the prince, especially this Prince, was very unwise.

Perfeyn's smile faded, and he glared across at the disheveled Arakin, who was helping Efscott carry the massive log.

"Well, aren't you just so amazing?" the Prince snarled. His eyes were vindictive and cold. "Perhaps you should put more effort into bathing once in a while." Perfeyn dropped the apple and grabbed some grapes instead.

Luxurous stood between Efscott and Perfeyn. "Make him look royal," he instructed. "Victorious!" Luxurous struck a pose with all the flourish of a bad ballerina, lifting Gun Ronin high with one hand while gazing up at it with an ostentatious air. "Like this!"

Efscott nodded. "Oh, I see."

"He should be in a suit of armor. Something elegant, yet practical."

Efscott nodded obediently again. Luxurous held out Gun Ronin. "So anyway, start! Now!"

Efscott bowed his head and took Gun Ronin with reverence and genuine intrigue. He gingerly addressed Perfeyn, who was still fully reclined on the couch.

"Perhaps if Your Majesty could stand for but a brief moment, it—"

"Use your imagination!" blurted Perfeyn, sending a spray of half-chewed grapes out of his mouth.

The guards lowered their spears at Efscott's head, and he smiled meekly in return. He cautiously raised his mallet and placed the tip of Gun Ronin against the large, bark-covered block of timber.

Perfeyn rolled over, turning his back to them all, making it even more difficult for Efscott to carve his likeness. And within seconds, Perfeyn was fast asleep, snoring blissfully. The lightest of gasps escaped Efscott's lips. Not out of disgust, only genuine distress over how he could solve this dilemma. Luxurous did not seem to have any intention of intervening and gave another irritated flutter of his hand at Efscott.

"Hurry up now," said Luxurous. "He'll probably roll over again in a while so ... just start with his back."

The guards shuffled in closer with their spears, and Efscott nodded, but his face seemed to grow paler.

Arakin weighed all this up. His eyes flashed to a large candelabrum on a nearby stool, and he raced over and grabbed it, then approached the sleeping Prince. The guards quickly leveled their spears at Arakin's face instead, and the King also stepped forward, eyeing him warily.

Arakin moved the candelabrum to the left and right, pretending to work the light on Perfeyn.

"We just need a bit more light," Arakin declared with an affable smile. "A flattering light."

Arakin struck the same pose that Luxurous did, holding the candelabrum high while continuing to pretend that he was shining a light on the Prince. In fact, what Arakin was providing, of course, was a model for Efscott to work with. It was a smart way of ensuring that he would not offend the royals by proposing that he, a feral orphan, would be worthy of modeling on behalf of the Prince. Arakin adjusted the angle of his body, hoping to hit the right pose for Efscott. He turned so that he was now facing Efscott and Prudence.

"Perfect!" said Efscott with immense relief.

Prince Perfeyn stirred slightly, then returned to snoring. Arakin held his pose, and Efscott slowly raised the golden blade of Gun Ronin up to the wood, then held it still for a moment. It hummed as sunlight gleamed across.

"This blade is unlike any other," hushed Efscott. "Whatever we carve today, with this blade and this wood, will be something special."

Arakin met Prudence's gaze, and they shared a smile.

Efscott tapped his mallet against Gun Ronin's handle, driving the blade smoothly through the timber.

CHAPTER TWENTY-SIX

The Shaping of Things to Come

Luxurous returned to his throne, slumped into it, and took a deep breath. He eyed the Witch and Minus, who stood close by. "So, the main issue at hand," said Luxurous, "is how do I enslave the rest of mankind with this new bounty I have acquired?"

Minus bowed. "I can confirm, Sire, that even just one chest of your gold could buy an army of the fiercest attack elephants from the far east. You could crush any army. Conquer the world! We really should—"

"No!" the Witch snapped, interrupting him. "We need all this extra gold to create the Duja army. You will conquer all mankind with this, Sire. You don't need elephants. Or men!"

Luxurous drew a deep breath, placed his hands together, and pensively rested his fingers against his lips. "The Witch is right, Minus. No elephants for the moment. Besides, supernatural demons are more fun, wouldn't you say? There is that sense of … ominous uncertainty." Luxurous looked up at the Witch. "But I can definitely control the Dujas, can't I?"

"Total control! Much more obedient than your current army of humans. Mortal man is flawed with so many personal wants and needs."

Luxurous glanced sideways down the eastern corridor at the treasury room. The door was open and stationed with several guards. A slow, constant line of weary townspeople lumbered in with their wire baskets of gold, dumping their contents onto the massive pile in the center of the room. A veritable mountain of glistening wealth reached the very rooftop.

Luxurous grinned and clapped his hands together. "Wonderful!"

Minus glared at the Witch, who shot a withering look back at him.

In the treasury, the Blacksmith emptied his bucket onto the mountain of gold.

The Witch addressed Luxurous. "That is the last bucket of gold, Sire. All the lead is mined from these lands. It will soon be time to conquer more lands. Lands defended by strong armies. And you will need the greatest of all armies to beat them."

The Blacksmith plodded wearily out of the room, with his head bowed, as the King surveyed with delight the giant pile of gold through the doorway behind him.

"If you want me to create the Duja army," continued the Witch, "I must start now. I must pour one thousand buckets into the wishing well."

Luxurous's eyes narrowed as he pondered this decision. "Very well. Yes!"

He nodded and called out down the corridor, "Blacksmith!"

The Blacksmith stopped and turned. "Sire?"

"Take it all upstairs! All of you!"

The Blacksmith stared back at the giant gold pile in total disbelief.

"And hurry up!" yelled Luxurous.

"Yes, Sire," replied the Blacksmith, with a hoarse voice born of exhaustion and mournful submission.

Luxurous stood, adjusted his cloak, and strode toward Efscott, passing Minus, who was still scowling with apparent indignation over Luxurous preferring the Witch's idea instead. Minus's eye twitched frenetically, and his mouth fidgeted as if he was restraining an avalanche of furious monologue.

And the Blacksmith—now a broken man—plodded back into the treasury room with the human chain gang of townspeople following him.

Luxurous came to Efscott's side and eyed the wooden log incredulously.

"You idiot, you're making him look fat! He looks like a tree."

The large branch still resembled a tree, of course, because Efscott had only trimmed off a few of the smaller branches in the short space of time he'd had.

"I have only just started, Sire."

Luxurous leaned in, and his eyes narrowed. "You better work faster, Carpenter. All of you! Have it done by sunset tomorrow, or you're all being fed to the crocodiles."

Efscott, Arakin, and Prudence bowed their heads obediently. "Yes, Sire," they replied in unison.

Efscott returned to carving the wood, but now quicker than before, his earnest expression underlining the fact that he was indeed devoting his utmost attention to the task.

"Tell me," said Luxurous, "is the chisel good?"

"It is indeed, Sire," replied Efscott.

"Why?" asked Luxurous.

Efscott paused for a moment, unsure how to answer, as Luxurous eyed him inquisitively.

"Well, Sire, Ash timber is usually stubborn and challenging to cut through—dense and resistant—and yet this blade cuts cleanly through, like none I have ever seen. This wood and blade seem to be made for each other."

"Very good," said Luxurous impassively, looking over the log again before turning and ambling out of the room.

Efscott returned to carving into the wood while Prudence tidied the area around him. She casually picked up a thick branch from the floor and studied it carefully, then took a whittling knife from Efscott's toolbox. Arakin noticed that Efscott looked over to her with some surprise.

"You won't carve it all in time, Father," she said softly. "I'll work on the sword."

Efscott nodded. "A good idea, child."

Prudence began carving away with slow, deliberate strokes, becoming a picture of absolute concentration. However, she still allowed herself an occasional glance up at Arakin, who stood firm under the weight of the candelabrum. She would always smile and return to her work. Despite the numbing fatigue that Arakin felt from aching hunger, parching thirst, and no sleep for two nights, these smiles from her seemed to ignite an enigmatic warmth and resilience deep within him.

***

Ash watched intently from the safe confines of the forest as dusk encroached. He was standing tall upon Slipnor's nose as the wolf perched upon a large boulder. From here, they had a clear view of the throne room's main west window.

"They're safe!" declared Ash with relief. "But I still think they should have let me come along to meet these royals. I can understand why they didn't want your help, old boy. You have no training in deportment. And to be quite honest, Fluffy, you smell. I, on the other hand ..."

Ash puffed his chest out proudly. Slipnor, clearly bristling from the barb, shook his head and sent Ash tumbling from his nose and bouncing off the branches of the bushes below.

"That's no way to treat your commanding officer. I could have you court-martialed for that!"

Slipnor cocked his head and barked dismissively, making it quite clear that he didn't take Ash's authority seriously.

***

Efscott and Prudence labored into the night, and Arakin maintained his pose with the candelabrum held high, but he was beginning to tremble slightly under its weight. The candles had burned halfway down.

Perfeyn continued his slumber upon the Grecian couch, oblivious to everything, and Arakin eyed him with a degree of envy. He was now aching for sleep more than he was food or water and could feel the blood draining from his head. He wondered if he would soon simply collapse. He took a deep breath and bit his lip, hoping the dull sense of pain would help keep him lucid. *This would all soon be over*, he reminded himself.

CHAPTER TWENTY-SEVEN

The Last Sun

The sun rose, bringing a new day with it, but some people felt the weariness of an extra day or more upon their shoulders, having not slept at all. The Witch had spent the night overseeing the depositing of gold into the wishing well on the tower's rooftop floor, forever urging the townspeople to quicken their pace.

The King entered via the second stairwell, yawning and adjusting his sleeping robe. Unlike most people, he had enjoyed a long, blissful sleep.

"Goodness," he declared. "It takes a lot of time to build a Demon Army from Hell, doesn't it?"

"Indeed," grumbled the Witch.

***

In the throne room, Prince Perfeyn rose groggily from his slumber and studied the bustle of activity around him through sleep-tangled eyelashes. He looked like someone who had enjoyed a night of good rest. He sleepily grabbed a handful of the purple grapes and called out to the nearest Guard.

"Bring me some poached baby monkey! I'm quite hungry."

Perfeyn pulled a grape seed from his teeth and examined it, then flicked it at Arakin, hitting him square in the face. Arakin felt a sting of indignation but kept his composure, even as the hot candle wax dripped on his hand. He flinched slightly but did not falter or complain, maintaining his regal pose, as always.

Perfeyn giggled. "I had the best dream ever!" he announced. "I shot a unicorn with my longbow. Right through the bum. It made the funniest noise when it was dying."

Arakin refrained from frowning and making direct eye contact with him, then noticed all the guards nodding congenially to Perfeyn in polite acknowledgment of the fact that he was sharing a thought with them. Efscott and Prudence did likewise, and Arakin realized that this was the safe thing to do. The smart thing to do. He did the same but couldn't help wonder what sort of person took so much pleasure in sharing such an unpleasant dream. Obviously, the same kind of person who liked to spit seeds in the faces of others.

***

As the sun journeyed across the sky through the course of the day, Efscott and Prudence continued to carve tirelessly. Arakin maintained his tiring pose with the candelabrum, and the townspeople ferried their buckets of gold up to the rooftop floor. Perfeyn found all this work particularly tedious to watch and was soon falling asleep once again, while all around him toiled and suffered.

***

The end of the day was drawing near, and Arakin noticed Efscott working with a greater sense of urgency. The sculpture was taking form, but Efscott needed to be quicker if he was to make the sunset deadline.

Arakin's arm was beyond numb from having held up the candelabrum for so long. Rife with pins and needles coupled with fatigue, it created an odd sensation that he had no arm, while still leaving a sense of pain where it once was. His neck was aching, his shoulder was cramping, but he knew what was at stake and dared not move. Even though Efscott was in the final stages of completing the statue, Arakin still got the sense that every detail was important. And this meant he needed to hold his pose, no matter how uncomfortable. Efscott nodded to him, and Arakin nodded back. All was well; they would make it through to the end together.

***

Perfeyn rose from his day slumber and took in his surroundings begrudgingly.

"Urgh, you're still here," he grumbled.

Efscott smiled politely in return. "Yes, Sire. At your service, Sire."

Perfeyn eyed the eastern corridor where the chain gang of townspeople lumbered onward, heaving their buckets of gold from the treasury up to the top floor. Arakin saw an old lady struggling with hers and winced with pity. Perfeyn set about devouring another bunch of grapes and noticed Arakin's reaction. The Prince scowled and flicked a grape at Arakin's head to grab his attention.

"Your small, peasant brain wouldn't understand," snarled Perfeyn as he methodically turned the gold ring on his middle finger. "My father and I wish to be surrounded by gold.

213

Forever. For its beauty can only be matched by us. By kings. By gods!"

Arakin had never heard someone refer to himself as a god before and certainly had not expected it from a boy about his age wearing a tunic covered in grape stains. He noticed his brow furrowing into a frown and quickly restrained the reflex, so he didn't agitate Perfeyn.

"The witches from my homeland are far more clairvoyant than the silly Oracles of your lands," said Perfeyn sharply. "And they have said that 'the one true king will be of King's Gold.' Do you see now?" Perfeyn gestured toward the townspeople who trudged down the corridor toward the treasury with their heavy burdens of gold. "I am surrounded by it! I *am* of it!" Perfeyn thought for a moment. "And … so is my father, I suppose. But for me, more so. I'm smaller, so there's more gold around me, relatively speaking."

Perfeyn's eyes flitted over at Arakin, who stared back blankly. "It's math," snapped Perfeyn. "You're very simple, so you wouldn't understand."

Brunt, the Blacksmith's son, limped into view next and fell in the middle of the corridor. A Guard kicked him, and he limped onward to raucous laughter from Perfeyn, who turned to Arakin. "That's funny! Don't you think? His fat wobbles when he is kicked."

Arakin took no joy in it, though, despite a lifetime of being bullied by Brunt. It was appalling to him that someone could take pleasure in seeing any human belittled and dehumanized, and it made him feel quite ill. Perfeyn scowled upon sensing this.

"Don't you think?" repeated Perfeyn, who was clearly waiting for his answer in the form of acquiescence. But what could Arakin say? He shrewdly deflected instead.

"Your statue is almost finished, Sire," Arakin replied enthusiastically.

Perfeyn's fierce gaze slid across to the statue, and he was immediately impressed.

Prudence, perched on a ladder, applied touches of gold paint to the statue's hand as Efscott gave a final stroke with his sandpaper to the smooth, pale, ash grain on the upper arm. He nodded to Arakin, who lowered the candelabrum in his trembling, cramp-ridden arm. Efscott noticed Perfeyn scrutinizing the statue and bowed to him, then promptly grabbed a paintbrush.

A Guard approached and carefully poured a bucket of gold nuggets into a small pot at the base of the statue. The pot was suspended on a brace over a fire that burned brightly within an iron pan. The new nuggets melted quickly, topping up the molten solution, and Efscott dipped his paintbrush into it, followed by Prudence, who promptly ascended her ladder again.

***

Upon the rooftop floor, the Witch gazed into the well, her eyes fixed on the flurry of gold nuggets that were continuously poured into the depths of its green-black waters.

As the townspeople deposited their baskets of gold into the well, a Guard stopped them to examine their faces. If they had been weeping, which was most of them, he scraped the tears from their cheeks with a blunt blade. He quickly but carefully transferred those teardrops into the Witch's large black bottle, which was strapped around his waist in a leather harness.

Another Guard swept up the gold dust that had fallen on the floor. And this, too, was tipped into the well. Nothing spared nor wasted. Every drop of misery. Every speck of gold.

The Witch waved her hands over the wishing well, and a shimmering light emitted from the waters that now bubbled and hissed. Her eyes turned jet black.

"What do you see?" asked Luxurous excitedly.

"The well grows strong. I see more—indeed, by sunrise tomorrow, we will be able to raise the Duja. It will destroy any army led by mortal man."

"Wonderful!" hissed Luxurous. "And then all the gold that remains in the world shall be mine. And all shall worship me!" He took a deep breath and beamed. "It's turning out to be a pretty good day on the throne."

Her eyes narrowed, and she examined the waters of the well more closely. Something clearly concerned her.

"What is it?" whispered Luxurous.

"A fractured image—powerful and evasive—but I recognize this pattern. Something with strong magic is nearby. Yet it tries to elude me."

"Can you see it?" asked Luxurous with growing anticipation.

Her eyes narrowed. "The Prince's statue!" she declared.

"What about it?"

"The blade that carves it. You must keep this close. It has great magic! Greater than even I saw."

Her eyes widened, her jaw dropped slightly, and she released a quivering breath. "It is … Gun Ronin! The King Maker!" she declared.

"Gun Ronin? You mean, there's actually a *real* one?" Luxurous gazed vacantly into space for a moment, digesting the information, then spun on his heel and made for the stairwell. "Guards!"

***

216

Perfeyn was munching on a plum when Luxurous stormed into the room.

"Where is it?" barked Luxurous.

Efscott turned innocently to face him. "Sire?"

"Gun Ronin! The chisel thing! Give it to me!"

Prudence and Arakin shared a tense, knowing look. Prudence put her paintbrush down and picked the gold sword up from a stool, then apprehensively handed it to Luxurous.

He snatched it from her and examined it, this time with far greater reverence, holding the flat of the blade against his open palm.

Perfeyn craned his neck. "Gun Ronin? So there is a real one after all?" he asked, with a mouth full of plum.

"Yes," replied Luxurous. "And this shade of gold matches my shoes too. Very pretty!"

"And look, Father! My statue! Isn't it wonderful?" Perfeyn pointed to the completed carving that had been painted in gold.

Luxurous marveled at it. "Ah, yes! A thing of beauty. We have both won something of gold today, my son." He inspected the statue more closely. "And the arms ... they look so strong. The wings of a king, my son, the wings of a king. "

The Witch shuffled in and again inspected Gun Ronin. She gave a thoughtful nod to Luxurous, thus confirming its authenticity, and he beamed like a child receiving the promise of eternal candy.

He offered it to her, "Hold it. Make sure its magic is real."

"There is no need, Sire. Its magic fills the room. Holding it makes no difference. Being one foot left of the sun is no different than being directly before it when standing so near."

She did lean in, though, admiring its exquisite design. Then she took a step back, nodding once more, but this time as if to appreciate being in its presence. She allowed her eyes to rise and rest on the statue of Perfeyn, taking it in for a moment, then stepped closer.

The sun was edging toward the horizon now, pushing light through the western window. It glided up the statue as the sun set lower, bringing it to life with bursts of brilliant, radiant gold.

"Impressive," muttered the Witch. Her eyes drifted over the statue, then settled on Efscott with a mix of approval and curiosity. "In fact ... beyond impressive," she mumbled to herself.

Perfeyn nodded appreciatively.

"This stirs something within," the Witch continued in a hushed tone. "Have I seen it in a dream? A premonition? It is meant to be, that is certain."

"It is marvelous, isn't it?" said Perfeyn with a proud, self-important grin.

"Beyond marvelous, in fact. Perhaps ... because it is covered in King's Gold ... yes."

Arakin found himself surveying the statue with growing awe. Unlike the Witch, he had never seen anything like this before in all his life. It was an object that fused a moment in time with something eternal in such a beautiful, grand way. It seemed so appropriate now that his tree, his home that had always wrapped its branches around him like nurturing arms, would take on this majestic form. Perhaps indeed, the magical properties of the ash wood within the statue could inspire Perfeyn to be a great leader after all, and not only be courageous but also inspire courage in others.

Perfeyn sauntered closer to the statue, casually spitting a large plum seed at Arakin's head as he passed. Arakin felt his fist clench and jaw tighten. *Maybe the inspirational effect of the statue took time*, he wondered, feeling his cheeks flush warm.

Luxurous addressed the guards. "Take it to the town square!"

The Royal Guards nodded and carefully heaved the statue onto a trolley, then gingerly made their way out with it to the rumbling of wooden wheels on the stone floor.

Efscott bent over to move a hammer out of their way, and Prudence feigned to assist, but instead she whispered something into his ear. It was unnoticed by everyone else in the room, except Arakin. Efscott tensed up upon hearing her words and looked at her with apparent anxiety. He glanced furtively at Luxurous, then returned to tidying up his tools in a somewhat self-conscious way, as if he was trying not to draw attention to himself. Arakin was curious to know what Prudence had said, but now was clearly not the time to ask.

Luxurous drew his old sword out of his gold scabbard, tossed it aside, and slid Gun Ronin into it.

"Interesting," said the Witch softly.

"What's that? I mean, I don't need my old sword now, do I?" asked Luxurous.

"Not that. Your scabbard. It cloaks the magic aura of Gun Ronin when you sheath it."

"Oh," said Luxurous with some concern.

"Evidently the lead base that King's Gold comes from," she said, gesturing to his scabbard. "But I think it's a good thing. A bright light attracts moths and other vermin. The safest home for it is invisibility."

"Very good," said Luxurous, adjusting his belt. "Plus I don't like moths—of any kind."

"Indeed," she said with a bemused expression.

Luxurous made to leave, then turned back to Efscott. "Well, good work," the King said casually. "Now clean up, and you may go back to your home-carriage-shack thing."

Efscott put on a brave smile and bowed. Prudence and Arakin did likewise.

Luxurous turned and flicked his coat in a grandiose manner, sending up a cloud of sawdust in his wake as he departed.

All Ends and All Begins

Prince Perfeyn approached the window and stared pensively out at the setting sun.

"You made the statue just in time. Pity, in a way. I've never seen someone fed to a crocodile. We just introduced it." Perfeyn eyed Prudence with a sinister glance and added, "Imagine a pretty little thing like you being pulled apart in seconds."

The morbid delight in Perfeyn's voice made Arakin's skin crawl.

Perfeyn strolled over to the southern window and leaned on the wall in repose, gazing at his gold statue in the distance, which was being erected onto a stone monolith in the center of the town square.

Arakin helped Efscott pack up, and after some time, everything began to feel as if the danger had indeed passed; the job was done, and the doorway out of here to a safer place was now so close. He wasn't even sure if he would try and retrieve Gun Ronin. It had served its purpose by solving this urgent dilemma and had proven that it was indeed a thing of magic, for which he would be eternally grateful. They had freed Efscott, and the job was done. They would all return home, and he would finally drink, eat, and sleep—sweet blissful sleep. And he would laugh and play with Ash and Slipnor. And he would find a new shawl for Prudence, to replace the one that was now cut in sections from Gun Ronin's razor-sharp blade.

It was at this precise moment that Arakin's gaze absentmindedly lingered on the last item of food in Perfeyn's fruit tray. An apple. And Perfeyn noticed this. The tone of his voice was almost convincingly sympathetic. "Oh, you poor thing. Have you not eaten in a while?"

"No, Sire," answered Arakin meekly.

Perfeyn's tone grew cooler. "Why not? You have food rations."

"I … gave them to my … dog, Sire."

"Well, you're stupid, aren't you?" asked Perfeyn, his voice brittle.

Arakin felt his jaw clench but maintained his composure. "Yes, Sire," he replied respectfully. "I have a happy dog though," he added. Arakin knew immediately that it was a foolish thing to say. Perhaps it was because he was so tired— everything around him felt a bit unreal, and the words just slipped out. It was not intended to usurp Perfeyn. It was only the truth, but it would most likely be interpreted as disrespectful.

As suspected, Perfeyn seethed at the reply, and his expression hardened. He snatched the apple from the bowl, and approached Arakin, holding it out. But when Arakin reached, Perfeyn dropped the piece of fruit intentionally. And with a plop, it landed into the pot of molten gold.

"Oops!" said Perfeyn. "Butterfingers."

Arakin watched sadly as it sank into the hot, liquid metal.

Perfeyn's expression grew dark. "But I'm going to make you rich, Orphan Boy. Take it out."

Arakin hesitated briefly, then nodded and knelt down, grabbing the submerged apple by the still-exposed stem and pulling it out. Heavy drops of gold dripped back into the bucket, and the apple's gold exterior became an even glossier sheen as it cooled and hardened slightly.

"Eat it," ordered Perfeyn.

Efscott and Prudence looked as if a sharp lesion of anxiety had paralyzed them. Prudence took a single step forward. "Sire, no!" she pleaded. "This will kill him!"

Perfeyn met her gaze, and an unexpected smile swept over his face, disarming her. "Question me again, and I will have you fed to the crocodiles," he declared calmly.

He moved closer to Prudence, then struck her cheek hard with the back of his hand. His ring connected firmly, leaving a red welt on her face. Efscott flinched with indignation but managed to control his anger. Arakin, however, became overwhelmed with rage and instinctively stepped toward Perfeyn, but then he restrained himself, still fuming.

The rumble of distant thunder rolled toward them.

Perfeyn glared at Arakin for even contemplating retaliation—for frowning and for taking a defiant step forward. He leaned toward Arakin and whispered coolly into his ear, "I see how you look at her, Orphan Boy. I know you like her. And if you don't eat this apple, I will tell my father that she burned me. She will be fed to the crocodiles in an instant, with no ceremony, no pause, and no final wishes."

Perfeyn grabbed the same candelabrum that Arakin had been holding, then brought the flames maniacally under his own chin. The curling light cast his face in an even more haunting air.

"Now! Before the gold hardens!" Perfeyn grinned viciously and brought the flames closer to his face. "Oh goodness, is it getting hot in here, or is it just some crazy peasant girl trying to burn me?"

Prudence stepped forward, but Efscott held her wrist. Two guards spun quickly and leveled their spears at her.

Arakin realized he was out of options. What a horrible and final twist of fate. His shock and fear were soon overridden with calm resignation; it was the end of the road, but what a road it had been. What a journey. What an adventure. He could refuse to bite into the poisonous apple and win his life, but it would kill him in worse ways to see them hurt Prudence. Ash knew the woods well and would take care of Slipnor, though it broke his heart to leave them behind.

Arakin gazed through his weary eyes at the apple. And within its reflective skin, he could see Efscott and Prudence. He smiled sadly.

"Why do you smile?" grumbled Perfeyn with genuine curiosity.

Prudence's and Arakin's eyes met through the reflection. "A lost orphan I may have been," whispered Arakin, "but in the end, I found my family."

And with that, he bit into the apple. He expected it to be scalding, but instead, it was oddly void of any temperature. The texture was soft and malleable, and the apple beneath was crisp and light. He anticipated the molten gold to harden within his mouth, but it did not. Astonishingly it dissolved, blending with the soft acidic juices of the apple. But immediately after swallowing, his chest tightened, his head felt lighter, and he felt a tremendous swelling pain in his stomach, shooting out like fire through every vein in his body to every limb and every organ.

Arakin, sweating heavily now, stiffened his resolve and bit once more into the apple, lifting his head to defiantly meet Perfeyn's gaze. Perfeyn stepped cautiously back and continued to watch with morbid fascination.

Prudence sobbed and shrieked. Again she tried to move forward, but Efscott took a firmer grip of her. He too wept. Thunder rumbled in the distance, and Arakin took a third and final bite.

"How is it, Orphan?" hissed Perfeyn.

Arakin's face turned pale, and his eyes drifted in and out of focus, but he could still make out Prudence reflected in the small portion of golden skin that remained. His voice softened.

"The finest I have ever known."

Arakin hoped Prudence would understand that these final words were meant for her. There was so much more he wanted to say, but time and circumstances clearly prevented that. His vision faded; he felt his body folding forward, falling, and connecting with the cold stone floor. He tried to move, but his body remained motionless. The only movement now was the distinct presence of the molten gold coursing through the chambers of his heart, then hardening, tightening, and restricting its movement, slowing its beat, slower still, and slower.

Efscott gasped in pained disbelief at the sight of Arakin on the floor, and Prudence screamed with grief. Arakin could hear her, but only faintly. She sounded so distant, and the stone floor now seemed so much colder.

And for a brief moment, no one moved. The room was still.

Perfeyn looked at his candelabrum. "Wow, this is actually *really* heavy," he exclaimed with total indifference to the dying figure of Arakin before him.

As Perfeyn plopped the candelabrum back down on the table, a single drop of hot wax fell onto his hand. He hissed and retracted it quickly, forming a fist.

Prudence, bereft, stared helplessly at Arakin. She stepped back, away from the guards, and away from the nurturing buttress of Efscott's arms. She pulled at her hair, shaking as tears welled in her eyes. Chokingly she drew a long breath that was punctuated with sobs. And at the peak of that inhale, she closed her eyes for a moment. It was as if she was perched upon a momentous decision. And then her eyes sprang upon, and she spoke. Just three simple words.

"Fianray tor gianrus."

Perfeyn stared at her, perplexed. "Have you gone spazzy or something?"

Deafening thunder cracked overhead, sending deep tremors through the walls, floor, and air around them. Perfeyn cowered, and even the guards flinched. This rumble was louder and closer than any other they had experienced.

Efscott turned her by the shoulders and pleaded, "Child, no! They will kill you!" Efscott apparently knew what Prudence was doing, even though others did not. Not yet, anyway.

Prudence met her father's gaze and smiled mournfully, repeating softly, "Fianray tor gianrus."

All ends and all begins. An anicient language. A powerful spell.

The air bristled with electricity. Perfeyn gazed at his arms as the hairs raised upward. Specks of dust floated up around them.

Thunder cracked again directly overhead.

***

226

Upon the rooftop floor, Luxurous and the Witch ducked instinctively, crouching by the wishing well as a lightning bolt ripped across the sky, dangerously close.

"What manner of lightning is this?" yelled Luxurous.

The Witch glared up at the low-set purple clouds. "Magic! A White Witch is near! She is making her vows."

"Well, she's not very subtle about it, is she?"

Another lightning bolt shot down from the sky, striking the floor just inches from them, and Luxurous leaped back with a shrill yelp. At the impact zone, there was now a smooth, circular hole over three feet wide. Stones, however, did not fall away into the throne room directly below because they were instantly incinerated. A cloud of grey dust floated gently down instead.

***

In the center of the throne room, Prudence looked skyward through the large hole in the roof high above and declared once more, "Fianray tor gianrus!"

A lightning bolt shot through the hole with a deafening crack, hitting Prudence in the center of her chest and holding her in its firm, beaming grip.

Prince Perfeyn yelped in horror and jumped backward, losing his balance and skidding across the floor on his bottom. The guards froze in terror. No one had ever taught them how to fight a lightning bolt.

Prudence did not seem distressed though. The lightning bolt hummed now as it pulled her upward. She calmly craned her neck and held her arms slightly out to the side with her palms facing up. She paused in space and remained levitated five feet above the floor.

*****

Through the hole in the tower floor, Luxurous could see Prudence below in the grip of the lightning bolt, and again, he yelped.

The Witch hissed, then bellowed out, "White Witch!"

She snatched the broomstick from the nearby Guard and held it in front of her snake.

"Bitten wood arise, now this broomstick flies!"

The snake bit the broomstick, sending venomous, green veins shooting through its handle, which twitched into life. The Witch leaped on the broomstick, straddling it as if it were a horse, and with a whoosh, flew off the roof. She climbed quickly into the sky and arced around, aiming now for the large window of the throne room.

*****

The lightning bolt retreated through the hole in the roof, and Prudence dropped gracefully to the ground. Meanwhile, the Witch accelerated toward her at a ferocious speed via the open window. Prudence spotted the attack and threw her hands up in front of herself.

"Slide and stop that Witch now drop!"

Arcs of electricity jumped wildly between Prudence's fingers and thumbs. She flicked her wrists, and with a crack, the electrical arcs vanished, and the giant, dopey Executioner was forced sideways across the floor under Prudence's spell, sliding before the large open window—the same one the Witch was flying through. With a resounding thud, the Witch collided into his stalwart back, bounced off the rear wall, and toppled to the ground. The Executioner burped upon the impact, but otherwise appeared as if he had barely felt a thing. The Witch, on the other hand, wheezed violently in a state of delirium.

Prudence rushed to Arakin's pale body, weeping as she placed a trembling hand on his forehead.

The guards, meanwhile, ran to Perfeyn's side to see if he had been hurt.

Prudence knelt beside Arakin and whispered tenderly, "Tears are proof that you are missed. So take my life within this kiss." She bowed her head and kissed him lightly on the lips, and as she raised her head, a single teardrop fell from her eye, landing on Arakin's top lip.

The Witch, still winded and unable to speak, was beckoning the guards and frantically gesturing toward either Prudence or Arakin. The hesitancy of the guards' steps and their uncertain glances at one another made it clear they were not sure what the Witch was motioning them to do.

Prudence continued her spell, gazing down upon Arakin's impassive face. "Come to life, for life you bring. Breathe again … my Arakin."

Her eyes closed, and she collapsed onto the floor beside him, utterly exhausted.

Perfeyn scrambled to his feet, his eyes flashing from the hole in the roof, the storm clouds above, and finally Prudence. "What are you doing? Stop this!" he screamed.

The Witch drew a short, shaken breath and croaked urgently, "Her power is drained! Grab her! Gag her quickly! Gag her!"

Two burly guards lumbered in, grabbed the semiconscious Prudence, and forced a leather gag around her mouth.

Meanwhile, Arakin's lips showed signs of life as they regained a healthy color. His face and body followed suit, and his eyelids twitched.

The Witch rose shakily and took a rigid step forward when her body suddenly shuddered involuntarily. Her eyes flitting over herself with an expression of horror underlined the fact that something was taking over her—a force she could not control.

"Curses! Curses!" she yelled.

Arakin's eyes sprang open. They found their focus upon the figure beside him—Prudence—locked in irons and being dragged away.

Arakin tried to move but found that his body was still in a state of shock, paralyzed and numb. He took a deep breath, and thunder rumbled outside, and the Witch was suddenly flipped upside down. Luxurous trotted in and had to look twice upon seeing his inverted necromancer levitating in space.

"What on earth—"

He ran toward her, but she was suddenly whisked away and sent hurtling around the room by a supernatural tornado.

"Oh, *do* stop flying away from me!" yelled Luxurous.

She flew around Arakin three times, swinging in closer with every spin, among a gust of embers that spewed from the fireplaces.

Arakin tried again to move, finding this time that his limbs responded. He lifted his head and wearily rose to one knee. The Witch came to a sudden stop directly in front of him, upside down, his face before hers.

Luxurous eyed them both warily. "What is this?"

"The golden apple this boy ate, so three wishes he can make!" declared the Witch.

Luxurous spotted the apple core lying on the floor and yelped even higher and louder than before. "How?"

"I gave it to him," answered Perfeyn, "but he died!"

"You what?" blurted Luxurous.

The Witch snarled, "Fool! Don't you remember the first lesson I taught you?"

Perfeyn shrugged.

The Witch sighed and yelled, "He who eats the golden apple, wins the wishes three!"

Perfeyn shook his head. "I thought you said, 'he who eats the golden apple, drinks the Witch's pee.'"

Luxurous and the Witch stared incredulously back at him.

"I just assumed it tasted bad!" he blurted out in his defense. "That's why I made him eat it."

Luxurous slapped his own forehead in utter disbelief. "Idiot!"

"Fool!" yelled the Witch.

"Well … you mumble a lot!" fumed Perfeyn indignantly.

Arakin searched for Prudence through eyes that struggled to focus. He found her again and stood.

The Witch was forced to levitate with him so that her face stayed in front of his. The Executioner grimaced as her butt, in billowing pantaloons, passed his face. The Witch pointed at Arakin.

"A wish this boy did win. This wish shall now begin!" she snarled with apparent resentment.

Lightning cracked overhead, and the Witch and Arakin were swept upward by a spinning paranormal force, up toward the large hole in the roof some forty feet above, among a stream of glowing embers.

"Oh, come on!" blurted Luxurous, realizing he had to run up the eight floors of steps again. He sighed melodramatically and trotted after them.

CHAPTER TWENTY-NINE

One of Three Wishes

Having seen the supernatural storm clouds overhead and the commotion that ensued, the Four Generals had made their way hastily to the castle. They were now charging up the master stairwell from the courtyard, with their swords drawn and with another eight formidable warriors close behind.

***

On the tower floor, two guards locked Prudence into heavy chains that were fastened to the two stone columns at the rear. Efscott rushed in, only to be grabbed and restrained by two other guards. Luxurous staggered in behind, utterly exhausted from all his running.

At the wishing well, the inverted Witch hovered before Arakin. The Generals charged in, but the Witch held up a hand, commanding them to stop. They did so but kept their swords at the ready. The Witch snarled at Arakin with burning contempt.

"Three wishes possible," she hissed. "But you may only choose one."

"Tell me," he replied softly, his voice raspy.

She pointed to the well. An eerie light emanated from within, and the water rose, taking the shape of a scroll that unfurled a liquid parchment.

"The first wish: you may ask for gold. And all the lead you find will be turned to gold. You will be wealthy beyond your wildest dreams."

Luxurous gasped in horror.

An image took form within the wavering water scroll. It was Arakin, sitting upon a gold throne, with piles of gold at his feet and a giant hall filled with gold behind him. Beyond the castle in which he sat, thousands of people toiled in the lead fields. Various races but all equally miserable.

The Witch continued, "The second wish: you may ask for beauty. To have two arms. To be so handsome that all will love you."

In the waters, Arakin saw an image of himself with two arms, walking through a village, surrounded by admirers, beautiful girls among them.

Arakin's eyes narrowed. "What is the third wish?"

"No one ever chooses the third wish."

"Tell me."

"The gift of freedom. You may wish to free all those who suffer now because of those who made a wish before you. The King's wish is killing these lands. You can stop it, and the land shall not be turned to white dust."

Arakin stared at the water scroll. In it, he saw an image of the King's army marching away from town. Water ran through the creek once more, clear and magnificent. The townspeople were happy and free.

The Witch continued, "His army will be released. Farmers will have crops that grow once more. You will free both man and land from slavery."

Luxurous brought his hand to his head, feeling slightly faint.

***

The townspeople had gathered near the mouth of the drawbridge far below and were listening intently. The supernatural element of the events above them formed an amplification of sorts, allowing them to hear everything quite clearly. The air was electric, charged with witchcraft and pervaded by the pungent, hot metal-infused water that wafted down from the wishing well.

***

The Witch continued. "But this third wish is different, for it comes at a price."

Arakin stiffened, and the Witch chuckled. Glowing orange embers still circled majestically in the winds around them.

"Should you choose this wish, then everything most precious to you will be taken away. You will be stripped of heart, for no person from this day forward will ever love you. You will be stripped of flesh, for you must give up that which is most dear to you."

She pointed to his arm.

"Your only arm."

***

The townspeople below all sighed, realizing they had just lost their chance.

"She really needs to work on her sales pitch," grumbled the Potato Farmer.

***

Arakin stared intently into the water scroll. He could see an image of himself walking down a long, desolate road, shirtless and with no arms.

"They will laugh at you," drawled the Witch. "You will not even be human to them, but a snake, a wretched snake with neither fangs nor venom to protect you. Not even your Ash Forest will be safe as home."

***

Down at the drawbridge, the exasperated Potato Farmer turned to the townspeople behind him and blurted, "And we're dead. Thanks for playing."

***

On the outer edge of the Ash Forest, Ash stood on the branch of a tree, with his gaze fixed on the proceedings taking place on the castle rooftop. Slipnor stood below, attentively gazing up to him for an update.

"I can't tell what's going on. Just boring chitchat by the looks of it, with a very cranky ... upside-down floating Witch. Hmm, have to admit ... haven't seen that before!"

***

At the wishing well, Arakin remained pensive.

235

The Witch's eyes turned black, and she searched for truths within his eyes.

"And oh, how much you have always wanted to have two arms." She leaned in farther upon seeing something else. "But even more than that. What you yearn for most ..."

And then she saw it: his weakness, his yearning. She pulled her head back, savoring the revelation. "What you yearn for most is to have a family. To be ... loved."

Arakin self-consciously averted his gaze downward.

The Witch continued. "Even when you were invited into the house of friends, you refused because you were ashamed. Of who you are. Of what you are. Different!"

Prudence lifted her head and opened her weary eyes, looking directly to Arakin, but he wouldn't meet her gaze. He felt small and ashamed. The Witch was right. These were indeed his fears, and the final wish she offered would indeed mean he would lose everything so that others could gain so much—their freedom, their happiness. The townspeople among them. The very people who had made his life a misery. But his selflessness would mean that the pain of so many would be alleviated. Prudence, Efscott, and the land among them. Arakin's mind buzzed with overwhelming emotions and fleeting thoughts as if his mind was filled with frantic fireflies trying to escape. All of it clouded by the incredible fatigue he felt. A numbness that ran so deep.

Luxurous and Perfeyn sidled anxiously up to the inverted, hovering Witch. Luxurous bent over and whispered conspiratorially into her ear, "Can't we just throw him into the crocodiles?"

"He must receive his wish," she whispered back, "or your body will be ripped inside out by the forces of magic."

"Well, that's a tad inconvenient," he hissed.

"But there is one loophole," she added with a grin. Luxurous raised an eyebrow inquisitively, but he was not to receive his answer right now. Arakin had made up his mind, and the Witch was drawn closer back toward him, hovering directly in front now.

"What is your choice, forest boy?"

Arakin, pained and defeated, but defiant replied, "I choose the third wish."

She smirked and grunted. It was not the reply she expected.

Arakin continued, "To free the people. To free the land."

All who heard were stunned by his choice. Efscott and the Four Generals stood rigidly in shock and reverence.

The townspeople below couldn't believe their ears. Their gasps were followed by murmurs of joy and disbelief. This meant they would be freed.

Luxurous winced.

Prudence gave a mirthless smile. It was as if she was unsurprised by his decision—as if it was already familiar to her.

The water scroll fell back into the well, and the Witch rotated in space, returning her to a non-inverted position. Her feet floated down to the floor, and she raised her staff. The air buzzed with electricity around her.

"Then so be it!" she snarled.

She beckoned to the Guard who held the large black bottle of tears. It was as big and heavy as a melon, with many years of misery collected within. They were a potent ingredient in the Black Witch's repertoire and were only ever used for exceptional spells. It would all be used very soon. But for the moment, only one drop was required.

The Guard brought it to the well and paused, awaiting the Witch's command. She held up one finger, and he nodded, tipping very slowly until one single drop fell from the bottle's lip, falling into the well with a tiny plop. She gestured toward the gargoyle on the well's rim, and the Guard placed the bottle down upon it. The anticipation was apparent upon everyone's faces. Nothing happened immediately, and the Guard wondered if something was wrong, so he leaned forward, peering into the well.

With a deafening bang, lightning struck the center of the well, an inch from his head, sending up an explosion of water and knocking the Guard backward onto the floor.

Arakin felt a burning eruption of pain flash outward from his heart in all directions, then swell back to where it began. He bent over, clutching his chest, and the Witch leveled her staff at his head. Her whiny, croaking voice gained a booming quality as she cast her spell.

"When the sun next rises, you'll find no joy, for no person will love you, oh forest boy. So heal the land and free all man, change for change, your arm be damned!" She drew a deep, guttural breath and spat out a fireball about the size of a fist, that roared through the air and hit the well dead-center with a splash and a hiss. The Witch raised her staff then ceremoniously jabbed the head of it in the direction of the well.

Arakin cried in pain and buckled over. The well water bubbled, steamed, and glowed brighter, then a plume of water shot up from it and took the shape of an ax.

It pulled back, cocking for the strike, and swung down at Arakin's arm with a sizzling whoosh. Upon contact, the water exploded in droplets around him. The water took a glowing serpentine form and wound around his arm, squeezing harder and harder.

Arakin watched in shock as his arm withered away, narrowing under the pressure that squeezed tighter and tighter. He moaned, slightly incoherent, and all who bore witness would later swear that as he fell to his knees, they heard the distinct sound of a distant falling tree.

His arm was gone. The water fell to the floor, and thunder split the air overhead.

Arakin, buckled over on the floor and covered in sweat and water, lifted his trembling head and gazed across at Prudence.

The Witch circled him and stepped in closer. She was sizing him up. But for what?

With a blinding snap, her snake lashed out and bit him hard on the neck, sinking its fangs deep into his flesh and flexing its jowls as it injected him with every ounce of venom.

Arakin's eyes widened, and he convulsed. Prudence and Efscott gasped and instinctively tried to move toward him, but both were still restrained, one by shackles and the other by guards. Pound too reacted with surprise and indignation. He tightened the grip on his broadsword but relinquished it again, just as quickly, with a look of sad resignation.

The Witch leered down at Arakin. "No wooden splint to save you this time, was there? By morning you will be dead. Consider it a favor."

He heard her cackle, but it seemed so far away. The venom was already coursing through his body and strangling his senses. His face and pupils turned a pale grey.

Luxurous grinned and stepped closer, feeling that it was now safe to be nearer to the spectacle of Arakin's demise.

He muttered through the side of his mouth to the Witch, "Not a bad loophole. Not bad at all."

Luxurous stepped to the front edge of the tower, addressing the townspeople below. He pointed at Arakin and bellowed loudly, "Let this be a lesson to all of you! Eating the golden apple is a noble endeavor entrusted to kings alone and not to be trifled with by riffraff and degenerates!"

Arakin eyed the shackles on Prudence's wrists and frowned. His gaze shot back to the Witch.

"Free her," he said hoarsely. "You promised!"

The Witch grinned, clearly relishing the detail she was about to impart. "But my dear," she crooned facetiously, "I promised to free all *mortals*. And she is not mortal. She is a witch. And I have plans for her."

"No!" cried Efscott. He stepped toward Prudence but was immediately pulled back by Pound and Dinara. Unlike before, though, there was a demeanor of compassion in their actions. They were free men now and were not under the charge of the King, whose wages previously secured their loyalty. Regardless, they clearly did not want to tempt fate by antagonizing the Witch, whose powers were beyond their comprehension. She apparently still terrified them.

Arakin fell to the floor as the sun sank beyond the horizon, and the cold blanket of night clawed its way across the land.

CHAPTER THIRTY

Fall's Early End

A sh, still viewing events from his vantage point in the forest, shuddered in disbelief.

"No ... Arakin," he muttered in a hollow voice.

He placed a hand against the trunk of his tree to steady himself, totally bewildered.

***

Upon the rooftop floor of the castle, the Witch flicked a dismissive hand. "Take him away. I have work to do."

One of the Royal Guards stepped toward Arakin, but Pound intervened. "Do not touch him!"

The Guard stopped, and Pound walked to Arakin's side. "He shall be carried by Generals," declared Pound with mournful reverence. He sheathed his sword and met Efscott's gaze. "And family."

Snow fell gently, and this seemed to concern the Witch.

Luxurous noticed this and scanned the sky. "Snows early around these parts."

"It shouldn't," croaked the Witch.

"What do you mean?"

"An early snow often foreshadows a great supernatural change taking place in the vicinity."

Luxurous shot a look across at Prudence. "Her vows, perhaps, yes?"

"She is shackled and gagged now," replied the Witch, "so poses no threat. Her vows are done."

"The boy—"

"The boy ate the golden apple, but my darling pet took care of him."

Luxurous's eyes flitted across to the well. "My Demon Army from Hell!" he exclaimed enthusiastically.

"Perhaps," she mumbled.

Pound knelt beside Arakin, who was still breathing, hanging on to life by a thread. Perfeyn was not too far away, savoring the spectacle as if it were a form of entertainment, and unable to hide the slight grin.

"Why?" Pound asked Arakin. "Why do this for us? For your townspeople? We did nothing for you. And yet you free us all."

Arakin was so exhausted that he could barely move his head. His gaze could not meet Pound's. But his words did. "Because I should. Because I can," he whispered.

Arakin's reply seemed to resonate powerfully with Pound, who gazed pensively back at Arakin, without breathing for a moment, in total silence.

"You are a true warrior, Arakin," said Pound softly. "And more."

Pound scooped Arakin's lithe body up in his thick scar-ridden arms, then crossed the floor and handed him carefully over to Efscott.

Efscott took a step toward the Witch, but again Dinara and Pound stopped him.

"There is nothing you can do," said Pound to Efscott, his tone consoling.

The Witch snapped out of her own introspection and met Pound's gaze as if she knew what he was thinking. "A treasure awaits you, oh mighty Generals. But if you and your men want the gold that magic has promised you, then you must leave now!"

Pound and Dinara ushered Efscott off the floor. The other two Generals, Yan and Pularax, and their other men were close behind. Efscott turned one last time at the exit, the threshold of the stairwell. He met Prudence's gaze and trembled, utterly bereft.

"Child. Dear child," he croaked.

Prudence looked warmly back, and Efscott tore himself away, then descended the stairwell, his head bowed, his eyes streaming with tears, and his shivering body clutching Arakin's tightly to his chest.

The eight soldiers who had accompanied the Generals also made their exodus, leaving only the two Royal Guards with Luxurous, Perfeyn, the Witch, and Prudence. The Royal Guards looked awkwardly at each other, and then to the Witch.

The first Guard pointed to the exit with his thumb. "Umm—"

The Witch answered their question before they finished it. "Yes! Leave! Now!"

The guards scuttled away, and the space on the tower floor now seemed particularly wide and open.

Luxurous glared at Perfeyn. "Well done, idiot! Now I've lost my army."

The Witch intervened. "It matters not. Your Duja army will be far stronger."

***

The snow fell heavier now as Efscott exited the castle with Arakin in his arms. The Four Generals walked with him but stopped at the threshold of the drawbridge.

Efscott crossed the bridge alone, toward the crowd of townspeople that parted before him and then followed silently as he returned to the village.

Arakin's breath was weaker, shorter, and shallower now, and his eyes were partly closed, but through a peculiar hole in the low-level clouds he could make out the shape of the moon, perched above the town, a giant silver orb, bathing them all in a cool light. It seemed so large and impossibly close, suspended just inches above the rooftops. It was as if the heavens and earth shared the same space at this very moment. The clouds folded slowly over the gap, obscuring the moon, and Arakin's eyes closed, his breath faltered, and he felt the cold sting of the snake's poison constricting his heart. And it beat no more. His body hung totally limp in Efscott's arms, and the Carpenter sobbed quietly, continuing his trek toward town, with small tufts of snow collecting on his shoulders and on the cold frame of Arakin's body.

***

Ash still watched from his vantage point in the branches and fell back into a sitting position with overwhelming dismay. "Arakin," he muttered. He glanced down mournfully at Slipnor,

244

who was looking back up at him, shuffling on his front paws and impatiently waiting for news.

Ash placed his hand on the left side of his chest as if to quash an aching within. He ran his fingers over the snake's bite marks, and his eyebrows contracted slightly as if a great revelation dawned on him. He tapped his fist lightly upon his chest two times.

***

The Blacksmith guided Efscott to his home and a cot in the corner. Even Brunt came to his aid with a demeanor of admiration and mourning, placing an extra cushion upon it before politely moving aside. Efscott lay Arakin down upon the small bed and stood slowly. Sir Sudley came to his side and placed a tender hand on Arakin's shoulder.

The melancholy townspeople gathered outside the door, paying their respects at a discrete distance, with the grandiose golden statue of Prince Perfeyn towering over them from behind, adding insult to everyone's injury. The snow fell heavier now, collecting in small patches on their heads and shoulders. A number of the townspeople stared curiously up at the sky.

"An early winter," said the Baker.

Suddenly, there was a commotion at the back of the crowd.

The townspeople gasped, stiffened, and trembled upon seeing what approached from behind—a giant white wolf. Slipnor!

Driyetta, the Baker's wife, immediately fainted, luckily falling straight into the arms of her husband.

"Kill it! Kill it!" the Baker hollered.

A number of the townspeople picked up rocks, and Slipnor stopped. The townspeople took aim, and suddenly Ash leaped

245

up out of the fur on Slipnor's neck, landing on the wolf's head. The townspeople froze, wide-eyed and wide-mouthed in terror.

"Easy there!" yelled Ash. "Oh … wow," he declared with genuine shock. "You people sure are ugly up close."

The Baker fainted with Driyetta still in his arms, and they fell to the ground with a dull thud.

The others kept staring at Ash without blinking.

Ash put his hands on his hips and took a deep breath. "Well, let's just agree on this. It's been a crazy week for all of us."

They didn't seem any calmer by his affirmation.

"And I know I have some explaining to do, folks. But in the meantime," Ash stiffened as if fighting the urge to weep, and pointed to the Blacksmith's door, "get out of my way. My brother is in there." Ash sat back down on Slipnor's neck, and the giant wolf walked onward. "So … we're coming through now. Stay calm!" he said, his tone sounding more hopeful than authoritarian.

The wide-eyed crowd parted for them.

"Nothing to see here! Move along!" added Ash.

***

Back at the castle's lower courtyard, outside the corner stables, a figure moved in the shadows, wheezing and groaning while loading a hefty bucket of gold onto a carriage. It was Minus. A wind blew the carriage's tarp off, revealing another ten buckets of gold beneath. Minus yanked the tarp back down and glanced anxiously left and right.

"Treasurer and Manager of Poo, indeed!" he snorted.

He scampered to the driver's seat and flicked the reins. The four horses strained under the load but managed to make their way out of the gates, building slowly to a trot.

"You have not seen the last of me, Ashville!" declared Minus, snapping the reins again.

***

Inside the castle, a long line of soldiers on horses snaked up through the stairwells to the treasury room and the pile of remaining gold. It was less than a tenth of the size it once was. Most had been poured into the wishing well to create the Duja army, but what remained was still a veritable fortune. The Four Generals assisted in the duties of pouring two substantial portions of gold into each horseman's saddlebags.

Each rider nodded with gratitude to the Generals and guided his horse out, the footfalls of the hooves now heavier as the horses braced themselves under the load.

***

Upon the rooftop floor, Luxurous stepped to the rear edge and disdainfully eyed the first group of soldiers making their way into the courtyard below. They formed themselves into ranks, awaiting the Generals and their final evacuation as one.

"All my remaining gold! Gone!" Luxurous snarled.

"It matters little," said the Witch firmly. "You will soon have the most ferocious army in the world. You will conquer all."

Luxurous glared indignantly at Prudence, bound to the stone columns beside him. "I'd like to kill that little meddling witch right now," he grumbled, slowly drawing a dagger from his scabbard.

"Wait!" yelled the Witch. "The blood of a White Witch shall feed our army. But we must wait until the last Duja has risen."

"How long does that take?" grumbled Luxurous.

247

"Funnily enough, the same amount of time as cooking a rat's head casserole."

She pulled a giant hourglass from her cloak and plopped it onto the rim of the well. The granules in the top bulb began trickling through the narrow neck and into the base. She pointed the head of her staff at the well, and her eyes turned jet black.

"Now you start, you will gestate, you will soon rise, and bring your hate!" declared the Witch, finishing the spell with a jab of her staff. A short blast of red, sinewy light shot from the head of it and hit the water with a moderate splash, then spiraled rapidly down like a snake into the depths of the well. A boom resonated when it hit bottom, and the red light burned brightly for a few moments, then subsided. The Witch's eyes returned to their normal color, and she gave a devious, self-satisfied grin.

Prudence craned her neck, and for a moment, her eyes twitched.

"What's wrong with her?" asked Luxurous. "Is she going spazzy or something?"

"She does go spazzy!" declared Perfeyn in a shrill voice.

"Visions!" said the Witch. "She sees glimpses of the future."

Luxurous's eyes narrowed as he studied Prudence with a mix of disdain and curiosity.

The Witch picked up the large black bottle of tears from the rim of the well. She grinned sardonically as she popped the cork. "And the tears of thousands I add to thee. To make you full of misery! Arise! Arise! Arise!"

She poured it all into the well, which glowed bright green as it boiled and hissed. Luxurous grinned and glared back at Prudence.

She calmly met his gaze, though, and this seemed to unnerve him.

CHAPTER THIRTY-ONE

Ash Inspires

Deceptively light footfalls from behind prompted Brunt, Efscott, and the Blacksmith to turn their heads. The sight of Slipnor's hulk sliding through the doorway with Ash standing on his head held them fixed in united shock.

"My goodness!" hushed Efscott.

Ash jumped off Slipnor, landing gracefully on the floor. "Hey … Dad," he said with a sad grin. Efscott smiled warmly back. "I think we can save Arakin," he continued, "but we have to be quick!" Ash pointed to a large bundle of bracken tied to Slipnor's back. "Ash wood. It draws the venom out."

The Blacksmith's eyes narrowed. "How do you know this, devil-toy?"

"I'm the living proof," chided Ash. "And it not only draws it out, it also makes the wood come alive. And my name's not devil-toy. It's Ash! Fatty!"

The Blacksmith looked duly reprimanded and offered nothing in the way of reply. Efscott had quickly moved to Slipnor's side and was placing his hand on the bracken, preparing to untie and unload. But a thought came to him, and he gazed through the open doorway.

"What is it?" asked the Blacksmith.

"Something even better," replied Efscott.

***

On the castle's rooftop floor, a demonic growl resonated from deep inside the wishing well. The castle shook, and the Witch snickered.

Luxurous grinned maliciously at Prudence and sneered, "Not so smug now, are you?" He skulked slowly up toward her. "My grandfather killed the last of the dragons. And my father killed the last of the wizards. And so, here I am. What's my legacy? Well, I'm the guy who has killed all of the remaining White Witches. Except for you." He pointed his long, bony finger at her. "Guess you're lucky last!"

***

Efscott rushed out of the Blacksmith's cottage and into the town square, pushing through the crowd. He cut a line straight to the statue of Perfeyn standing regally tall, stabbing the sky, resplendent in indestructible gold skin and bathed in the cool moonlight.

Efscott slammed his hands against the stone monolith upon which the statue was pinned and tried to push, but it wouldn't budge. Ash was close on his heels and joined in. Unsurprisingly, it still didn't move.

The townspeople all shuffled anxiously back, clearly worrying that they might be assigned guilt by association and, therefore, still incur Luxurous's wrath. All but one: Sir Sudley. He stepped forward and reefed an iron pike out of the ground,

250

the same one upon which Efscott's execution notice still hung. He sidled up to Efscott and levered the pike under the monolith with all his might. It moved. But only an inch.

The Potato Farmer waved a disapproving finger. "There'll be hell to pay if the King sees you doing that! He still has a Witch. And she's got a temper!"

Efscott, Ash, and Sir Sudley kept pushing. And this time, the stone monolith moved farther, leaning over slightly, more and more. The entire structure bowed forward with a creak and groan, like a mast as its sail took hold of a stiff breeze.

"Watch your toes!" yelled Ash, and with all their might, they gave another hard push. The statue passed its center point of balance, and now gravity worked in their favor. Over it went. The gold sword, held high, scraped across the night sky in a wide arc as the statue and monolith careered downward, falling with a mighty thud. It sent snow billowing upward and townspeople diving out of the way among a ripple of yelps and cries.

***

Prince Perfeyn watched aghast from the castle's rooftop. "Father! My statue!"

Luxurous spun on his heel and came to the edge of the tower, seething upon the sight of the felled royal sculpture.

"Send the soldiers after them!" pleaded Perfeyn.

"The soldiers have all gone, child," said the Witch impassively. "They have received their severance pay. Neither you nor your father has any sway over them."

Luxurous glanced beyond the rear edge of the floor and down into the courtyard. The army of four hundred was commencing their exodus on horseback with their heavy

251

saddlebags of gold. Luxurous puffed out his chest and straightened his tunic with a firm tug. "They will always listen to a king," he said proudly, sidling up to one of the pillars where Prudence was chained.

Luxurous eyed Pound in the front of the line and yelled with the most commanding and regal tone he could muster, "I say there, General, attack those people in the village … now! Your King commands it!"

Pound brought his horse to a halt, and the army behind him also stopped, including the other three Generals. "We have no king. We have gold!" declared Pound, eyeing Luxurous calmly.

"And what is a general without a king?" screamed Luxurous. "What purpose does *he* serve?"

"I expect he'll just enjoy being rich. That's all," said Pound with a grin.

"And what of your pledge to the heavens? You will serve the King who brought order from the chaos, and light from the darkness! Empty words, it seems?"

"You are the chaos and the darkness!" Pound bellowed at Luxurous, his face reddening with rage. "And your father was even worse! At least you were just a greedy idiot. But you're more like him every day. Hollow men with a need to fill your souls with the misery of others. Aye, when I was a young lad, I did indeed have foolish ideals … to think that one day I would meet a king worthy of my sword, my army, my life. But in my years, I have seen that all kings are selfish men, cold and heartless, no love of the land or the people. Pure poison! Aye, I'll take ya money. I'll be needing it to make sure I keep my kin far from your unholy army."

Pound flicked his reins and urged his horse onward at a leisurely pace. The other three Generals rode to his side, and they exited together.

"How dare they?" seethed Perfeyn. "And how dare those peasants desecrate my statue."

Luxurous was absolutely fuming. He lifted his chin proudly and strode over to the southern end of the floor. "Well topple it they may," he hissed, "but they shall not break it, for it is coated in King's Gold. The only thing that can cut it is the indestructible Gun Ronin. Speaking of which, I shall repay General Pound for his insolence by introducing him to one of my bone-crushing gargoyles."

The clapping footfalls of hooves upon stone indicated that Pound and his men were approaching the exit of the barbican below the tower, and on toward the drawbridge, directly under Luxurous.

Luxurous drew Gun Ronin from its sheath. He eyed the hefty stone gargoyle on the tower's edge, perched directly above Pound, who now emerged from the castle's entrance. Luxurous's expression darkened, and he swung the sword hard at the gargoyle's base.

But with a thump and a thwack, the sword bounced off the gargoyle and struck the King in the face. He staggered back, clasping his nose and dropping the sword.

"Ow!"

"What trickery is this?" exclaimed the Witch. She scurried over to the sword and grabbed it, scrutinizing it frantically and in disbelief. She tapped her finger lightly on the blade, and it resonated as solid objects should, but she was frowning and could clearly tell that something was wrong. She ran her finger across its edge, then harder again, indicating that she was discovering it was not sharp—at all.

"Owww!" Luxurous howled again as he stomped his feet. A large red welt now appeared, running diagonally across his face.

"This is not Gun Ronin. A wooden sword! A trick!" the Witch screeched as she tossed it aside.

Prudence grinned, for she already knew this.

While Efscott had been carving the statue of Perfeyn, Prudence had been frantically shaping the wooden block at her feet into a wooden sword—a copy of Gun Ronin—meticulously cutting and sanding it to the point of replica perfection.

And while Perfeyn devoured his purple grapes, Prudence hurriedly painted the wooden version of Gun Ronin. She kept her eye on Luxurous as he descended the stairwell, then she ducked behind Efscott's back before Luxurous entered the room—and she switched the swords.

As Perfeyn devoured his plum, Prudence scampered up the ladder and placed the real Gun Ronin into the hand of the statue. Just in time, before Luxurous rounded the corner and entered the room.

And as the guards carried the statue out, Prudence whispered into Efscott's ear, revealing her secret. His eyes widened in horror as he watched Gun Ronin being carried away within the statue's fist, but he still managed to face Luxurous with a brave smile.

***

As the billowing clouds of snow around the felled statue settled, Efscott shot a glance toward the castle. Prudence's small, fragile shape was visible to all, still shackled to the pillars on the castle tower's rooftop. Efscott smiled sadly. Her risky plan had obviously shown incredible foresight.

Moonlight drifted across the sword within the fallen statue's hand, and it hummed. Efscott wrenched Gun Ronin by the hilt and slid it out of the statue's grasp with a bell-like ring. He gripped it firmly, lifted it high, cocked for a strike, and swung down at the figure with every ounce of strength he had. With a thunderous crack, he sliced cleanly through the statue's shoulder joint, separating the arm from the rest of the body.

Efscott cleaved at the second shoulder. And with another crack, it was Perfeyn who was now armless, at least in his statue form.

Although the majority of townspeople tensed in fright at this provocative display of rebellion, a few of them grinned and clenched their fists, as if they wanted to clap and cheer but refrained for fear of retribution from Luxurous.

The Potato Farmer was not smiling though. He was pale with fear. "You know what they call this? Treason! No other words for it."

Sir Sudley met his gaze. "How about poetic justice?"

***

Perfeyn bayed with indignation at the spectacle. "I will destroy you all!" he screamed.

Luxurous snatched the wooden sword from the floor and eyed Prudence with seething suspicion. "Smug little brat!"

He hurled the wooden weapon at Prudence, but it missed her head and bounced off the pillar, then flew back and hit him in the face again with a thwack.

He howled again, "Owwwww!" a second red welt now swelling up, crossing the first, and forming a red *X* across his face, with his nose at its center point.

A sudden, ground-shaking roar from the wishing well provided an immediate distraction from his pain and offered solace in the form of imminent revenge. Luxurous gingerly approached the well and peered into it. A pair of glowing gold eyes peeled open, deep within the dark waters. The Witch grinned, and Luxurous leered at Prudence. "When my Demon Army from Hell rises, I will send them into town to where your father is. And your boyfriend! Did you foresee this?"

Prudence nodded calmly, clearly not as unnerved by his threat as he'd hoped.

Luxurous stormed up to her. "Then why are you smiling, halfwit?" As he glared at her, his face twitched slightly, but not from rage. It was the look of someone a little unsure of himself. Prudence, on the other hand, remained stoic.

"What else did you see?" Luxurous asked, with a hint of anxiety creeping into his voice. "Tell me!" He pulled the gag slightly away from her mouth and pointed his knife at her throat. "And no spells," he reminded her, pushing the knife a little harder into her soft skin.

Calmly she met his gaze, and her tone was relaxed as she spoke. "I saw a boy who would save me. With golden sword, he would be king. He had two arms of strongest gold. They call him … Arakin."

Luxurous's face twitched again, like a rabbit's. He shoved the gag back over her mouth and stepped away cautiously.

"You just love to rhyme, don't you?" he mumbled irritably. "You crazy witches."

***

Efscott now cradled the two severed gold limbs in his own arms, with Gun Ronin laid upon them, and made his way back into the Blacksmith's cottage with an air of reverence and purpose, as if providing an offering to a deity.

Slipnor lay beside the cot, looking forlornly across at Arakin, then rose and backed away as Efscott approached, giving him space. Sir Sudley pulled his scarf off—the same one given to him by Luxurous many years ago. "We can use this," he said with a conspiratorial tone.

Efscott and the Blacksmith placed the timber cores of the statue's shoulders flush against Arakin's shoulder stumps and pushed. Sir Sudley wound his purple scarf in a figure eight around Arakin's torso and the shoulders of the gold arms, pulling everything tightly together in a series of skillful knots. Ash gently patted Slipnor, who whimpered helplessly.

There was a murmur outside, and the townspeople turned. The shuffling sound of many hooves on the gravel had grown louder. The Four Generals and their army were approaching slowly through the shadows of the night.

Many of the townspeople scurried away into their homes, no doubt fearing it was a task force sent on a retribution campaign because the statue had been defiled.

The army formed a circle around the Blacksmith's cottage, with the Four Generals taking the prominent positions near the front entrance. They took off their helmets and bowed their heads, sitting there, quiet and still.

"What are they doing?" whispered the Baker, who had stayed near the Blacksmith's front door.

"A gesture of respect to he who freed them," Sir Sudley replied softly. "Arakin."

CHAPTER THIRTY-TWO

Born of Winter's Night

Upon the castle's rooftop floor, the water in the well boiled more fiercely.

"The Duja rises!" declared the Witch with malicious delight.

The Duja's large granite hand reached slowly from the steam and water, then clasped the rim of the well with a loud crunch. Its body was a haggard grey carapace of stone with radiant molten gold deeper down, visible between the many cracks throughout it.

Prudence cringed, and her eyes flashed helplessly down at the Blacksmith's home far below. There was no movement though. No sign of Arakin.

Luxurous grinned imperiously at Prudence. "Good luck with your boyfriend."

***

Inside the Blacksmith's cottage, a bright green color suddenly pulsed through Arakin's veins. It flowed toward his shoulders— and into the ash wood core of the golden arms.

"It's working!" breathed Efscott.

***

Meanwhile, the Duja's second hand rose from the water and clasped the well's rim. Prudence looked to the horizon. The sun was creeping over it. Then a sound split the air. It was the Duja, roaring from within the well, sending a spray of hot water upward.

Its head rose through the shimmering shroud of steam. Its face was flat with haunting deep-set eyes and bright, molten gold glowing within. It growled, exposing huge stone fangs dripping with black oil, then heaved its hulking mass from the well with its four long arms.

The creature stood erect upon the rim of the well, nine feet tall, towering over everyone.

"Your first Duja," cried the Witch jubilantly. "He is Dujara, the General of your Duja force."

Dujara crouched, sprang upward, arced through the air, and landed deftly on top of one of the southern facing pillars, crouching low and surveying the village below with a menacing growl. He was a mangled body of callous rock that moved with sinister, catlike grace.

***

Upon the cot, Arakin's golden hand twitched. And so did his eyes.

"That's it, my boy!" encouraged Efscott.

259

Daylight spilled into the room, and Arakin's eyes opened. He took a deep, gulping breath. Ash smiled with utter relief but was knocked sideways when Slipnor's tail sprang into a frenetic wagging. He spun across the floor and hit a nearby wall with a bump, but his frown from the impact was immediately replaced with another beaming grin. Arakin heaved his exhausted body up and tried to find focus through the haze of death's sleep that he had risen from. It felt as if this place he was returning to had a dream-like quality to it, and the one he had temporarily visited, though more vivid and real than anything, was already fading. Already forgotten. An eternity closed beyond the veil of here and now. He did not belong there—not yet. There were things left undone. Prudence. He stood, as quickly as his stiff, tired body would allow him.

***

Arakin stepped onto the threshold of the Blacksmith's doorway.

The crowd had been gazing in horror at the Dujara above the castle and were equally flabbergasted to discover Arakin now standing before them. They burst into excited mutters amongst themselves, affirming how incredible it was that the ash wood had successfully drawn the snake's venom out of his blood. Their response was a relief to Arakin, because it showed they did not believe he was rejuvenated through evil witchcraft, an argument he didn't need right now. Others gingerly made their way out of their homes, craning their necks curiously among a flurry of enthusiastic murmurs, shocked and bewildered by his return.

Pound, Pularax, Dinara, and Yan dismounted their horses and approached Arakin, regarding him with intrigue and wonder.

260

"You have a habit of cheating death," said Pound crisply, standing before him now with the other three Generals beside him.

"He learned to dodge a lot of things growing up in the Ash Forest, including death," said Sir Sudley as he came to Arakin's side in the doorway.

The rising sun reflected off Arakin's arms and threw a dancing array of glittering gold light over the confounded faces of the townspeople and the Generals in front of him.

Although Arakin's mind was still foggy and his senses quite numb, he could clearly feel the coolness of the air against the gold, armor-like skin of his brawny arms. He also sensed the warmth of the ash wood in their core. The snake's venom had bound with the wood's sap, creating blood of sorts for these alien limbs that were now linked to him. But perhaps they were not so alien after all. He had always felt he was a part of the forest, and here he was now, with arms chiseled from Grandastal, the grand tree that had protected him for so many years. Arakin felt an overwhelming power and calm flow through him as he realized something: he was not only a part of the Ash Forest—the Ash Forest was now a part of him.

This rapid montage of thoughts transpired in less than a few heartbeats, and as Arakin gained his bearings and filled his lungs with air, his thoughts went swiftly back to Prudence. Efscott came to his shoulder, and Arakin asked anxiously, "Where is she?"

"The tower," said Efscott, his voice breaking.

Arakin felt as if his blood had turned to ice. He eyed the castle and took two rigid steps toward it, clenching his fists tightly, the sound of metal grinding upon itself resounding as a result.

"The Demon Army from Hell rises quickly," said Sir Sudley in a sympathetic voice. Sir Sudley could clearly identify the look of overwhelming compulsion in Arakin's hardened face. "You won't make it alone."

"He's not alone," declared Ash, dusting himself off and coming to Arakin's side, with Slipnor close behind.

Pound bowed his head and returned to his horse. The other three Generals did likewise. They all shared a similar stride—a plodding gait of sorrow, of lost magnificence. And although they had won riches beyond their wildest dreams, a part of them looked broken.

"Let's go," hushed Arakin to Ash and Slipnor.

"Wait!" called Efscott. "They'll slice you to ribbons. You need armor." He eyed the fallen statue of Perfeyn. "Unbreakable armor." Efscott strode toward the fallen figure and drove Gun Ronin into the chest plate, then sliced and peeled open the gold armor surrounding the torso with the speed and finesse that only a Master Carpenter possessed.

Sir Sudley surveyed the unsettled crowd, then rounded on Arakin. "Talk to them," he whispered, placing a gentle hand on Arakin's arm. "You will need an army behind you."

The rage burning in Arakin felt like it could only be quelled by sprinting immediately to Prudence. But he knew there was something in Sir Sudley's words: a pearl of wisdom he knew he should listen to, despite his primal urges.

Sir Sudley nodded knowingly at Arakin and then turned and darted through the crowd, calling out to Efscott as he passed, "I'll get some bindings."

Arakin moved passed the throng of people toward the center of the road and onto a small, broken portion of the stone monolith, two feet high. The townspeople promenaded around it, gazing up as he addressed them. "Help me! Please! If we fight them together, we can win!"

***

Upon the castle's rooftop floor, Luxurous spotted the commotion in the town. And then he saw the figure at the center of everyone's attention. He squinted and leaned forward, grimacing. "That's not him, is it? The armless orphan boy?"

"It is," blurted the Witch in disbelief, "but he has … arisen."

Luxurous's face twitched with exasperation and shock. "Oh, come on! Just die, for goodness sake!" he screamed.

He turned to the Witch and howled incredulously, "What is *wrong* with kids these days?"

"My arms!" shrieked Perfeyn, his voice constricted with fury. "He dares wear *my* arms?"

The Witch's eyes narrowed, and she gazed dreamily into space, seeing something invisible to the rest, then declaring ominously, "His arms are from the woods, and his blood flows strong with magic. A sacrifice is pending now, with a son whose fall's not tragic."

"Nope. Didn't understand a bit of that," said Luxurous, throwing his arms despairingly out to the side. "But thanks for the pep talk," he blurted in a deadpan tone.

Several more Dujas leaped from the well.

The Dujara pointed below, ordering them onward, and the new arrivals bounded obediently over the edge of the tower floor, plummeting eighty feet down to the moat. They crashed through the drawbridge and landed in the shoulder-high water with a colossal splash. The crocodiles wasted no time, darting in and biting hard while Luxurous watched with morbid fascination. The Dujas brushed the crocodiles aside with the utmost of ease, though, and moved nonchalantly past. They trudged up the embankment, feet thumping loudly, finding sync with each others' stride. At the top where the inclined leveled out, they formed an army-like regiment in front of the castle, where they waited perfectly still. Luxurous grinned and shot an approving glance to the Witch, who nodded in return.

The icy water covering the Dujas quickly turned to steam, billowing ominously up in curls of thin white cloud, heated by the hot molten gold beneath their stone shells. The Dujas surveyed the town with haunting dead eyes of blazing gold, void of life, yet filled with malice and a wanting for battle.

***

Back in town, in the place known as the Empty Heart, which was more crowded than ever before, there was a growing unease. The army's horses shuffled nervously on their hooves, clattering over stone and snow, eyeing the distant Duja army with abject terror. And while their riders offered calming assurances, it was clear that they were equally anxious.

"I thought battle horses felt no fear," said the Blacksmith warily to Pound, whose horse, while less jittery than most, was still shifting on its feet nervously.

"They've not seen the likes of this army. Ever," said Pound.

A number of the townspeople wasted no time and bolted to their houses, where they began frantically packing bags in preparation for their exodus. Others just stared in horror.

"An army from hell," croaked the Baker. "It really has been a week of firsts," he added with a surprisingly indifferent tone, as if the events over the last few days had exhausted his capacity to be astonished by anything.

Arakin felt his fists and jaw clench tightly. He took a deep breath and addressed the Generals and the crowd with greater conviction. "If we fight, we make sure that you are never enslaved again. For slaves are what you were. Robbed of land. Robbed of choice."

Sir Sudley, flushed and panting, pressed through the crowd with a leather tunic over his arm and a knife in his hand. He sidled up to Efscott, who eyed the garment and nodded appreciatively. "My grandfather's," said Sir Sudley, catching his breath. Efscott, now in a lather of sweat, peeled back the last layer of gold plating, handed Gun Ronin to Sir Sudley, then collected the hefty pile of gold sheets. He strode up to Arakin and placed them on the edge of the fallen stone monolith.

Sir Sudley came to the base of the monolith, and with one hand on the flat of the blade and the other on the sword's hilt, he regally presented the handle of Gun Ronin to Arakin. Arakin stared at it for a moment, then took it with a friendly nod. He was surprised that he could feel the subtle warmth of the metal grip, which was afforded by Efscott's body heat while laboring with it. This was contrasted by the cold air on the back of Arakin's hands and arms. His limbs, while artificial, were clearly very much alive.

Sir Sudley pointed to Arakin and bellowed out, "Behold, Gun Ronin! In the hand of he who claimed it!"

A hush fell over the crowd, followed by a wave of murmurs. Yan, the Harromaen General from the Kingdom of the Sun, regarded Arakin coolly. "You will need more than a magic sword, child. The age of magic is dying," he declared with a crisp, raspy voice.

"And we are not dressed for battle," added Dinara, the Cuttorian General from the Dominion of the Deserts, his voice calm and measured. "We are dressed for returning home. Our gold weighs down our horses. They cannot run."

"We all hoped that a king might bring us order from the chaos, Arakin," said Pularax, the Yurrandar General from the Empire of the Wild Plains, his voice deep and resonating. "But this wish was as futile as magic itself. This is the age of every man for himself. You and your people should flee. Leave this land. Leave this King." Pularax eyed the castle thoughtfully and the pillars where Prudence remained chained. "We all lose something in war, Arakin," he added sympathetically. "To survive, you must know when to retreat."

Arakin felt his heart sink. If he could not convince the Generals to help him, it would be impossible to persuade the townspeople. He glanced over at Pound, the Baertic General from the Realm of the Far North, with futile hope. Luxurous had clearly bestowed a slightly higher rank on Pound than the other Generals, which seemed to be respected by all, and would make him a particularly influential ally. Regardless if this was still the case, Pound's impassive expression offered Arakin little promise.

Sir Sudley finished cutting his leather tunic into long straps. Efscott raised the first piece of gold armor to Arakin's chest, readying him for battle, but Arakin raised a hand. "No! On Slipnor!" said Arakin firmly as he patted the giant wolf, who had come closer and was affectionately burrowing his forehead into the boy's chest.

Efscott and Sir Sudley hesitated but then nodded dutifully. They began fastening the various gold plates onto Slipnor with the long leather straps, and Slipnor, a seasoned battle wolf, showed his pedigree, staying perfectly still as they worked around him.

Arakin stepped up to a higher portion of the monolith block, broken in length but not width. He was almost five feet above the heads of the crowd. Ash made his way to Arakin's side, standing close to his ankles and as tall as a ten-inch man could, with an expression of stern conviction.

Arakin sheathed Gun Ronin on his back, within the folds of Sir Sudley's purple scarf. He eyed the castle anxiously. His stomach tightened, and his heart beat faster. If he couldn't convince anyone to support him, he would need to launch an attack alone, a futile assault, without a doubt. But he would not abandon Prudence. How long did he have though? And so he decided—he would wait no longer than the time it took to armor Slipnor.

Arakin gazed earnestly over the one thousand faces before him, then bellowed in a commanding voice that grabbed everyone's attention. "This army of demons is said to be indestructible, yet all things do end, as all things begin. How will we live, though, in that moment between? For even if you flee, know that this army's reach is eternal." Arakin surveyed the faces of the townspeople before him. Fear and defeat were etched on their faces. His gaze settled on Pound, who regarded Arakin with compassionate resignation.

"This land is damned, Arakin," said Pound, with a surprisingly sorrowful tone. "Our gold gives us our direction, and it points us home. We have no king." He gave a respectful nod, turned his horse, and gave a gentle flick of the reins, coaxing it onward at a steady walking pace. The other three Generals did likewise.

Their soldiers parted for them and followed—an ocean of men, moving with fluid, regimented perfection—all exiting south, leaving Arakin and the townspeople behind. Arakin found his eyes fixed on Pound's back for a moment as a sense of hopelessness swept over him. He snapped himself out the gaze and surveyed the faces around him.

Arakin's throat felt tighter and drier, but he spoke louder now. "Luxurous's conquest is inevitable. His army will find you and those you love."

The three dwarves were nearby, having handed some gold shavings to the Potato Farmer in exchange for his Clydesdale. Arakin's words clearly struck a nerve with them, causing them to pause as they prepared to mount the giant horse. They glanced thoughtfully at one another.

Arakin continued, "And if you refuse to be enslaved, then an early grave is where they send you. But perhaps you yearn for more. To write a book perhaps, like Busk, from the Northern Tribes."

The surprise was apparent on Busk's face as he pulled his horse to a halt and looked over his shoulder at Arakin, who now addressed the column of men to the right: the Cuttorian tribes. "Or perhaps like Omar from the East," yelled Arakin, "you would just like the opportunity to express your feelings."

Omar, the giant of a man, stopped his horse. A single tear ran down his cheek, and he looked over at a fellow soldier, smiling like a gleeful child. "He knows my name," Omar croaked softly.

Pound stopped his horse and looked over his shoulder, regarding Arakin with greater intrigue. And so did the other three Generals. Their entire army came to a standstill.

Arakin had everyone's attention now, and he felt an overwhelming sense of urgency sweep over him as beads of sweat formed on his brow despite the frigid air. He needed to race toward Prudence, but he also needed to evoke action among those before him. His mind ran wild with what he might say. *Had the years of listening so attentively to people afforded him an insight into their higher needs,* he wondered? A key to their empathy and foresight?

Arakin stood taller and eyed the crowd with impassioned calm. His voice rang clearer than ever. "Our lives are but a brief moment in time defined so greatly by how we share it. Should it not be shared well?"

Arakin felt a rush of warmth swelling in his chest, and he bellowed out crisply, "Instead of an unwanted life of fighting, in which you create no life at all, why not create the life you've wanted, that is worthy of fighting for!?"

A fog of silence settled over the crowd, who gazed in awe at Arakin. Were they inspired enough though? It seemed their fear of the Dujas was more overwhelming, leaving them frozen in terror and too subjugated to cheer. The Baker, however, had a slight tear in his eye and was nodding pensively. But he, too, refused to move or speak. He bowed his head despondently.

Efscott and Sir Sudley finished attaching the makeshift armor to Slipnor with the leather straps, and they stepped away. Slipnor looked absolutely menacing.

Arakin looked over the silent crowd once more, then took a deep breath. Now was the time—he could not waste another heartbeat—so he gritted his teeth, then leaped onto the giant wolf with Ash clinging to his trouser leg. Ash bounded up to Slipnor's shoulders. Arakin turned to Efscott and stated emphatically, "I will save her! Alone, if I have to."

Efscott nodded. His calm façade belied his rage within. "We'll be behind you! Even if no one else is," he said resolutely. Sir Sudley nodded and came to Efscott's side.

The Baker pointed to Gun Ronin. "Does it talk to you … this Gun Ronin … does it say anything?"

"No. It's a sword," replied Arakin matter-of-factly.

The slightly embarrassed Baker nodded and pursed his lips together.

Arakin glared up at the castle. "But *I* have something to say … to the King! Charr!"

Arakin grabbed Slipnor's shoulder fur tightly with both hands and gave a firm tap of his heels against Slipnor's side. The giant wolf bounded off the stone monolith as if it were a springboard, traversing the heads of the crowd before him. Upon hitting the ground, he broke into a sprint, with Arakin and Ash hanging on tightly. They headed straight for the castle, cutting through the sea of people that parted for them.

Ash climbed higher onto Slipnor's neck and closer to his ears. "You can do it, boy," he hushed. "You can get us there. Run like the wind."

Efscott and Sir Sudley trotted after them—Efscott with a mallet in his hand, and Sir Sudley with his tattered spear.

CHAPTER THIRTY-THREE

Crashing from the Sky

Luxurous spotted Arakin, and his eyes narrowed. He clenched his jaw as his eyes flashed to Prudence. "Oh, he's coming to save you, is he?"

Prudence grinned beneath her gag, and Luxurous drew his dagger out once more.

"I'm going to cut your throat, you smarmy little brat," he threatened with rage as he stormed up to her and pressed his knife against the soft flesh of her throat, this time pushing the point in and breaking the skin.

"Stop!" screamed the Witch.

He paused.

"We can only pour her blood into the well when the last Duja has risen," the Witch declared, "and it must be fresh!"

Luxurous backed away from Prudence and bared his teeth at her. "You'll get yours, girly."

The Dujara eyed Arakin warily as he continued his charge up the town's main street and into the clearing, the no man's land between the village and the castle, which was now covered in a thin blanket of snow.

The Dujara leaped from the column onto the rooftop floor, where he grabbed three of the giant, iron candelabra with spear tips in their centers.

***

In the town square, the Potato Farmer stood up on the fallen monolith to get a better view of Arakin's progress. He turned to the Blacksmith beside him. "So how are we supposed to know if that's the real Gun Ronin? Seems everyone's got one nowadays."

***

At the edge of the castle rooftop, the Dujara hurled the three candelabra straight at Arakin with ferocious power and accuracy. The center one moved fastest and shot ahead.

Arakin guided Slipnor deftly to the side, dodging the first. While drawing Gun Ronin, he sliced at the second, cutting it in half. Suddenly, the base plate of the third and final candelabrum broke, curved in the air, and spun toward them—a deadly flying disc coming from one direction and a sharp spear from the other. But Arakin sliced both cleanly in half with lightning-fast speed, and the pieces deflected away in a shower of sparks and a crack like thunder.

"Yikes!" declared Ash, ducking instinctively.

The broken pieces tumbled and spun past Efscott and Sir Sudley, who ran some hundred yards behind them.

***

Back in the town square, the Baker raised an eyebrow. "Have to admit, I haven't seen that before."

***

On the castle rooftop, Luxurous gaped in astonishment and outrage. "How can he do that?" he screamed at the Witch. "That's not normal, is it? Is it?"

The Witch stepped to the edge beside Luxurous, eyeing Arakin's formidable charge with a degree of trepidation.

"He has returned from the dead," she croaked, "and he brings with him the power from that world."

"Well, that sounds like fine-print to me," seethed Luxurous. "Are you a witch or a lawyer?"

Luxurous glared across at the Dujara, standing between the front two columns.

"Kill him! Now!" hollered Luxurous, his veins pulsing in his neck while pointing at Arakin.

The Dujara roared, and the army of three hundred Dujas who were assembled in front of the moat charged toward Arakin with an ear-piercing cry, drawing their swords of gold-infused stone from scabbards within their thighs.

"No! It is too soon!" protested the Witch.

"It's never too soon to kill an orphan!" yelled Perfeyn, as he swaggered up to his father, his expression rife with glee.

***

Pound and the other Generals had not taken their eyes off Arakin as he continued his solitary charge into battle. The army behind them had fanned out to the sides, giving them an open path ahead and a clear view.

"He races to a fight he cannot win!" said an astonished General Yan.

"What courage!" stated General Dinara.

"What a boy!" added General Pularax.

"What a king!" declared Pound with reverence.

The sudden ring of a sword being drawn prompted Dinara, Pularax, and Yan to turn.

Pound now held his broadsword tightly in his right hand. His left hand moved to his saddlebag, where he unhooked its center hole from the saddle horn. He yanked the bag sideways, sending it over his horse's shoulders to the ground, where it landed with an almighty clank. The gold burst out and sprawled across the snow. A hundred lifetimes of fortune for Pound—discarded in the time it took for a single breath.

Pound stared fixedly at Arakin, who continued his charge into battle. "We once served a King who saw the cost in everything yet the value in nothing," yelled Pound. He turned and faced his men and aimed his broadsword in Arakin's direction. "I see a new King! And he is pointing the way!"

Pound looked across at the other Generals, who met his gaze, nodded, drew their swords, and cast their bags of gold aside. All of their soldiers followed suit. A thunderous roar of gold hitting the ground resounded as four hundred men cut their gold bags free. Their treasure flooded the earth, and the sunlight reflecting from it danced over them.

The townspeople watched with astonishment. And yet not one of them ran for the discarded fortune. Instead, the Blacksmith picked up his giant hammer, the Potato Farmer grabbed his pitchfork, and the rest of the townspeople did likewise, seizing whatever was near: sticks, rocks, a kitten that issued a soft meow. The Baker, thankfully, put the kitten back and picked up a rolling pin instead. Just an accident—he always was a tad excitable. And shortsighted.

Pound stood up in his stirrups and bellowed out at the top of his lungs, "Who will fight with me this day?"

Yan, Dinara, and Pularax roared heartily, jabbing their swords into the air. Pound met their gaze and gave a nod of deep appreciation and respect, which they returned. The army of four hundred also roared in support, creating a chorus of rage that split the air.

Pound looked back toward Arakin and bellowed out fiercely, "Protect the King!" He dropped back in his saddle, dug his heels into his horse, and charged forward.

His men cheered even louder, with thunderous exuberance, and followed, holding their swords high.

Pularax, Yan, and Dinara also roared and led their own men into the charge. "Charrrrrrrr!"

The townspeople watched in awe as the army galloped past them, displaying far more fury and enthusiasm than they had done on the day they attacked the village. The army disappeared quickly down the main road in a cloud of swirling smoke.

The Baker took a deep breath, raised his rolling pin, and squeaked, "Yarrrr!" He ran onward into battle, following the horsemen—totally alone, with the townspeople watching in silence.

Then, in unison, the townspeople pumped their fists and weapons into the air with a combined "Yarrrrrrrrrr!" And they, too, charged forward, following the Baker at their own idea of high speed, hobbling under the weight of their large bellies, huffing and puffing, slow but resolute.

***

Watching this from the castle rooftop, Perfeyn glanced incredulously across at the Witch. "You said that at sunrise, no mortal would love him," he yelled. "And yet, they follow him into battle!"

275

The Witch still stood at the rooftop's edge and scowled. "They do not follow him for love," she grumbled.

"Then what? Fear? Greed?"

She eyed Arakin with a mix of wonder and contempt. "Courage," she declared. "The truest of kings inspire courage."

Luxurous sighed and threw his hands up. "Well, that sounds like more fine print to me! Thanks a lot!"

The Dujara roared an order to another Duja as it rose from the well. It leaped across the floor and with unbelievable force smashed the eastern column with its fist. One deafening crash followed another as the column toppled over, broke into thirds upon hitting the floor, then rolled to the rear, scattering debris in its wake. The middle section plummeted over the edge and plunged through the open stairwell, severing the only route of entry and exit. It then smashed through a small wall on the royal quarters' level and landed with a thunderous bang in front of the main door in the courtyard, thus blocking it.

Luxurous flinched and stiffened. "I say, aren't they house-trained?"

"They are protecting you, My King," informed the Witch.

The Duja seized the upper third of the pillar, hoisted it above its head, took a few strides forward, and hurled it at Arakin with a roar.

"Goodness!" blurted Luxurous with a mix of fear and admiration.

Six tons of stone and gold now flew toward Arakin, howling through the air.

Perfeyn bristled with joy by this show of unbelievable force. "Yes! Yes! Squash them!" he cried.

***

276

Arakin charged with Slipnor and Ash over a slight rise in the snow, and upon his descent on the other side discovered that three hundred Dujas were racing straight for them, just seventy yards away. Only now did he spot the stone column spinning toward them. He moved Slipnor to the left, but the column snapped into four pieces in midair—too many to dodge—and a collision was imminent. With a colossal thump, one of the pieces hit the ground and clipped Slipnor hard. He somersaulted forward with a yelp, sending Arakin and Ash flying through the air as well.

Arakin hit the snow and rolled forward, sending up a spray of white powder. He lifted his head to check on Slipnor, who had taken the worst of the hit and was sitting back in the snow, dazed but still conscious. Arakin searched frantically for Ash but couldn't see him.

The Dujas had spread out slightly, the snow impeding their collective, coordinated speed. The first arrow formation of their charge was heading straight for Slipnor. Just fifty yards away now.

"Slipnor!" wheezed Arakin, trying to scream through winded lungs.

Arakin hauled himself to his feet using his right arm. The first time he had ever used it, he realized. At first, it had felt so foreign, but once instinct kicked in, it became more natural. He staggered toward the advancing Dujas to block their attack on Slipnor. Adrenaline took over, dissolving the delirium from the shock of his tumble; he was now more alert than ever, in full command of his senses and totally aware of the incredible strength in his arms.

Arakin drew Gun Ronin and collided with the Dujas. He deflected the first several blows with the same speed and deftness he demonstrated in the Ash Forest when facing the

Venus Mantraps and spiders. His agility made him a problematic adversary for the Dujas, who had been built for dealing with brute force. They swiped and missed numerous times. Arakin swung hard with Gun Ronin, and it chipped into the nearest Duja's sword. Another blade came swinging in from the side, and Arakin clipped it in a sweet spot, slicing it cleanly in half. With furious energy, Arakin ducked, turned, cleaved, and chopped, slicing into their arms, legs, and blades, cutting two more swords in half and dodging their constant attempts to grab him.

Regardless of his blindingly fast assault, Arakin was quickly outnumbered. With a bone-crunching punch, one of the Dujas knocked him onto his back. Another two Dujas sprang forward and pinned his arms down, and another three Dujas roared with jubilance as they swung their swords down at Arakin's throat.

But the blur of their swords was swiped away by the blur of something else. With a whoosh and a smash, a large force slid into view from behind Arakin like a giant wave. Horses were leaping over his head as the Four Generals and their entire army charged over the rise behind him, vaulting from its apex, clean over Arakin—an airborne cavalry to the rescue. They smashed into the Duja Army in a crunching crescendo of metal and rock. Their mortal roars of wrath formed a surge of human thunder as they pushed the Dujas away from Arakin.

Slipnor was still looking dazed, with his butt firmly planted in the snow. He regained his bearings, then heard a muffled moan and quickly stood. Pressed into the snow directly under his butt was Ash, wincing, spread-eagled.

"Oh, that was not a pretty sight!" Ash groaned.

Slipnor looked over his shoulder at Ash, who abashedly declared, "Let's agree not to tell anyone about this. Like … ever. Okay?"

Several Dujas had slid through the army's charge and bore down on Slipnor and Ash. Just ten feet away now. Ash drew his tiny sword and assumed a strong defensive stance.

"Come on!" he yelled at them defiantly.

Suddenly, a colossal horse came flying overhead—a Clydesdale. One dwarf steered while the others swung giant iron hammers, smashing the Dujas back away from Ash and Slipnor.

Arakin sprang to his feet and ran with the horsemen, straight for the Dujas, who received a flurry of vigorous and audacious hits from the Army of Man. The tables quickly turned, however, with the advantage of surprise now spent. Although the Dujas were fewer in numbers, their power was overwhelming. They swung mercilessly with their swords and fists of stone, delivering an absolute beating upon the Army of Man. Humans and horses were sent tumbling through the air.

One particularly vicious Duja eyed Arakin with sadistic glee and stormed toward him. General Yan galloped in from behind and smacked the Duja on the head with his sword, but it merely bounced off. The Duja turned, not even hurt, but distracted— and that was enough. It swung at Yan with its sword, but Arakin blocked the blow. Pound stepped in and stopped the strike from the Duja's other hand. A thought occurred to Arakin as his eyes flashed across the Duja's stalwart torso that loomed so menacingly close. Each Duja shared a similar cavity in the same area of their body. Perhaps a weak spot, small though it was, but all creatures had them. Arakin seized the opportunity, spinning on his heel and driving Gun Ronin through the narrow crack on the Duja's left chest area.

The Duja convulsed and threw its head back as gold veins appeared on the surface of its stone carapace, glowing now, white-hot. Yan swiped his sword through its waist, above the hip, where the joints opened up slightly, providing exposure to its inner gold core. The Duja's body fell apart into a pile of rocks, covered with molten gold! Arakin, Pound, and Yan nodded to each other. A shared eureka moment.

"We fight as one!" declared Arakin. "And aim for the heart! It's where they're weakest."

Pound stormed toward the next Duja and swung at it with his broadsword. The Duja blocked it with its stone arm and hit back with its blade, but Pound blocked the blow with his shield. Yan raced in, stabbed the Duja through the crack over its heart, and Pound swung again with his sword, slicing the Duja in half. Dinara and Pularax noticed this, as did the Blacksmith. They all jumped into a similar style of tandem teamwork. The entire army of soldiers and townspeople followed suit upon seeing their comrades' success with the technique.

Arakin's eyes flitted around as he tried to get his bearings amid the chaos, and he spotted a flash of familiar white between the horsemen: Slipnor, sprinting toward him, with Ash standing tall upon his shoulders, pointing the way.

CHAPTER THIRTY-FOUR

Doorway of Fire, Windows of Time

Luxurous fumed upon seeing the Army of Man gain the upper hand, which had now been joined by the ragtag army of townspeople, a collective of odd shapes and sizes, dressed in the most unmilitary-like clothing and wielding makeshift weapons. Disparate, peculiar, yet fighting as one. While they did little in offering brute force or overwhelming attack, they provided numbers and a valued distraction to the Dujas' coordinated attack. And that was enough.

Perfeyn bristled beside Luxurous. "They're being beaten, Father! Your ugly Duja army is being beaten!"

Luxurous spun toward the Witch. "You said no army led by man could beat this Duja army."

"They are not led by man. They are led by a boy—returned from the dead—from Vadoria. The Under Land. Him!"

She pointed to the battlefield below. Slipnor was emerging from the northern end of the melee with Arakin and Ash on his back, cutting a line through the blanket of snow, charging straight for the castle. The Witch appeared paler than usual, as though filled with a nameless dread.

"It was he who brought the early winter," she muttered. "He ate the golden apple, he absorbed the snake's venom and journeyed into Vadoria in that window of time when he was deceased. And now he rides with a vengeance straight for here, for her!" The Witch pointed at Prudence, and Luxurous groaned.

"This is really turning out to be a very frustrating morning for me," snarled Luxurous at the Witch, "and I'd appreciate more solutions, if you don't mind. What can we do about him—"

"He has no way to get up here anyway," seethed Perfeyn. "The stairs are gone, and the doorway's blocked. The courtyard will be a graveyard to anyone stupid enough to enter. If he even makes it that far, which he won't." Perfeyn grabbed a discarded longbow and quiver from the floor and had it armed and cocked in no time. He aimed at Slipnor.

"Say goodbye to your happy dog, Forest Boy," Perfeyn hissed, then fired his arrow.

***

It was an excellent shot, and the arrow hit Slipnor's chest hard. But it bounced feebly off the gold armor with a snap and a twang.

Ahead of them now, one hundred Dujas clambered out of the moat, seething with bloodlust. Arakin tightened his grip on Gun Ronin and braced himself. Slipnor sped up and jumped high, arcing through space, traveling cleanly over their heads, and landing with grace and explosive speed.

One of the Dujas from the castle's rooftop had eyed the great wolf's approach and had already leaped from the tower's edge to intercept him. It landed with an ear-splitting crack directly in front of them, blocking their entrance.

Slipnor feigned a move to the left, then dodged to the right, throwing the Duja off-center and creating the opening he needed. He breached the gates.

The Duja turned and took chase. But Arakin cut the chain that held the heavy grill of the iron portcullis, and it came crashing down, stopping the enraged Duja, which smashed face-first into it.

****

Perfeyn snatched the handle of the giant oil pot behind Prudence. It was four feet wide and filled to the brim. He pulled the lever ever so slightly, and a flame-capped drop of oil tipped over its edge and hit the stones behind her, splattering against her heel. "I should just tip this on you!" he hissed.

His eyes flashed to the courtyard, where he could see the shadow of Slipnor entering the ground directly below him. He grinned at Prudence and, with a firm push of the lever, tipped the oil out.

****

The flame-infused liquid poured down toward Slipnor, Arakin, and Ash, but it missed them by inches, erupting into a wall of fire behind. Despite missing the downpour, Slipnor's lower back still managed to connect with a few droplets from the splash, setting his coat ablaze in three small patches. He yelped and spun around helplessly. Ash was quick to act, shooting past Arakin with handfuls of snow he had scooped from Slipnor's neck. He smothered the fire with these and finished off the final flames by throwing his chest onto them. Ash rose with black soot smeared across his chest and face.

"Woah, heartburn," he croaked.

Arakin's eye flashed skyward. He spotted the form of Perfeyn retreating from the edge of the tower while hissing. Arakin anxiously surveyed the courtyard; the only entrance leading to the tower was blocked by massive doors, barricaded and fortified by an iron door two feet thick, and now with a giant pillar of stone before it. The stairwells beyond it that led to the tower rooftop were destroyed anyway, so these doors offered no solution.

"No way up! We're trapped!" snapped Arakin.

Another Duja jumped from the tower's edge with a roar, landing with an earth-shaking crash in the courtyard. It bounded up quickly and sprinted straight for them. Arakin braced himself but noticed a new threat in his peripheral vision. He dodged and sliced, cutting an arrow aimed directly at Slipnor's unprotected shoulder, fired by Perfeyn. Then another arrow.

"Watch out!" yelled Ash.

Arakin felt an incredible force hit him in the upper arm, a sword swung by the Duja, hitting him with a clank and sending him tumbling to the ground. The Duja had closed in faster than Arakin had thought. Arakin was unscathed, though, and quickly shot to his feet, defending the next blow and fighting back, hard and fast.

Perfeyn kept firing arrows at Arakin, and Arakin kept slicing them with Gun Ronin or deflecting them with his gold arms. Meanwhile, he took a pounding from the Duja. He was faster and more dexterous, but couldn't match the Duja's power.

Slipnor pounced with a growl and knocked the Duja off-balance, buying Arakin the brief window of opportunity he needed. Arakin delivered a perfectly aimed killer blow into the narrow crack of its chest and followed through with a slice through its midriff. The Duja tumbled apart into a pile of rocks covered in hot, molten gold.

Arakin eyed Perfeyn retreating out of sight, then spotted the broken pillar teetering on the roof's edge. His eyes flashed back to the rising heat from the burning oil and the molten gold. He looked at Ash—a eureka moment—and they spoke at the same time.

"Thermals!"

***

Luxurous's eyes flashed from the courtyard to the battlefield, and then to the Witch. With a flush-red face, clenched fists, and gritted teeth, he screamed maniacally, "I don't like losing, Witch! Do something! Anything! Now!"

She eyed him coolly, then pointed her gnarly finger at the hot, bubbling waters of the well. "But how badly do you wish this, Sire?" A light of green and gold suddenly flickered within the well. "You will gain all the gold and kill all mankind. All will be yours that gets left behind."

Luxurous met her gaze. She clearly scared and intrigued him.

Her eyes narrowed. "I'll unleash all of hell, but what must be done is that you give me the life … of your one, only son."

She pointed to Prince Perfeyn standing at the tower's edge. He turned and lowered his bow. "Are you absolutely mental?" he blurted.

Luxurous weighed this all up and gazed into the flickering light within the well, which now turned orange and red. His eyes widened with horrified delight at what he saw and heard. The screams of many echoed from within—the sounds of hellfire—and the sights of the world he apparently wanted.

Perfeyn stiffened. Luxurous grinned at the Witch. The water in the well slowly began to turn, faster now, becoming a powerful whirlpool and generating an incredible suction force. Luxurous needed to lean back, to maintain his balance.

***

Down in the courtyard, Ash gave the thumbs-up to Arakin and released his parachute, which immediately unfolded and lifted with a whoomp, carrying him upward, fast and unwieldy. He pulled on the strings, gaining reasonable control, and followed the wall of the castle's central tower by maintaining an elliptical flight path.

Arakin sheathed Gun Ronin on his back and took the coiled wizard's rope from his shoulder.

Ash brought his parachute under greater control and steered toward the gold standard on the rooftop's rear pillar, where Prudence was tied. He flew quickly and smoothly toward its center and nodded cockily to himself. "Yeah, like a pro, baby," he said softly.

But the suction created by the well's whirlpool tugged him suddenly across as he neared the standard, and with a clang, he slammed face-first, on his right side, into the golden wreath of thorns.

"Argh! Are you kidding me?" he whispered hoarsely as he wrapped his arms around the standard.

The wind from the well's whirlpool also fanned the flames of the fire that burned beneath the oil pot directly behind Prudence. The fire now inched dangerously closer toward her.

***

Arakin spun his grapple hook at a faster pace, preparing to unleash an almighty throw. He searched the rooftop anxiously for a sign of Ash.

"Come on, Ash. Where are you?" Arakin whispered.

He maintained his composure but couldn't help glancing over his shoulder at the front gates. The news wasn't good: several ferocious Dujas were smashing on the front portcullis relentlessly. It began to crack at the sides with every punch, gradually pulling itself away from the hinges. The Dujas roared with the anticipation of getting their hands on Arakin.

***

Ash bounded off the wreath onto the top of the gold fist. He hadn't been spotted by anyone yet. Crouching down, he drew an arrow and aimed down over the edge.

"Yes," exclaimed Arakin softly, and he threw his grapple hook up, fast and high.

Ash fired down at the hook, and with a swish, his launched arrow pulled the string from his shoulder with it. His arrow sailed downward and hit the rope at the base of the hook with a slight pinging noise. A perfect shot.

***

Unaware of all this, Luxurous stared intently into the roaring whirlpool, and the Witch came closer to him.

"Only you and I shall walk the earth. You shall never need to share your gold ever again," she said quietly.

Luxurous gazed dreamily into the well. "And the one true king will be of King's Gold," he hushed.

Suddenly, he seemed to snap out of his reverie and looked across at the Witch. "That sounds like a pact with the devil!"

The Witch narrowed her eyes—was he getting cold feet?

Luxurous grinned. "I love it! Sign me up!"

The Witch grinned, and Luxurous cast a sinister glance at Perfeyn. "Here's your hot whirlpool bath, boy!"

Luxurous stormed over to Perfeyn, grabbed him, and heaved him over to the well's edge. "Father, are you bonkers?" screamed Perfeyn in a shrill tone while putting up a futile struggle. With another firm twist and shove, Luxurous sent Perfeyn over the edge and into the well's whirlpool with a splash. The Prince's peculiar cry of indignation resonated as he was sucked swiftly down, spinning wildly, into the crimson depths, "You're both poo!"

Luxurous groaned. "I shouldn't be surprised that he could talk under water." His glance set hard upon the Witch. "This better be worth it." He eyed the hourglass near the well's rim and smirked— it was getting lower. Time was running out for Prudence.

***

The commotion around the well made it easier for Ash to remain undetected. He had seized the opportunity and jumped off the pillar, aiming for the large iron ring bolted at the back. He fell cleanly through it, pulling with him the string he held. Upon landing, Ash quickly surveyed things left and right with the gusto of a Special Forces soldier who took his job very seriously. Then he sprinted to the broken pillar.

Ash tied the string to a rock, fed it through the iron ring on the broken pillar, and tossed it over the edge. Down it fell, pulling the string and rope with it.

In the courtyard below, Arakin finished tying his end of the rope around Slipnor's chest and waist, just as he did in the lava river. The plates of armor that Efscott had belted to Slipnor made the job much easier this time though.

The grapple hook flew through the upright pillar's ring above, just fitting through, and then through the ring on the broken pillar, teetering on the tower's edge.

***

The Witch pulled the snake from her neck. "Absolutum dominion!" she snarled. The snake seemed to suddenly realize its fate and tried to wriggle free. But the Witch hurled it into the well, and it was sucked quickly into the glowing red depths below.

The well glowed brighter now as if it was relishing the two recent offerings that had been poured into it.

"Is this going to take long?" grumbled Luxurous.

With a zap and a splash, a lithe shape shot upward from the water; a long white vine covered in thorns flailed wildly, twenty feet high, and many others exploded out of the frothing well to join it. Hundreds of them. With a whoosh, they all ignited in flames.

Luxurous stepped back apprehensively, shocked and delighted at the same time. "Good grief!" he spluttered.

Several of the burning, thorny vines lashed out at Prudence but couldn't reach her. Then one did, cutting her face with a whiplike flick. Prudence, for the first time, appeared genuinely terrified, and she pulled frantically on her wrist shackles. But to no avail.

Her eyes widened. She had noticed something else—the last grains of sand in the Witch's hourglass had fallen through. Time was up. The Witch turned to her with a sinister grin.

An ominous groan and rumble emanated from the well, and the entire castle trembled.

289

***

A groaning tremor rippled out from the base of the castle, violently shaking the ground beneath the armies fighting in the snowfields. The earth cracked in sections, forming deep, narrow gorges that yawned open beneath their feet, as far as three feet wide. Only the Dujas seemed unperturbed, while all others were clearly horrified. The townspeople were particularly distracted, shrieking and yelping. In contrast, the soldiers maintained a shaky focus on the battle, casting sporadic, fretful glances at their new enemy—the very ground they stood upon.

***

At the castle's gates, the Dujas pounded their heads and fists on the portcullis. One of the hinges snapped under the force, and the bolt of another popped out. Only two hinges remained, and they were quickly breaking under the newly acquired strain.

Arakin heaved down on the rope, and the grapple hook pulled on the broken pillar above. It lifted ever so slightly and teetered back down. He needed to pull harder, he realized, but it was so heavy.

A thunderous clank from behind meant only one thing: the Dujas had smashed the portcullis clean off its brace. They came charging in, roaring with bloody fury and heading straight for Arakin, blindingly fast.

Arakin pulled hard on the rope again, leaning desperately into it. The pillar rose farther this time. Hopefully, it was enough to create the momentum needed. He let go, and as he had hoped, the massive column tipped slightly over the tower's edge. Slowly, slowly, it leaned farther down.

The Dujas were closing in on Arakin, and the closest one lunged for him with its four long arms outstretched. The pillar plummeted off the edge.

"Yes!" cried Arakin.

It pulled the rope down with it, and yanked Slipnor and Arakin upward, escaping the Duja's reach by an inch. Arakin leaped onto Slipnor's back, and upward they flew.

Luxurous noticed movement in his peripheral vision and spun, spotting Ash tiptoeing toward Prudence. Ash became as still as a statue and as wide-eyed as an owl. He knew he was in trouble. Luxurous's expression darkened, and he grabbed a rock from the floor, then hurled it. It whizzed past Ash's face, and he broke into a sprint.

Luxurous hollered as he stormed toward him. "Wretch! Rat! Whatever you are!" Luxurous grabbed a larger rock and threw it. Although it missed Ash, it did block his path. He was trapped. Luxurous bore down on him. "Or perhaps I should call you ... kindling!"

Luxurous now brandished an even larger rock in his hands. He lifted his arms high above his head, poised to crush Ash— until an unexpected voice from above caused him to halt.

"His name is Ash!"

Luxurous twirled and to his horror saw Arakin sitting tall upon Slipnor, high above the gold fist standard, behind Prudence.

"And he's my brother," added Arakin defiantly. He drew Gun Ronin from the sheath on his back. "And by the way," he gestured to Prudence, "she's with us!"

Luxurous, looking suddenly pale, dropped his rock and scampered back behind the Witch for protection.

Arakin leaned down and sliced the vines that were coming in for another attack on Prudence. They whistled and writhed as they hit the floor.

The Witch scowled and hissed, then drew herself up taller and gripped her staff more tightly, the knuckles of her hand whitening. "All hell rises, and all hell comes! Drink all her blood, and hell has won!" she roared.

The floor shook, and the thorny vines suddenly came together to form a giant hand, with Prince Perfeyn's royal insignia ring clearly visible on its middle finger. It seemed he was still around in some form. The thorn-hand clenched tightly, then opened. It flexed, twitched, and morphed, taking on a new shape that caused Arakin to stiffen in terror. A giant snake.

***

Down on the battlefield, flames exploded from the cracks in the ground, setting many of the fighters alight. The soldiers and townspeople patted their sleeves and leggings into the snow to smother the flames, but the Dujas seemed far from concerned. In fact, they became more robust, striking now with even greater force. Their demonic bodies were engulfed in fire that flickered highest upon their shoulders and heads, and they roared louder, with even greater enthusiasm.

"Demons of hellfire! Reapers of the apocalypse!" stammered the Potato Farmer. And then with a mumbled "Sod it!" he dropped his ax, spun on his heel, and bolted back toward town. Many of the townspeople followed suit, fleeing in a mad panic.

Pound gazed up at the castle and stiffened upon seeing the giant thorn-snake. His face was ashen, and his breath still. He looked very much a man poised on the precipice of a monumental decision. Then he took a deep breath, gritted his

292

teeth, and bellowed to his men with a hoarse roar, "A true king will never abandon his men—nor true men, their king!"

The color came back to Pound's face, and he returned to swinging at the fiery Dujas. And Pularax, Dinara, and Yan joined him. Everyone else who remained on the battlefield did likewise, fighting harder than ever before, clearly going beyond themselves, with a passion beyond rage and a rediscovered vigor beyond exhaustion. They were fearless and united, determined to be there for Arakin as he was for them.

CHAPTER THIRTY-FIVE

King's Gold

Up on the tower, the thorn-snake spotted Prudence and gave an ear-piercing hiss. It heaved itself out of the well and moved toward her, its long, forked tongue darting out and flickering.

Arakin, still on the pillar above Prudence, stood motionless, paralyzed with fear as the snake inched closer. Its haunting, pale eyes surveyed him ruefully as steam curled from its mouth. The thorny vines that formed it were packed so tightly that it now seemed more like a serpent that had once impersonated thorny vines, rather than the other way around. Its huge fangs glistened in the sunlight as its jaw gaped wider.

"Ash, am I seeing the world's largest snake coming straight for us?" hollered Arakin. "Or is it just a hallucination because I'm so tired?"

"That one is definitely real!" croaked Ash. "I can see it too."

Arakin remained frozen to the spot for a moment, then slid awkwardly off Slipnor. Trembling, his face grew pale and sweat-ridden, and an icy weight seemed to fall from his chest into his stomach. He was so terrified he could not feel his legs; they may as well have not been there. And then a thought occurred to him: what did that matter, for he was once the boy with no arms, and yet here he was.

"Perhaps you have to lose something to truly find it," he whispered to himself, remembering the quote from Efscott when Arakin had returned his stolen chisel to him. Arakin braced himself, gritted his teeth, took a deep breath—and launched himself off the column, diving at the snake.

He soared through the air and landed lightly between the snake and Prudence. He swung fast with Gun Ronin, directing a mighty blow at its snout. But to his astonishment, the gold sword bounced off its callous hide, almost throwing Arakin backward.

The Witch cackled. "Something wrong with your sword, boy?"

The snake lunged for Arakin, but he dodged it. It snapped again, and he somersaulted elegantly over its head.

Ash cheered ardently. "Yeahhhh! Now it's dancing-angel time!"

But when Arakin landed, he lost his footing, tripped, and fell flat on his face.

Ash continued, "Okayyy, spoke too soon again."

Arakin realized he was sliding toward a deformity in the floor—a shape, a hole. The hole formed from the lightning strike summoned by Prudence. Arakin jammed the pummel of Gun Ronin into the stone floor, acting as a spark-erupting brake. He came to a stop and peered over the edge into the throne room forty feet below, then rolled over onto his side, immediately feeling a crushing force around his ribs.

The thorn-snake had lunged again, lightning fast, and locked its jaws around Arakin's waist. Its fangs narrowly missed puncturing his flesh but still acted as robust claw-like grasps around him, locking him within the crushing jaws that squeezed tighter and tighter.

Arakin felt at least two of his ribs break with a loud crack, and the others felt poised to do likewise. He winced and groaned as a nauseating pain radiated from his sides through the rest of his body, searing his mind with blinding agony, obliterating his confidence, and overwhelming him with a sense of helplessness.

"No," he hushed to himself, a command to his body that it must refuse to give in, a reminder to consciousness that he needed to stay present. There was never a perfect time—there was now, there was only now. He had to act. He had to stay focused.

Arakin regained composure through his fog of pain and delirium and unleashed a series of ferocious strikes at the side of the snake's face with Gun Ronin. But again, the sword simply bounced off. The Witch blurted defiantly, "Not even Gun Ronin can cut the thorns of hell, boy! Only Witches possess such magic."

Slipnor, who had been continuously barking, bared his teeth, saw an opening, and jumped off the standard, hurtling through the air and landing behind the snake's head. He bit ferociously into its white-thorned hide, but the giant serpent flicked him off violently, sending him tumbling across the floor—and over the edge. His front paws found traction, and he hung on. Just. But he was slipping and began scraping desperately on the smooth stone floor. It was a deadly eighty-foot fall.

The snake smashed Arakin against the stone pillar by Prudence's left side. It shook so violently that it sent the gold standard above toppling off, narrowly missing Prudence's head and landing instead in the vast empty oil pot behind her with a deafening clang.

Luxurous ducked instinctively from the force of the hit, then did a double take when he got a closer look at the purple scarf tied around Arakin.

Befuddled, he asked, "Is that my scarf?"

The thorn-snake pummeled Arakin into the northern pillar with such force that Arakin was knocked from its jaws, spinning like a top. A momentary twitch of his hand saw Gun Ronin flung from his grip, and it slid across the floor with a bell-like scrape—toward Luxurous. Arakin was struggling to stay conscious and tried to stand. But his limbs wouldn't respond.

"My sword!" declared Luxurous with glee as he grabbed it. Wasting no time, he bounded across the floor and directed a deadly swing at the back of Arakin's neck. There was a slight swish-thwack noise, and Luxurous suddenly recoiled in pain, then leaned back and buckled over while grabbing his left buttock, missing Arakin totally with his attack.

Ash had fired a tiny arrow into Luxurous's butt and was preparing to shoot another, but Luxurous turned on him quickly and lunged forward to stomp on him. But Slipnor dove in— back in the game, having hauled himself over the edge—and he bit deep into the King's ankle and flung him sideways.

"Yeah! Meet my fluffy buddy, Your Majesty!" rejoiced Ash.

Luxurous lost the grip on Gun Ronin as he spun through the air, sending the sword across the stone floor toward the rooftop's edge.

Arakin's eyes blazed widely as he pulled himself up and dove for it.

Gun Ronin disappeared over the edge. Out of sight. But a hand followed it quickly. Arakin had slid across the stone floor to intercept it and reached out just in time. He pulled his hand back over the edge with Gun Ronin firmly in its grasp.

The snake lunged and seized Arakin once more in its jaws. He groaned under the vice-like grip and felt his flesh tear as its fangs pierced his stomach and chest, warm streams of blood now seeping from the wounds. But he was determined to keep a hold of Gun Ronin and maintain focus.

Luxurous pulled himself wearily from the floor. "Get my sword back. Knock it out of him!" he hollered.

Arakin glanced over at Prudence, and it was now that he noticed a single strand of gold herb protruding through the buttons on her top. His eyes flashed to hers. She nodded fervently, her eyes wide.

Arakin screamed, "Ash! Get the gag off Prudence!"

Ash nodded, sprinted across the floor, and frantically climbed one of the pillars that Prudence was shackled to.

The Witch, though sluggish at walking, proved wicked-fast at spitting fireballs. She hocked one up in a split second and spat it straight at Ash. With a whoomp and a pow, she scored a direct hit on his butt. The force knocked Ash off the pillar and sent him somersaulting over the edge, disappearing, with his scream fading away fast. There were no thermals on this side of the tower to help whisk him back up.

Arakin cried out in horror, "Ash!"

The Witch inhaled gruffly and spat another fireball, this time at Arakin. But he deflected it with his golden arm, sending a splash of fast-dying flames dancing through the air.

The thorn-snake pummeled Arakin into the pillar by Prudence's right side, again hitting it so hard that the gold standard toppled off into the giant pot behind her. The first standard had already melted, fueled by the furious flames beneath the giant metal bowl. The boiling liquid gold splashed up as the next gold standard fell in, sending splatters of burning gold over the lip of the pot and down, dangerously close to Prudence's feet and hands.

Arakin was unable to breathe under the pressure of the snake's massive jaws, his mouth now bitter with the taste of his own blood from either a puncture wound to his lung or lacerations in his mouth—he couldn't tell. A short, sudden coughing fit suggested the former. His head was spinning, and his eyes were blurring; he had been deprived of sleep and food for four days, and he was being pulverized into nothing by a creature more powerful and terrifying than he could ever imagine. Arakin could feel the deceptively appealing peace of sleep now pulling him into darkness—sleep, pure sleep. But in that blanket of illusory calm wrapping around him, there was thought, just one thought: *Prudence*. If he failed, she would suffer a horribly painful death. He could not surrender to the pain, fear, fatigue, and resignation that erupted within. But even in this state of defiance, he could feel his vision dimming, blacking out. The world around him was fading away.

"Prudence," he mouthed softly as if willing himself back into coherence.

A bright, stabbing flash of the sun above Prudence grabbed Arakin's attention and offered lucidity by way of an idea. It was sunlight reflecting on the shackles around her wrists. Arakin realized now there was a way he could free Prudence without getting to her.

He spotted a figure rising behind the Witch. It was Ash, levitating swiftly over the edge of the tower floor, grimacing, with his butt on fire. The heat of the flames was feeding the rise of his parachute, pushing it upward. It was the ultimate case of turning a bad thing into good. Portable thermals, very convenient, despite the significant discomfort of having your bottom on fire.

Ash was fervently chanting to himself, "Take the pain, use the heat, take the pain, use the heat."

Arakin smiled with delight through the haze of crushing fatigue.

Ash landed on Prudence's shoulder and reached for her gag.

The snake smashed Arakin into another pillar, clearly relishing the process of torturing and toying with him.

Ash pulled down hard on Prudence's gag, and she wasted no time. "Serpentine distraxi!" she cried immediately. Her words cut the air like a thousand bells. A simple spell that was aimed at buying just a fragment of time.

The thorn-snake paused for a moment and glanced back at her. A big mistake on its part.

Arakin's eyes narrowed. He cocked his arm and threw Gun Ronin. It hurtled toward Prudence and ricocheted off both pillars, whizzing over her head and Ash's. It was a direct hit on both shackles.

Ash ducked, shoving his flaming-bottom down into the snow that had accumulated on Prudence's shoulder, smothering it. Steam rose, and he grinned.

Gun Ronin flew back to Arakin's metal hand. His fist enveloped its handle once more with a loud clang. Those years as a boy who had no one to play with had come to fruition; bouncing acorns off trees in the forest had, like so many other things, given him a skillset upon which he drew.

Luxurous smirked sardonically. It seemed that Prudence was still bound in her shackles. Still entrapped, perhaps?

But the smile faded swiftly from the King's face as the shackles fell from Prudence's wrists with a jangle. She was free. Her eyes narrowed.

Luxurous's reddening face was alight with malice as he bellowed with rage at the snake. "Finish it! Swallow him whole, then rip off her head!" The snake cocked its head and smashed Arakin onto the floor with a bone-crushing force.

Prudence's eyes glowed pure white, and her hair floated upward as she concentrated in earnest on her next spell.

The Witch's eyes widened with horror upon seeing what Prudence reached for—the tufts of gold leaf in her chest pocket. "No!" exclaimed the Witch with dread.

Luxurous and the Witch both broke into an awkward, hobbling sprint toward Prudence, who slapped both palms together and crushed the leaves with three firm turns of her hand. Luxurous drew his dagger. This time he looked intent on driving it all the way in.

The snake tossed Arakin high into the air and opened its mouth wide, preparing to swallow him.

Luxurous reached out to grab Prudence's hand and thwart her spell, but with a thunk, a tiny arrow hit his nose, and he slid to a stop, wincing in agony. Ash was already loading his bow with a new bolt; he fired, scoring another direct hit into Luxurous's snout with a louder thunk.

"Ow! Owwwwww!" Luxurous squealed.

Prudence threw the thistles of gold herb high with both hands. They flew ethereally upward, then down onto the snake. Prudence held her arms before her, her palms facing the enormous white monster, her fingers splayed wide. "Thistle meet the thorn of hell, bind with it, and turn to shell!"

The thistles glowed bright white, and with a resounding crack, the snake suddenly stiffened, then crystallized, its hide of thorn-riddled vines glistening as they turned to ice, with flashes of gold light rippling over it.

Arakin, still plummeting through the air, dove into the snake's giant, gaping mouth.

Prudence continued, "While ten heartbeats are all we get, we'll spend it well with no regrets!"

Arakin spun around and came to a halt, deep inside the transparent snake's throat. His feet were now in line with the top of the well. He stabbed Gun Ronin outward, and with a booming crack, the gold blade cut easily through, into open daylight.

The Witch had reached Prudence and wrapped her hands tightly around her throat but flinched upon hearing the noise of the breaking ice. She spun to see Arakin cutting effortlessly through the snake's entire neck, in a circular motion, causing ice fragments to explode outward like a spray of solidified sunlight. The giant snake head peeled off from its own neck and fell, shattering into thousands of pieces with an incredible crash, leaving Arakin standing in the clear with his feet straddling the well and steam billowing up around him.

Two dark scarlet patches of blood stood out on his torn, pale shirt, but they had begun to dry already, a good sign that the bleeding from the snake's puncture wounds had ceased. The pain was also far less excruciating.

Then the fabric of his torn shirt fluttered outward, and the Witch's eyes widened upon seeing Arakin's wounds more clearly, her expression now an odd mix of disbelief, horror, and wonder.

"He will be of King's Gold," she hushed.

Arakin followed her line of sight and discovered what astonished her: two round patches baring a distinct gold sheen were changing to his normal skin tone. His flesh was healing at a phenomenal speed with the aid of the gold inside him. The gold he had eaten.

But the snake was also recovering quickly; a chattering and creaking noise where its head had fallen heralded that Prudence's spell was wearing off. The thousands of ice fragments rapidly morphed into their vine state once more, and the thorn-snake's head retook shape. It rolled away toward the tower's edge—still lifeless and seemingly harmless. But as the last flickering beads of gold light faded from it, marking the end of Prudence's spell, the snake's huge, dead eyes flickered with life again. It convulsed, glowing red hot then sprang around and lunged ferociously and instinctively at Arakin.

Arakin leaped out of the way, landing dangerously close to the hole in the floor. He teetered over it for a moment, then jumped across the chasm.

The snake, meanwhile, bounced off the wall of the wishing well, flipped around, and rolled rapidly and uncontrollably toward Luxurous, the Witch, Prudence, and Ash.

Prudence didn't hesitate or flinch. She simply ran—straight for it—with Ash still on her shoulder.

"Ummm ... what are we doing?" yelled Ash.

The answer came via action as Prudence slid past the shock-ridden Witch and Luxurous, who now had their backs turned to her. Prudence sprang upward, somersaulting elegantly over the snake, plucking Ash from the air as he spiraled out of control.

"Oh, we're like dancing angels," he crooned.

Prudence landed elegantly beside Arakin, who watched in amazement.

"Good jump," he said softly.

She blushed coyly and daintily bobbed up and down.

"All in the knees, right?" asked Arakin.

She nodded with a grin and placed Ash on his shoulder.

They both eyed Luxurous and the Witch warily as the snake head came to a halt between them. Its sinewy tough flesh vibrated momentarilly, returning again to its ghostly shade of white, and it blinked hauntingly up at Luxurous and the Witch, then morphed once more into the shape of a giant human hand.

"Yesss," hissed the Witch with maniacal joy. "Lose your head but find your hate, squeeze them dead, oh hand of fate!"

The giant hand twitched sporadically, then rose quickly, preparing to launch across the floor at Arakin and Prudence, who braced themselves for the renewed attack.

But in its haste, the hand knocked the pot of molten gold hard, rocking it backward and bending one of the axles. On its forward swing, it popped off the broken shaft and tipped forward—enough to launch its entire contents.

Luxurous and the Witch ran to escape it, but when a drop of the molten gold hit the tip of the hand's finger, a reflex reaction caused it to retract, curling fast into a fist and grabbing Luxurous and the Witch within its vice-like grip.

The Witch shrieked with guttural rage.

"Oh, poop!" blurted Luxurous.

And the wave of molten gold covered them entirely within a few heartbeats. It was over so quickly. Luxurous, the Witch, and Perfeyn were dead. Foiled literally by their own hand.

As horrific as this demise was, they both had rather comical expressions of surprise on their faces, frozen in time forever within their carapace of gold.

The thorn-hand's upright position meant that its wrist lay flush with the floor, giving it the appearance of reaching out from the ground. Luxurous and the Witch were captured in a pose where their arms reached upward and out. Together, the three of them formed an image uncannily similar to Luxurous's own standard of the fist clutching the thorn wreath.

The Witch's arm moved slightly. But it promptly seized up as the gold cooled and hardened in the bite of the early winter's air.

The sound of magic gold ensconcing the Witch and severing her power resonated in the form of a great groan followed by an almighty crack, issuing outward like a thundering wind, cold and powerful, fleeting but reaching far.

***

In the center of the field, Efscott had been knocked to his back by a fierce Duja. Sir Sudley ran in and swung a club at the Duja's head, but the wooden weapon shattered into pieces upon impact. The Duja barely flinched, then bore down upon Efscott with its sword. Efscott rolled away just in time, but the sword in the Duja's other hand was the one he couldn't dodge. He was pinned against the blade of the first one. It looked like the end for him.

The Baker, who had also remained with the warriors to fight, let out an almighty sneeze.

The booming noise emanating from the castle like a wave hit them all, and the Duja above Efscott froze, then tumbled apart into a pile of lifeless rocks. Its sword fell from an absent grip toward Efscott and landed blade-first in the snow, just an inch from his face.

Every other Duja befell the same fate. With a tremendous crack and a mighty rumble, they all fractured open and toppled apart, hitting the snow as a pile of grey rocks and molten gold.

The Baker gazed around in amazement. "Did I do that with my sneeze?" he asked breathlessly. "Perhaps I, too, have magical powers."

305

The entire battlefield was now a field of gold at the feet of mortals. Steam rose like a ghostly curtain as snow and molten metal came together.

Pound, Dinara, Pularax, and Yan glanced across at each other, sharing similar expressions of euphoria and relief. They had chosen their king, they had stood their ground, and they were victorious. The Four Generals gazed up at the tower, and the warriors around them did likewise. Up on the top, they saw Arakin, accompanied by Prudence, Ash, and Slipnor, who all stepped to the edge.

Arakin raised Gun Ronin above his head, with the blade pointed skyward.

And the disparate army of embattled warriors and townspeople below jabbed their own weapons skyward with a deafening cheer. The Baker sneezed again and looked anxiously around. Nothing happened. "Perhaps not," he mumbled.

The huge cracks in the earth closed up with a rumble, smothering the fires that had belched from within.

And then there was silence.

Everyone on the battlefield then broke out with more cheers and laughter as they embraced each other and tended to their injured comrades. The battle was over; it was finally sinking in. They were victorious. They were free.

The women and children who had fled town were at the top of a slight rise to the south, gazing back in disbelief. Their cries of jubilation could be heard even on the battlefield as they dropped their belongings and ran home.

High above on the castle rooftop floor, sunlight gleamed across Gun Ronin, and the blade hummed.

CHAPTER THIRTY-SIX

You Have my Sword

Upon reuniting in the castle's courtyard, Arakin, Prudence, Efscott, and Sir Sudley embraced each other, with the Generals huddled close around them.

Everyone converged on the town and met in its center. The townspeople who had fled now ran with arms wide open toward loved ones who had returned from fighting, then they turned to embrace the soldiers, expressing their tearful gratitude for protecting their family members.

The town buzzed with euphoria and a celebratory mood, but it didn't stop Arakin and Prudence from immediately tending to the injured in whatever way they could. Prudence's advice on herbs afforded effective remedies, while Arakin's presence alone bolstered a cheerful glow in every person he came in contact with. Ash rode Slipnor close behind them at all times, like a worried older brother keeping a wary eye on them.

A group of excited children approached but then hesitated, terrified to come any closer yet fascinated by Slipnor and Ash. Arakin beckoned them on with a smile, and they gently reached out to pat the giant wolf, whose armor was now removed. The children barely reached his upper leg, so Slipnor leaned into their rubs, clearly enjoying it, and the children giggled and cooed with glee.

Meanwhile, many townspeople dug into the earth of their gardens, retrieving small wooden boxes and leather bags. From these they withdrew dried fruits, biscuits, cider, ale, and other delicacies. They had kept these treasures hidden from the army, and even each other, rationing it for their own survival.

But now was a time for sharing.

Platters of food and beverages were carted around town for all to enjoy. Arakin and Prudence munched on handfuls of Driyetta's warm, toasted cranberry biscuits and gulped down malted milk drinks, chuckling as they watched Slipnor ravenously devour a series of meat trays that the young children kept offering him.

"He likes the grilled crocodile best of all," said a young girl.

The snow had stopped falling, and sunlight peeked around the clouds, bathing the land in warm light as a festive spirit swept over the town.

The fighters—soldiers and townspeople alike—all regaled each other with their battle stories. The Baker held court with over thirty wide-eyed children, and he proved to be a compelling storyteller. Still brandishing his rolling pin, he reenacted his swipes and parries with great flourishes and grand posturing. His audience laughed, clapped, and hurrahed on every enthralling update.

The injured were now determined to join the festivities, and it wasn't long before they had all limped and hobbled into the heart of the party. Their stories received the greatest oohs and ahs. Busk, the writing enthusiast from Pound's army, was among the injured. He sported a large bandage on his leg, but his mood was infectiously jolly, and he soon produced a small wooden flute from his jacket, leading the way in tune, with many others joining in.

The Four Generals ambled among the throng of fighters, congratulating them on their courage. Pound caught the eye of a boy staring fixedly at his necklace, a leather strap with a wooden-horse figurine dangling from it. He recognized the child. It was the boy from the town's square, whose tear-streaked face had moved him after the toy raid. Pound thought for a moment, then yanked the necklace off and handed it to the child, who at first seemed terrified. Then the boy took it, smiled, brought it to his chest while clenching it in both hands, and ran to his mother with delight, showing it to her proudly. Pound turned to discover Arakin smiling at him.

"A kind-hearted General, after all," said Arakin.

"Well, it tended to chafe anyway," said Pound with a wave of his hand, turning slightly red as the other Generals slapped him on the back.

Talk throughout the town drifted from battle stories to tales of home and family. The soldiers were soon lamenting those they missed, and they expressed their admiration of Ashville, revealing that they considered it a place worthy of calling home. The townspeople were delighted to hear this and encouraged the idea.

Efscott, Sir Sudley, and the Blacksmith set up a series of fire pits around the village to keep the revelers warm. The largest was lit in the center of town, a huge bonfire that burned brilliantly. Arakin, Prudence, Slipnor, and Ash came to Efscott's side, joining the small group around it, including Sir Sudley and Mrs. Sudley. The Blacksmith and Brunt were also there and greeted them with a nod. Driyetta stepped in, giving Arakin a gentle nudge, offering a platter of more sweets presented regally around two laurel wreaths. She gestured to the biscuits upon which a ring of yellow berries was embedded, then placed her hand tenderly on Arakin's shoulder, looking reverently from him to Prudence.

"We call them Royal Crowns," she said.

"Thanks so much, but I don't think I could eat anything else," laughed Prudence.

"Me either," said Arakin, placing his hand on his belly.

"Taking a crown right now would be most appropriate, I would think," came a booming voice behind them.

Arakin turned to see the Four Generals emerging from the crowd.

"We have been talking," continued Pound.

Arakin searched their faces for a clearer sign of their mood, which was hard to gauge. They seemed so serious; were they angry with him for some reason?

They stopped in front of him.

Driyetta automatically offered them the platter. "Oh. Would you like a biscuit?"

"No. But we would like a king," replied Pularax, flashing a warm smile, his eyes fixed on Arakin.

"An official king, appointed by Generals. A master and commander," said Dinara.

"And we would make this place our home," said Yan. "Assuming the Chief of Ashville would give us his blessing?"

The Four Generals looked to the Blacksmith, whose mouth was crammed full of biscuits. He swallowed hard and nodded awkwardly. "Indeed I would," he croaked. "A fine idea. We would be ... honored." The Blacksmith was still frowning and squinting slightly, but it may have just been from the strain of swallowing a fistful of shortbread in such a hurry.

"A king?" said Arakin apprehensively.

"And that king is you," said Yan, grinning at Arakin. "To rule over these lands, these people."

"But I am … just a boy," said Arakin, totally bewildered. "I don't know how to be a king." His eyes flashed to Prudence and Efscott, hoping they'd agree with him, but they simply smiled warmly in return. "I'm an orphan from the woods," said Arakin more firmly. "I'm nobody."

"Nobody?" said Pularax. "The orphan boy who, for the betterment of others, surrendered love and kingdom, only to be surrounded by both? I say *that* is somebody."

"They say the truest of kings can inspire courage," said Dinara. "And that even in times of chaos, they unite kingdoms and unite man. For *this* king is wisest. And wisdom rules best. And here it is," he gestured around him to the town of disparate people, all bonding and sharing under the enchanting warm glow of dusk and firelight.

Those closest to the conversation had shushed others behind, and gradually a hush fell over the crowd. All eyes settled on Arakin and the Generals.

Pound took a step closer and spoke crisply. "Arakin, you created a bond where there was once fracture. You created honor where there was once shame. And you gave hope where there was once despair. It is now *our* turn to give."

Pound dropped to his knee in front of Arakin and bellowed, "You have my sword, My King."

"You have my shield, My King," boomed Pularax as he too dropped to one knee.

"You have my bow, My King," roared Yan, dropping to one knee.

"And you have my spear, My King," declared Dinara, who also took a knee.

A ripple of movement swept through town as the four hundred soldiers took a knee, the injured among them. They then bellowed in unison. "Yar!"

Driyetta jumped in shock, almost tipping the sweets off her platter. "Oh my," she whispered.

"And you have our armies, My King," said Pound. "What more could a king desire?"

Arakin looked across at Prudence. Her eyes locked on his.

"A queen, if she would stand by me," said Arakin. "For it was she who gave me life, returning me from the Under Land, and it was she who gave me purpose. What is a king without these?"

Prudence stiffened, but also grinned. Her face seemed to glow.

"I would indeed stand by you," she replied softly.

There was a wave of gasps, claps, and swoons throughout the crowd, particularly among the townspeople. The children especially were astounded, watching transfixed. The Four Generals beamed.

"Then we shall begin our quest," said Pound firmly, "to forge a crown that is worthy of you both."

"There is no need, General," said Arakin. He reached out to Driyetta's platter.

"Biscuit?" she said meekly, assuming he was trying to take one.

"No," replied Arakin with a smile, "but could I take these, please?" He placed his hand on the two laurel wreaths, and Driyetta nodded with a bashful grin.

"Oh, of course," she tittered.

"A fitting choice for the boy from the forest and the girl bonded to nature," said Pularax.

Efscott gave a slight start as if realizing that he was standing when he shouldn't be. He promptly lowered himself to his knee, and the Sudleys followed suit. Prudence, clearly feeling uncomfortable by the gesture, gave a subtle shake of her head. But he gave a courteous nod in return, smiling proudly, and gestured with his hand as if to say that it was all fine and this was how it should be.

Arakin gazed down at the laurels in his hand for a moment. "I only hope I can be a good king, worthy of this honor."

"You will not be a good king," said the Blacksmith, and all eyes turned to him. A ripple of murmurs followed, along with an awkward silence. The Blacksmith was still standing, as were the rest of the townspeople. But while their expressions were of intrigue and enchantment, he was stern and rigid. The Blacksmith puffed out his chest and took a step forward. "You will be a *great* king," he boomed, then dropped to his knee. "And we are honored to have you lead us. You have Ashville, My King!"

Brunt and the townspeople immediately followed suit, all taking a knee.

"A great king indeed," said Brunt.

Arakin was moved by his sincerity and equally moved by the genuine warmth from all who looked to him.

"But ... they are not bonded in marriage," whispered Driyetta to the Generals, still balancing her large platter of sweets while kneeling.

"It matters not," said Pound, "for they are bonded with magic, which clearly still lives."

"It does indeed," said Yan. Pularax and Dinara nodded.

Arakin placed the first laurel wreath on Prudence's head, and she did likewise with the remaining one, all the while grinning at each other. Ash was still seated on Slipnor's head and gave

313

him a gentle pat as he shuffled excitingly between his front paws. Arakin turned back to the Generals and nodded. He wasn't really sure what he was supposed to do next.

A roar of applause and cheers erupted as everyone rose to their feet.

Pound and Pularax grabbed several ales from a nearby platter and distributed them to Yan, Dinara, Efscott, Sir Sudley, Mrs. Sudley, and the Blacksmith.

"To the King and Queen!" bellowed the Four Generals heartily in unison as they raised their mugs. The soldiers and townspeople repeated the toast with exuberance. Jubilant music broke out once more, but even louder, and as day faded slowly into night, the town was lit up by hundreds of candles and lanterns as the festivities continued—contrasting groups of people, bound together with laughter.

It was clear that many were going to party well into the night, but the last few days had obviously been extraordinarily taxing for some. Arakin and Prudence were trying to hide their yawns, but it was clearly time to retire.

The Generals insisted on appointing a detachment of their finest soldiers to guard their new king and queen. "You never know when a horde of savages will charge into town," joked Pound.

The Baker and Driyetta had the largest house in town, and they offered three spare rooms for Arakin, Prudence, and Efscott, given that Efscott's shack had been destroyed. Arakin's initial reaction was to refuse and return instead to the familiarity of the Ash Forest, but he knew this was an old habit kicking in where a more lucid judgment was required instead. He needed to be here now for those who needed him, and he could not spend the nights detached from everyone else just because it was a comfortable routine. Besides, he might even like it. He gratefully accepted the Baker and Driyetta's offer.

It was the warmest, softest bed Arakin had ever felt, and it dawned on him that it was the first time in his life he had slept anywhere but in the Ash Forest. As far as he could remember, at least. He wondered why the feeling was not more peculiar, and he quickly realized that the branches of the great tree Grandastal were still with him, and therefore the Ash Forest was still with him no matter where he went.

Slipnor was curled up at the foot of Arakin's bed, a giant ball of white fur relishing the close proximity to the room's small fireplace, which crackled and flickered a rich amber light. The wolf's gentle snores were more like contended purrs. Ash had chosen the windowsill for his bed's location, mainly because of its safer distance from the fire. He had bashfully agreed to let Driyetta apply some linseed oil to his burned bottom, and he now pulled himself under the warmth of a thick tea towel. Arakin gazed up at Gun Ronin. He had placed it on a varnished timber sword-holder given to him by Pound and kept closely beside his bed. Arakin then glanced over at Ash, who was looking back at him.

"You were right before," said Ash. "You remember that day in the forest when you cut my strings off?"

Arakin nodded but was trying to remember what Ash was referring to.

"You said the next few days were going to be filled with high adventure," said Ash. "You weren't wrong." Ash seemed to fall asleep even as he was chuckling.

Arakin smiled and closed his eyes. He felt the comfort of fatigue wrap around him like a soothing cloak as he sank into the deepest and most blissful sleep he'd ever had.

CHAPTER THIRTY-SEVEN

Arise the Knights

The blade of Gun Ronin moved toward Ash's head, sliding through the air toward his neck. But Ash did not seem concerned. On the contrary, he was still, and his head was bowed.

The flat edge landed gently on his shoulder. Arakin lifted the blade and tapped it gently on Ash's opposing shoulder.

Ash was on one knee before Arakin, who spoke loudly and crisply with a mix of formality and genuine warmth. "Arise, Sir Ash! Arise a Knight!"

Ash rose to his feet, beaming with absolute pride.

"And join these knights," continued Arakin, "sworn to protect king, land, and people. For all time!"

Ash strutted toward Efscott, Sir Sudley, Pound, Dinara, Pularax, and Yan, who stood shoulder to shoulder, all adorned in purple ceremonial robes and gold livery collars. His fellow knights.

Arakin and Prudence also wore gold livery collars, but what set them apart from everyone else were the gold-coated laurel wreaths upon their heads. Elegant and majestic, without the formality of a typical crown. Slipnor stood to the other side of Arakin and also wore a gold livery collar. They all stepped to the edge of the tower, with the knights following close behind them.

The army and townspeople that had gathered below cheered in jubilation, a roar of absolute joy. They all stood close to the castle's main entrance, which was now void of a moat. It had been filled with soil, and from it grew a variety of flowers.

It was spring in Ashville. The snow had receded and was replaced with green fields, rich with crops. The air was alive with the smell of life, caressed with a cool breeze and warm sunshine.

The castle itself had been refurbished to a far more elegant form. The courtyard was now a garden for the people. The castle's rear chambers had been removed, revealing the grand waterfall that poured again, not into a chamber feeding into a well, but instead flowing through the center of the courtyard, feeding the creek once more.

Not far from where the drawbridge once stood, an elegant stone bridge traversed the creek, connecting the land on both sides of the clear waters that cut between the Ash Forest and the cottages.

The town had grown, not only in size but also in stature. The residents had once been content in their self-imposed solitary existence, but now this village was a real home to all and a genuine community. They had stood side by side in the face of terrifying adversity and come together as one.

More cottages had been built to accommodate all the soldiers. They had transported their families to Ashville to make it their home too. They had found the life worth fighting for in Ashville and the king worthy of that title in Arakin.

Efscott's old carriage, which no longer served as their living quarters, was parked in the castle's stable area. Arakin, Prudence, Efscott, Ash, and Slipnor were granted the honor of the royal quarters in the castle by decree of the Generals, their army, and the townspeople. This was their home.

The entire assembly was adorned in purple ceremonial gowns, soldiers and townspeople alike. They fanned out in two lines on opposing sides of the creek, then became unified as one group in the center of the bridge. Columns of purple speckled with flashes of gold. From Arakin's viewpoint, they bore an uncanny resemblance to the line of caterpillars he gazed upon before his adventure began—that day in the grove when he first laid eyes upon Prudence. So much had changed since then.

***

On the castle's rooftop, a butterfly fluttered by Sir Sudley's face, and he jumped back in fright.

Pound chuckled. "The first butterfly. Spring is coming," he added.

"So is something … very odd," declared Sir Sudley in a throaty tone, pointing to movement edging over the horizon, beyond the town's gates.

An ear-piercing sound split the air.

"Battle horns," declared Pound with concern, narrowing his eyes and stepping forward.

All eyes had similarly flashed to the eastern horizon, where Sir Sudley was pointing. To their bewilderment, an army of forty elephants and five hundred foot soldiers charged across the plain toward them, churning up a dust cloud in their stampeding wake.

Each elephant brandished long, menacing tusks that had been capped with polished, sharpened steel, and had three riders upon their back. Eight of these elephants also had two hollowed-out tusks strapped to either side of their shoulders. Ivory battle horns. The riders were blowing into the tapered ends to blast out the very note that had broken morning's serenity. The foot soldiers were indeed hardened warriors, but as they drew nearer, Arakin could tell that their armor was comparatively fragile, and their numbers relatively low. He also recognized something else: their leader.

Pound turned on his heel and made for the exit. "Knights, prepare for battle!" he bellowed, and the other Generals made to follow, but Arakin calmly raised his hand, and they stopped.

"Sire," hushed Pound as he stiffened.

"No need to raise the alarm, General," said Arakin. "This man will talk first. He's very pragmatic."

"Enough to pause an attack?" asked Pound.

"Enough to be a Royal Treasurer," replied Arakin with a mix of amusement and intrigue.

Pound and the other Generals grinned as it dawned on them what Arakin was suggesting. They squinted, trying to make out the shape of the person leading the charge.

The Elephant army stormed closer without slowing. Just thirty yards away now, and the leader was close enough for all to see. It was, as Arakin indicated, the King's old Treasurer, Minus, hunched over the reins of the first elephant, flogging its shoulders fretfully with a long stick. Ten yards from the gates now and Minus brought his elephant to a stop, raised his hand, and his entire army stomped to a thundering halt behind him.

As a fog of silence fell over the town, the enormous dust cloud created by the army swept forward, driven by the easterly wind, billowing high into the air and stretching toward the castle.

Minus's elephant reared up aggressively on its hind legs, its massive trunk whipping skyward and blaring a trumpet-like wail that echoed across the town. Minus, still composed and rigid in his saddle, bellowed toward the castle tower with brazen confidence, "People of Ashville, yield to me, for I declare myself your new *King*!"

As the dust cloud engulfed the castle, Minus grinned like a disdainful smoker who took joy in blowing his fumes into someone's face. No doubt he was expecting to see the gangly, buffoonish shape of Luxurous and the sullen, squat figure of the Black Witch soon appear on the rooftop.

But it was Arakin who emerged from the luminous dust cloud, a solitary figure before a billowing wall of grey-white, lionlike with his thick mop of hair wavering in the wind. Arakin moved to the tower's edge, and the remainder of his entourage bloomed from the dust behind him, stern-faced and stout.

Minus gave a start at the sight of them, and his face twitched as he took it all in. His elephant lowered itself back onto all fours, and Minus gripped the reins more tightly.

Prudence came to Arakin's side, and Slipnor stepped to the other, with Ash perched upon his head, standing tall, his hands on his hips. Efscott, Sir Sudley, and the Four Generals marched in with a swagger of rediscovered magnificence, coming to a stop behind Arakin.

"Minus," yelled Arakin, his voice resonating loud and clear across the land, "once esteemed Royal Treasurer and Manager of Poo, we have no quarrel." There was a ripple of laughter in town and some perplexed expressions on the faces of Minus's own soldiers. They were no doubt discovering more about their leader's past. Arakin thought for a moment. "However ..."

Everyone watched Arakin closely, especially Minus.

"… if you would like your old job back," he continued, "we do have toilets you can work on." The Generals chuckled behind him. "But if you choose to do battle this day, know that we will exact the same absence of mercy you afforded Efscott Borelle when you pressed for his execution."

Minus puffed out his chest and smirked, then placed a hand on his sword grip. If he drew it and pointed toward the castle, it would mean that he would inevitably give the order for his army to attack. But Minus barely had time to contemplate this action.

Upon the tower, Arakin ripped off his purple ceremonial robe. The Four Generals, Efscott, Sir Sudley, and Prudence did likewise, revealing that they all wore something more foreboding beneath: gold armor, elegant enough for ceremony but forged with the pure intention of function in battle. With a resounding chime, Arakin drew Gun Ronin from a leather sheath on his back and held it high above his head. The sun reflected brilliantly off the blade straight onto Minus's face, who squinted, bringing a hand up to shield his eyes.

The townspeople and soldiers of Ashville had been warily eyeing the castle for their cue from Arakin—and it came with this action. They followed suit, tearing away their robes, revealing that they, too, wore impressive gold armor beneath. Their earnest expressions and synchronicity in movement made it clear that these were a united people, prepared for any fight, sudden or not.

Arakin's entourage, the townspeople, and soldiers all simultaneously drew out formidable gold swords, eliciting a loud metallic chime. Like Arakin, they raised them high above their heads, sending a barrage of dazzling reflected light into the eyes of Minus and his army, then bellowed out in unison, "Charrrrrrr!" They were a thousand people roaring as one, scaring hundreds of birds into flight from the nearby trees, a dark cloud darting skyward, circling over Minus's army before flitting away.

Minus flinched in response to the deafening war cry, leaping slightly in his saddle, hunching his shoulders and blinking anxiously while shielding his eyes from the blinding, reflected light.

His army spent little time contemplating their next move and simply turned and fled to the thunderous roar of forty elephants and five hundred men making a terrified retreat, leaving Minus totally alone. He sighed heavily, and his face twitched once again, then he turned his elephant and urged it onward, following the retreat of the others, running into the luminous dust cloud formed by their stampede.

"Good idea turning all that King's Gold into armor," said Ash, taking in the glistening spectacle beneath them.

"Thanks," said Arakin softly.

Prudence grinned. "Definitely more practical than a giant, gold slippery-slide from the castle rooftop into the creek," she added.

Ash puffed his chest out. "Still ... would have been fun, though, wouldn't it?"

"It would," said Arakin with an affectionate grin.

Prudence chuckled good-naturedly, and Ash joined in as Slipnor sniffed the air, closing his eyes partially, as if curious and content. The slight upturn in his mouth gave the distinct appearance that he was smiling.

Arakin sheathed Gun Ronin, prompting everyone else in town and on the tower to do likewise, resulting in a reverberating chime. Arakin gazed out pensively at the retreating army and the horizon they raced toward. *Would more come this way*, he wondered. And what if they presented a challenge that he could not handle? What sort of king would he be then? He had proven he could lead an army into battle, but did he know how to rule? And at that exact moment, Arakin felt Prudence's hand brush against his. Her warmth was all-encompassing, so subtle, yet powerful enough to leave his head swimming, helping him release the doubts that led to eternal questions, bringing him back to this moment in time—to now.

And it dawned on him that for the first time in his life, he had a home. He had a family.

THE AUTHOR

About the author

This is Stephen R. Pratt's debut novel. He has worked for over twenty years in the film and TV industry as a writer and director. He lives on the Gold Coast in Australia with his wife and pet Moodle, and in his spare time, he loves ocean swimming and space exploration.

Connect with the author

I hope you enjoyed reading *Ash Forest (and the King's Gold)* as much as I enjoyed writing it.
I invite you to connect with me at: www.stephenrpratt.com
I look forward to hearing from you.

And if you enjoyed this book, please consider leaving a review on Amazon. It really does make a difference.

If you would like to discover more about Ash Forest, sign up for the newsletter at the website above. You can receive an array of exciting updates and insights, including a Discussion Guide. It will also allow you to be the very first to see the artwork for the upcoming books. Have your say, get involved, and dive into the adventure.

Pre-order coming books by Stephen R. Pratt

Ash Forest (and the King's Gold) is the first of a series. You will be able to pre-order the second part of the series, ***Ash Forest (and the Rise of the Vadorian Guard)***. Arakin and Prudence incur the wrath of King Luxurous's father, the Highland King, who is far wealthier than Luxurous and far more malicious.

Stephen R. Pratt is also writing the first book of a different series, ***Space Marine (and the Battle of Moon Rising)***, which will be available in 2022. Set ten years in the future, it follows a young boy who travels to the moon in a spaceship ill-equipped to handle the conditions, in a desperate bid to save his parents who have crash-landed on the lunar surface.